Redtown

ALSO BY LAWRENCE GULLEY

Buffington

The Peanut House

Cora Jean

Bayou County

The Pilgrim (Bessie's Story)

Brothers

Redtown

LAWRENCE GULLEY

Redtown
L.E. Gulley

ISBN: 978-1-943927-14-2

DEDICATION

I dedicate this book to my Lord and personal
savior Jesus Christ. Through Him all things are
possible. I also dedicate this book to Shelby,
Buddy, Pap, and Rumby, and all others who
are preaching the word of God.

In Memorial

Buddy, Dale, and Shandi.

CONTENTS

PRELUDE

L ong before we moved to Redtown, there was a killing of a prominent citizen in the town. Sometimes, believe it or not, someone needs killing for the betterment of everyone concerned.

In lieu of not being able to find the murderer, the adjacent town, which was just across the railroad tracks, built a huge bronze statue of the deceased that stands to this day in front of the Courthouse.

The person that did the killing was never discovered.

REDTOWN: A NOVEL BY L.E. GULLEY

Chapter 1

Daddy packed up everything we owned in a boxcar, including the chickens, mule, our dog "Black Boy," and the farming implements. We moved to Redtown, Alabama, on June 6th, 1951. We only lived ten miles from the town we were moving from, but by the time the train switched stations so many times, it took us all day to get there.

Mama was mighty worn out by the time the old boxcar squeaked and rumbled to an ear-piercing stop by the side of the old tin-top red clapboard house. All of us kids got busy helping her put up the beds, while Daddy put the mule in the stall and fed him. Then Daddy reassembled the wood stove.

We all had to rush while there was still daylight, for

the old house was similar to the one we had moved from; it wasn't wired for electricity.

The whole affair was exciting to us kids. From the best we could tell, the house was on the outskirts of a town, closer to civilization than where we had moved from.

Mama cussed and raised hell about how dusty the old house was, so we all knew what was ahead of us the next day. We knew we would be scrubbing floors and walls, getting things in order to suit Mama, who had always kept a spotless house. We didn't have much furniture to speak of, so by the time the kerosene lamps were lit, we had about half of our belongings out of the boxcar.

Daddy had checked the place out before we made the move, so he'd had time to repair the chicken pen and other odds and ends ahead of the time he brought the rest of us. By the time we got the chickens into the pen and untied their legs that very first night, it was good and dark.

The only drawback to the place was the water pump, which was about seventy-five yards from the house. Mama sent my brother Pap and me with a water bucket each to the hand pump. By the time we returned with the water dripping down our legs from toting the heavy buckets, we could smell bacon frying. We could tell Daddy had the old wooden stove assembled and Mama had started supper.

Thus, our new life in Redtown began. All we knew to start with was that we figured it would be more interesting to live by a town instead of far off in the country with no excitement to speak of. We had no idea at that time that before long, we would have more excitement than we wanted. We didn't know we would make an unexpected new friend, help solve a missing persons mystery that had law enforcement puzzled for years, and meet several truly crazy people.

To tell the gospel truth, that last one was no big doings, as we had our own brand of crazy right in our family.

Chapter 2

We called her "Big Mama," and she was my grandmother on my mama's side.

Before I tell you more about Big Mama, this is how the rest of our family was arranged.

There were five of us children, me being the fourth in line. Daddy had nicknames for all of us. My sister, Shelby, the oldest, was four years older than me; she was known as Shebby. William was next; he was called Buddy. Then came Pap. I don't believe to this day that he knows what his real name is, but he says his name is Jimmy. Next there's me, Lawrence (known as Lew), and last is my baby brother Karl (known as Rumby).

Us boys seldom wore shoes or shirts in the summers. Our skin was already dark, due to Daddy's Indian heritage, so by the end of the summers me, Pap, and Shelby were almost as dark as he was, yet Buddy and Rumby had blonde hair and green eyes like Mama.

Shelby, Buddy, and Rumby were sort of passive in nature like Daddy, whereas Pap and I were like Mama—we had a little fire to us, especially Pap. He'd fight at the drop of a pin.

Pap and I cursed like sailors when we'd get out of range of Mama, but Buddy, Rumby, and Shelby didn't. I'm almost certain Daddy heard us a time or two, but since he thought none of us had any sense except Buddy, he never mentioned it to us. Most importantly, he never told Mama, because she would have whipped us for sure.

Daddy was a small man; he never weighed over a hundred and twenty pounds. He was just about full Choctaw Indian, very dark skinned with raven-black hair, and he always had a smile on his face. I never heard him say a curse word or see him lose his temper. He never whipped us, and he only corrected us if we were doing something wrong concerning work. He did believe in that, and he kept us busy, mostly on the eighteen-acre farm that came with the house we moved to near Redtown.

Daddy was talented in many trades. He could carpenter, file saws, and mechanic. He couldn't even drive an automobile, but somehow knew how to fix them. He was a good millwright, which is what brought us to Redtown. He was hired as a millwright at Excel Furniture Manufacturing, builders of bedroom furniture.

Mama was far different from Daddy, with her blonde hair and green eyes. Her skin was as light as his was dark; her complexion was so fair that she almost looked anemic.

Mama was beautiful. She was fifteen years younger than Daddy, and I later learned that everyone wondered how Daddy got her and managed to hold onto her.

What Daddy lacked in temperament, Mama made up for, and then some. She had a red-hot temper, and had just as soon jump on a man as a woman. She stayed ready for a fight or a confrontation.

We were scared of her. I think Daddy was too. We learned early on to just stay out of her way as much as possible.

Mama had an uncanny ability to give her opinion on a

subject quickly, while Daddy, when you asked him a question on something, had to mull over it for a while.

Daddy would say, "Well, let me think on it for a while."

Mama would say, "Hell no, let me tell you what to do ..." and then she'd spit out advice like bullets: blam, blam, blam, blam—and it would be right, too.

Mama's folks lived about a mile down the road from us. Her Daddy, whom we lovingly called "Daddy Jim," was a wonderful, loving grandpa. He was a bootlegger, but no more honest of a man ever lived. He was like Mama, straight down the line with everything. He didn't hem or haw. He might have been a bootlegger, but he had the respect of people who knew him. He was as honest as the day was long, and he was called "Mr. Jim" by the locals.

Daddy Jim knew everything about everybody. I found out later that he thought moving us to Redtown was a bad idea—but by the time Mama figured out he was right, it was too late. We were already in it.

Daddy Jim, like two of his brothers, was drawn nearly double with arthritis. The three of them always kept their walking sticks handy. This was not only to assist them in walking, but in Daddy Jim's case, he also used it as a weapon. If the walking stick didn't work, he always had his little stacked-barrel derringer pistol on him at all times, and folks knew it. I once witnessed him shoot the first joint of a customer's finger off over fifty cents worth of bootleg whiskey. Once word of that got around, nobody else ever refused to pay Daddy Jim what they owed.

It was rumored that he had his hand in other illegal activities besides moonshine; I never knew for sure. All I knew was, he always seemed to have money when you needed it.

My grandma, who, like I said, we referred to as "Big Mama," was pretty much the opposite of Daddy Jim. She seldom allowed us in her house. We never ate a mouthful that she cooked, and were never invited to. About all I ever saw her do was sit down on the couch, file her fingernails, and read the Bible. She dipped snuff, but swore up and down she didn't. There'd always be a can nearby for her to spit into when she thought no one was looking.

Big Mama couldn't have told you the truth if her life depended on it, yet she could preach to you the Bible. She knew every verse. Instead of cursing, she'd spell the word out, whereas Daddy Jim would just let it fly. Cussing was a practiced art to him.

Like I mentioned, Big Mama was crazy, but we didn't know it at the time. We just thought she was a big liar.

Among some of the crazy lies Big Mama told was that she could fly, and often did, visiting other cities and even other countries in the middle of the night. She claimed that she was a composer of beautiful music, and that in fact she was the one that wrote "The Tennessee Waltz." She also told us that some of her deceased children would visit her every Sunday night, and they would go for walks in the moonlight.

Daddy Jim didn't pay her any mind, so we didn't, either. At times when she told a lie, she'd say, "Isn't that right, Daddy?" and he'd just say "Yeah, yeah, Mama . . . whatever you say."

Big Mama had two litters of children. She had my Mama and two more daughters, and then about twenty years later she had three more. Two of my uncles, Mama's brothers Willie Joe and Talmer, were only a couple of years older than me, and my last aunt, Sunshine, was a year younger than me.

For some reason Big Mama was mean to Sunshine, so the

girl stayed at our house most of the time. Between the crazy lying and the meanness, I didn't blame her a bit.

Sunshine was like all Mama's other sisters; she was a pretty little thing with long blonde wavy hair. She and my baby brother Rumby, who was the same age, played together coming up. Where you saw one, you saw the other.

It was strange to me that Mama and all her sisters were pretty, but Willie Joe and Talmer were as ugly as homemade sin. Both of them had thin limp brown hair, were very pale in complexion and didn't have a bit of muscle tone to their bodies.

Talmer and Willie Joe were twins, and they were too lazy to walk. They scooted around on their asses until they were twelve years old. Instead of making them get up and exercise, Big Mama would pull them around in a small hand wagon, claiming that her poor babies were too weak to walk.

When Willie Joe and Talmer were out of Big Mama's sight, us kids would whip them with limbs, and they'd jump from that wagon and run like scalded dogs. Turns out that even though they looked weak, they were plenty strong and fast when they needed to be; they just knew Big Mama would drag them around so they didn't have to make the effort to move on their own. They could just about beat Big Mama in the lying department, too. You couldn't believe a thing they said.

Daddy Jim acted as though Talmer and Willie Joe didn't even exist. Sometimes, if he was close to them, he'd shuffle his feet on the floor just to see them leap from their sitting positions and run. Of course, as soon as Big Mama was in sight, they'd fall down and act as though they couldn't walk again.

My brothers and I toted many a whipping from Mama on account of Talmer and Willie Joe. If we did anything wrong, she kept Daddy's razor strap hanging in a convenient place and she'd go to wailing away on our backsides, saying she'd beat us to death before she'd see us as sorry and shiftless as they were.

Chapter 3

It didn't take us long to learn that when we moved to Redtown, we wound up living on the wrong side of the tracks.

Hampton, the county seat, was on the opposite side of the tracks. We soon learned that everything was more modern in Hampton than it was in Redtown.

For instance, Hampton had a theater, along with larger stores, including a drugstore. It had doctors, paved roads and cement sidewalks. Several of the houses were bricked instead of the red-painted clapboard shacks that gave Redtown its name. Hampton had running water and electricity if you could afford it, which the majority of the residents could.

All the "big shots" resided in Hampton, along with anyone who had the money to live there. But if they fell on hard times, they, too, were forced to move across the tracks, where things were cheaper.

The city fathers of Hampton had jerry-rigged the town's map, so that the citizens of Redtown couldn't even vote in any of the city's elections, which suited Redtown's populace just fine.

We soon found out that the so-called "downtown district" of Redtown was just a couple of blocks behind where we lived. In fact, the land that went with our place ran right up to the back of the few stores and juke joints. Someone in the past had fenced the whole eighteen acres with what was now just a rusted hog wire fence, so we soon knew our boundary.

Mama made her first visit to the downtown section of Redtown the day after we moved there, just to get a few grocery items. She told all us to stay at home to keep an eye on things and also to watch after our baby brother, Rumby.

Mama didn't waste time getting back. She was carrying only one small paper bag, and her face was as white as a sheet. Me and two of my brothers were in the yard, and she told us to come into the house.

After counting heads, making sure we were all inside, she told us to stay away from downtown. "Everybody down there is crazy," she said.

"My Daddy was right! Why in the hell y'all's Daddy would move us here is beyond me. Y'all stay inside the fence, and from now on, make sure there's always two of you together," she added.

We didn't ask any questions, but we knew she was serious, because Mama didn't scare easily. But when we saw her go to the cedar chifforobe and take out her pearl-handled revolver, we knew just how serious she was this time.

We were all as scared of Mama as a rattlesnake, but after a few days of staying inside that fence, Pap and I couldn't stand it any longer. We jumped the fence and ran toward town, and as usual, Black Boy was trotting along with us. We were praying to get back before Mama missed us.

As long as I live, I won't ever forget that day, and the people we met in that crazy town.

There was only one intersection in the whole town, and

in the middle of the intersection stood a giant of a man. He was dressed in what we would later find out was a World War I uniform, complete with the doughboy hat and brightly polished brass whistle attached to a brown plaid string that hung across his shoulder.

We didn't see any cars coming by, but the giant soldier stood ready to blow his whistle and motion for any automobiles to come through in case one showed up.

From my brief observation of things as we were at the intersection, I soon learned that every building, including the houses, stores and other establishments, were painted the same chalky red color, which gave Redtown its name.

Just about the time Pap and I had gotten somewhat used to the sight of the Army man in the middle of the road, we noticed somebody else who was an even stranger sight.

Coming toward us by the side of the road was a middle-aged man walking a small poodle dog. The man and the dog were ordinary looking in every way but one: the dog was facing forward like a normal dog, but the man was walking backwards.

I blinked my eyes and looked over at Pap, who was standing stock still with his mouth dropped open. I nudged him a little and we started walking again as the backwards man moved past us. We looked away from him.

That was a mistake, as it turned out, because when we looked away from the man with the poodle dog, we looked straight into the eyes of the strangest person we met that day, which was saying a lot.

At the side of the road, right at the intersection, was a lady. Well, less than half a lady, actually.

All you could see was her head and a little of her shoulders, sticking up out of the red dirt by the roadway. She had dug a hole right at the main intersection, got down in that hole, and covered herself with dirt, leaving mostly only her head sticking out to converse with people as they walked to and fro from town. And converse, she did.

"Good morning, boys," the attractive-looking woman said politely, for all the world like she was meeting us at church or a tea party. "You're new in town, aren't you? What are your names?"

It was bad enough to see a giant soldier in the middle of

the road, and an ordinary-looking dog with an ordinary-looking man who walked backward; but when the woman by the side of the road, buried up to her neck in red clay, spoke to us and asked us who we were, that was it for us. Pap and I turned tail and ran as fast as we could, back toward the house.

In time to come, we learned that most everyone in the town was strange in one way or other. Like Sarge, the giant soldier in the roadway, and Mr. Bowen, who walked backwards one day out of the week, claiming that it would add years to his life. We didn't stay in Redtown long enough that first day to even meet Mr. Reese, who ran the gas station on the corner, and stuttered so badly that no one could understand a word he said, except possibly his wife, by whom he had sired fifteen beautiful blonde-haired daughters.

But none of these people, as different as they were from anybody we had ever met, would have such an impact on our lives as the woman in that red dirt hole.

Chapter 4

It would be some time before we went back into town; there was too much work to do at home. We were used to it by then, because we knew Mama had a thing about her house. She was a slave to it, and Daddy was the same way about the yard and fields. All us kids had to do our part to keep everything running the way they wanted it to be.

Back in those days folks didn't have grass or weeds in their yard; it was chopped or hoed up, then the yards were kept swept clean with a brush broom or yard rake. If you went by a house and saw grass or weeds in the yard, you automatically assumed the person living there was either lazy and shiftless or was too sick to get outside.

Daddy didn't want to see a sprig of grass anywhere, come plowing time for the fall garden. We always hoed from March to September each year, so by moving to Redtown in June, we had a lot of extra hoeing to do. The place, not being worked the previous year, had to be completely weeded.

The day after Pap and me made our short visit to town, Daddy sharpened all the hoes before he left for work. As soon as we'd eaten a little breakfast, Buddy, Pap and I hit the yard and started hoeing that grass.

Shelby and Rumby stayed inside with Mama. We sure didn't envy them, because anything beat staying out from under her watchful eye.

After we were through with the yard, we gathered up all the grass and threw some of it into the chicken pen, for they loved it. We gave the remainder of it to Pete, our mule.

The next day, we started hoeing the grass and weeds out of the farm land. In the meantime, Mama and Shelby worked at sweeping the yards down with gallberry brush brooms. By the time we came in for a quick dinner, we had to admit that the outside of the place looked better.

After we hoed for about a month, Mama couldn't stand

it any longer, and we started with the detailed cleaning of the inside of the house. All the floors and walls had to be scrubbed with a concoction of lye soap. It was some powerful stuff, for if a drop of it hit your skin, it would burn like fire. Mama told us to be careful and not let any of it get in our eyes, or we'd go blind.

Black Boy was asleep under the house as usual, and when some of that lye water seeped through the cracks and poured on him, you could hear his head hitting the floor joists as he made his hurried retreat out from under that house.

After we scrubbed every inch of the house with corn-shuck mops and rinsed everything down, it was clean enough to suit Mama. Next, we had to bring everything back into the house and set our few belongings back up after the floors dried. Then Mama remade the beds with starched sheets. Once all that was done, she stood back, crossed her arms, and looked everything over. When she finally nodded her head, I could tell she was satisfied.

We had about half of the field hoed by the time school started by the fall of that year. We'd stored the grass and weeds in the small barn for the mule to eat as fodder during the winter months. As soon as school was out each day, we knew we'd have to hit that field again. Daddy wasn't satisfied until all the grass was gone.

Chapter 5

Now, my older siblings hadn't clued me in on anything about school. All I knew was they hated it. My sister, who was four years older than me, had taught me my alphabet and how to write in cursive, by drawing or writing in the dirt with a pointed stick. I could read a little too. All of us were good at numbers; we learned it by playing seven-card stud or five-card draw.

How well I remember that first day of school. First off, we carried our lunch in brown paper bags. There was a deep culvert on the walk to school, and of course, we had to stop to throw rocks and other debris into it. Well, I wound up dropping my lunch bag into the rushing stream. Mama must've had a five-pound baked sweet potato in there, for it sank straight to the bottom, meaning I wouldn't have anything to eat on my first day of school.

Buddy showed me where my assigned room for the first grade was, then he left to go to his class, which was the third grade. Pap was in the second grade, and Shelby was going into the fourth.

Mrs. Carter, my teacher, was a plump middle-aged woman. She had all us form a line. She sat at her desk, and when it was our turn to step up, she asked us our names, then assigned a desk for each of us.

As I mentioned earlier, Daddy had nicknames for all of us. All I knew was that I answered by the name of Lew. I didn't know my last name, or anything that might be helpful to the teacher.

When she asked me my name, I told her "Lew."

"Lew who?" she asked, as she looked up from the thick book where she had written down the other kids' names.

I squirmed around for a few seconds, not knowing what to say. Then told her the only other thing I could think of, that I was Pap's brother.

"Oh, go find you a place at the back of the room," she said.

So I did, while listening to some of the other students snicker and laugh behind my back. The worst students had to sit at the back, with the smarter ones near the front of the room.

They wouldn't laugh long, though, as they found out by the end of the day that I may have been ignorant, but I wasn't dumb.

Along toward the middle of the morning, some of the young'uns got homesick and started crying, which only caused more of them to start. I'll have to admit, I had to choke back tears too, but Buddy had already warned me that if he heard that I even whimpered, he was going to tell Mama.

I was homesick and hungry, but my biggest problem was, I was hot and miserable in my new clothes and shoes that Mama had made me wear. The new shirt was stinging my neck, and since I was unaccustomed to wearing shoes, my feet were on fire.

Mrs. Carter had pulled up all the windows that she could pry up, but some of them wouldn't open. With the steaming temperature in the room mixed with the odor of all the new clothes, I was beginning to get nauseous. But then, Mrs. Carter asked if any of us knew the alphabet. Very shyly, I slowly raised my hand into the air, after looking around and seeing that no one else had raised their hand.

Looking surprised, the teacher asked "Lew, you know the alphabet?"

"Yes, Ma'am," I answered.

"Please stand and recite it for the class."

I was so nervous that I recited it too fast to suit her, so she asked me to say it again slowly as she wrote each letter at the top of the long chalkboard behind her desk at the front of the room.

She pointed out each letter with a yardstick ruler, saying it out loud one more time. Then she said, "Lew, move your desk up to the middle of the class."

After I moved my desk, other than being hungry, I suddenly didn't feel so bad anymore.

Well, we made it to dinner time, and by then half the children were crying and taking on something awful. Mrs. Carter threatened them with a paddle that she pulled out of her desk, so that slowed them down some.

After the other kids ate their dinner, she told us all to lay our head on our desk and take a nap.

There was this one little tear-stricken boy who dozed off holding an orange. Since I didn't have a mouthful to eat for my own dinner, and I had to sit there and watch everybody else eat, I noticed right away when his fingers relaxed and that orange rolled straight to my desk.

Mrs. Carter had her back turned to me, for she was dusting the chalkboard.

That orange was my dinner the first day of school.

After the nap, Mrs. Carter escorted all the girls to the bathroom, and she had an older boy in another grade escort us boys.

I'd never even seen running water, a urinal, electric lights or anything like that, so I just followed the crowd and did what the other boys did, trying to act casual like I knew what I was doing.

The last thing we did was wash our hands with a bar of Octagon soap. I knew the brand from the odor, because that's what Mama would scrub on our dirty clothes when she washed them.

The older boy that escorted us (whose name I later learned was Ralph) made sure to give us all a slap upside the head before we went out the bathroom door and lined up in the hall.

The girls took longer, but when they finally started coming out of their rest room, I could smell the Octagon soap on them too.

About the middle of the afternoon, we had play period; now, I liked that. It lasted a full hour, and I got to see my brother Pap. He'd pulled his shoes off and was running around with some boys, so I pulled off those hot shoes of mine and started running with the boys too. I was pleased to see Pap; seeing him made my day.

We didn't stay in the classroom much longer after play period before Mrs. Carter rang a little silver bell that she kept on her desk, telling us that school was out for that day. She reminded us all to take home the various pages of different objects that we had colored on our first day of school.

When she told us all it was time to go home, I remember some of the children looking at each other with a perplexed look on their face. I guess they'd figured we were in there for life. We didn't waste time getting our work so we could head outside.

The pupils that rode the buses were escorted out first, and the ones that walked to school went out after that.

I met Shelby, Buddy, and Pap in the hall. I noticed that Pap's new shirt was torn and a couple of buttons were missing, so I figured he'd been in a scrap. I also knew Mama would get him when we got home.

After we got outside, I noticed Black Boy was waiting on us, wagging his tail. I never did learn how that dog knew when school would be out, but he followed us to school each morning, and he was always there to follow us home in the afternoons. He was a good dog.

Pap pulled his shirt off and was carrying it along with his colorings, hoping to get away without it being noticed when he got home. Mama knew him pretty well, though, because right away when we walked in the door, she examined his shirt and then his knuckles before she whipped him.

When it was my turn, I told Mama what had happened at school when the teacher asked me who I was. I asked her to write my real name on a piece of paper so that I'd know what it was, so she did.

Then, Mama looked at the work I brought home and laughed, saying that it was pretty good for my first day.

Chapter 6

The next few days of school went very well. I was constantly raising my hand, and Mrs. Carter kept moving me up until I had dragged my desk to the very front row of the class.

My second week of school, the teacher escorted me to the principal's office. I was scared to death, for although he was a little skinny, he was a very gruff-talking fellow.

He asked me to sit at a desk in the corner of his office and gave me a test to take. I did real well on the arithmetic part. I'd learned my numbers from shooting craps and playing poker with some of Daddy Jim's customers. I pretty well understood most of the questions, so I answered the best that

I could. The hardest part to me was trying to hold a steady grasp on that big green lead pencil.

The next day, Mrs. Carter took me out of the first-grade classroom and escorted me to the one for the third grade, then gave me a note to take home to my parents.

Mrs. Kinsey was my third-grade teacher. I liked her; she wasn't as stiff and mean-acting as Mrs. Carter.

I soon learned, though, that I wasn't the wizard that I was in the first grade. I really had to work hard to keep up with the older kids. Some of the boys were ten or twelve years old; shoot, one of the boys named Rudy was already shaving! Of course, a few of them picked on me some because I was so small and young, but they soon learned that I'd fight back when it was play period time, so the bullying soon died down.

I toted a whooping from Pap a couple of times because I was a grade ahead of him, but we were always close, so that soon died down too.

Everything was going real well in school until the first of November, when I came down with the red measles and double pneumonia at the same time.

Now, poor folks didn't go to a doctor in those days unless you were dying. I stayed home and Mama gave me every homemade remedy that she knew of. By Christmas time I was so weak from fevers and such, I couldn't get out of the bed. All that I could hold down was peach juice.

Mama sent Buddy to Daddy Jim's three different times to get money for a doctor. Each time he was turned away by Big Mama at the door, saying Daddy Jim wasn't there. Finally, the people at the place where Daddy worked heard about my plight, so they took up a collection and Daddy called the doctor to the house.

I remember the doctor examining me, touching my wheezing thin chest with some kind of cold object that he carried in his briefcase.

He told Daddy that I needed to be in the hospital.

Mama told the doctor that they didn't have money to put me in a hospital.

"Aren't you Mr. Jim's daughter?" the doctor asked.

"Yes, but Daddy must be off on one of his deals or something. I can't get hold of him," Mama answered, wringing her hands.

When I heard about going to the hospital, I was too weak to say anything so I just started shaking my head no, thinking I didn't want to leave Mama and my siblings.

Dr. Redding took a deep breath and whispered to my folks that I probably wasn't going to make it anyway, and one thing was for sure, I certainly couldn't live long just drinking peach juice.

After Dr. Redding left, Mama sent Daddy to Manning's store, which was on the other side of the tracks. He brought back three cans of evaporated milk, more peaches and a small funnel.

I hadn't chewed food in such a long time that I couldn't swallow anything.

Mama mixed that milk with water and peach juice. I had to struggle, but I managed to sit up in bed. She stuck that funnel down my throat and poured that mixture down.

She did that three times a day, and I soon got to feeling better, but I still couldn't swallow any food.

There wasn't any sort of heat in that old shack but a fireplace in the living room and a wooden stove in the kitchen. It seemed like I stayed in that freezing bedroom forever, huddled under mounds of quilts, smelling nothing but the stench of Vick's salve that Mama smeared religiously on my throat and chest twice a day.

Bright and early one cold February morning, I remember waking up ravenously hungry. I called for Mama but didn't get an answer, so I swung my legs out of the bed to stand up and walk, but discovered I couldn't. My legs were so weak they wouldn't hold me up, and I collapsed back onto the bed.

Mama had an old straight-backed chair at the head of my bed, so I pulled it in front of me, and stood up grasping the chair. Putting all my weight on that chair, I slid it into the warm kitchen, one slow step after another.

I began looking around for something to eat. All I could find was some leftover biscuits from breakfast that Mama had stored in the top of the stove.

I knew there was some cane syrup on the table, but I didn't take time to stick my finger in the biscuit and pour syrup in the hole as we usually did when we wanted a treat between meals. I just stuffed some of the biscuit in my mouth and chomped down. I chewed on that piece of biscuit, trying to work up enough saliva to swallow it, for what seemed to me to be at least five minutes.

I finally managed to get the dry biscuit down, but as soon as it hit my stomach, I started retching and tried to vomit it up. Somehow, I held it down. I put the remainder of the biscuit in a saucer, got the syrup pitcher and poured syrup over it, and before long I'd devoured the whole biscuit. I then slowly slid the chair over to the water bucket, got the dipper and drank what must have been a half a gallon of that cold water.

I looked through the kitchen window and saw Mama at the pump. The big black boiling pot had a fire going under it, and I knew she was washing clothes. At least, I assumed it was Mama; she was wearing so many clothes and had such a thick head scarf on until she was unrecognizable.

I sat there in that chair and watched her from the unusually quiet room for about fifteen minutes.

Finally, I saw her take a long stick to dip the clothes out of the hot boiling water. As she dropped each piece into the cold rinse water, I knew all that she had left to do was wring the clothes out and hang them up to dry.

Rumby was playing near her, and I saw that he had several layers of clothes on, too. Every once in a while she'd jab at Rumby, just messing with him, and I could hear them laughing through the closed window.

I soon became too weak to sit there anymore, and decided I'd better try to make it back to my bed.

Mama and Rumby came in the back door in about thirty minutes. The first thing she did was to make up some of that milk and peach juice mixture.

When she came into my room, she couldn't believe that I was sitting up in bed.

"I don't think we'll need that funnel this morning," I said.

She stuck her cold hands to my face and didn't feel any fever. She looked up and clasped her hands together.

"Praise be to God," she said.

So I drank the mixture straight from the glass, and surprisingly, it had a pretty good taste to it.

After that I slowly made a recovery, but I remember the first time I walked by a mirror how my image startled me. I was so thin and pale! With my jet-black hair and dark eyebrows, the weight I had lost from being so sick, made me look gaunt and hatchet faced.

I later learned a boy in my class named Wayne had gotten the same illness that I did. His folks took him to the hospital, but he died anyway.

Chapter 7

By the middle of March, I started back to school. I was so far behind in my classes that I failed that year, and I felt so bad about it that it liked to have killed me.

Two good things came from me being sick, though. One, I missed out on breaking up the land with that mule, and two, when I headed back to school in the fall, Pap and I would be together in class.

By the summer, I'd gotten back into the swing of things, which meant plowing the garden and more hoeing.

Pete, our mule, was just like Black Boy—he was one of the family. That was the craziest mule; he loved Mama's biscuits.

The mule lot was right behind the house, and Pete would

bray and bray until one of us threw some of Mama's biscuits in there. Finally, Mama told Daddy that she wasn't cooking any more biscuits for a "damned ole mule," and she made Daddy move his pen to the back of the land, so the annoying braying wouldn't be as loud. It sure suited us, because we didn't have to tote his water so far; his lot was right near the water pump.

Daddy never planted cotton like the big farmers did. He mostly truck farmed. We had peas, butter beans, sweet potatoes, squash, tomatoes, and of course, corn.

Most of the corn was for feeding the animals, for Daddy had bought a big red sow hog which we named Rose. Then he bought a milk cow with long pointed horns.

Mama was scared to death of that cow. She put that cow in a small stall and put a small amount of grain in the trough for the cow to eat while Mama milked her.

Mama would put a short stool outside the stall, put a pail under the cow's udders and start milking. Every time that cow would switch her tail or move, Mama would jump and run. Sometimes the old cow would stomp her foot and turn the pail over, spilling all the milk.

After about a month of trying to milk that cow, Mama suggested killing the cow and eating it, because she wasn't going to try to milk it again.

Buddy, Pap, and myself took turns milking the cow. We sure enjoyed that fresh milk, too. Mama would make buttermilk and butter. The cow even produced enough milk for Mama to sell.

We didn't have refrigeration, but we had a small oaken ice box. Mr. Steadman, the ice man, would bring us a fifteen-cent block of ice three times a week, and it kept the milk cool enough so that it wouldn't spoil.

When Mama canned all the peas, butterbeans, tomatoes and other vegetables that she felt we needed, we'd sell the rest in Hampton. Folks in Redtown seldom bought anything, for they usually had them a small garden of their own.

Daddy dug about an eight-by-ten-foot hole, four feet deep, and lined the bottom with pine straw. When we dug our sweet potatoes, we'd lay them on top of that straw, then cover them with about a foot of more straw. Daddy then built a small shed over top, about four feet high with a small door. When we wanted sweet potatoes, we'd go into the sweet potato bank and get them, making sure to re-cover them with the straw, so that the cold winter wouldn't freeze them and cause them to rot.

Right before school started that next year, Rosie had twelve piglets and the cow had a calf. We were living better than I could ever remember.

Chapter 8

The worst time of the year for me was late summer, because when we were through with our gardening, we were hired out to pick cotton.

Pap could out-work Buddy and me. In pretty cotton he could pick four hundred pounds a day. I'd come in at about two hundred, and Buddy would pick about two hundred and fifty.

We'd usually get paid about two dollars and fifty cents a hundred. We used that money to pay our tuition for another year of school, our school clothes, books, and supplies.

I think I picked that cotton standing up, bending over, laying down and squatting. Boy, did my back and shoulders hurt!

Rumby and Shelby stayed in the house and helped Mama, but we knew that Rumby's day was coming, so we weren't jealous of him. Besides, I believe I'd rather have been picking cotton than staying at home, and Pap and Buddy felt the same way.

Saturday was my favorite day of the week. After we'd finish our chores, Buddy, Pap, and me would run the entire mile to Daddy Jim's. We always had a good time over there.

I loved to hear Daddy Jim play that big ol' Gibson guitar of his. He could draw a crowd picking "The Wildwood Flower."

But the music wasn't the main reason to go to Daddy Jim's; we mostly went to help him bottle his moonshine and hide it.

He'd make Willie Joe and Talmer hide in the back of the house, because if they saw where we hid the shine, they'd steal it and sell it for themselves, or either drink it.

When we'd finished, he'd give us a pint to sell for ourselves. We'd always go to the Courthouse in Hampton, and when we spotted one of Daddy Jim's customers, we'd meet them in the basement of the courthouse and sell it to them at a fifty-cent discount. Shoot, we'd still get two dollars, which was enough to get a loaf of bread, a wide slice of bologna and three RC colas from the Jitney Jungle store.

The Saturday matinee wasn't but ten cents each, so we'd go to the movies. They'd usually play Westerns on Saturdays. My favorite was "Hopalong Cassidy."

We always made sure we got back home in time to feed up everything and milk the cow.

Daddy didn't like the idea of us going to Daddy Jim's, but Mama told him that he couldn't just work us to death, that we had to have a little fun.

Daddy was a good man, but he believed in us working, for he worked all the time himself. When he wasn't working at the mill, he was doing something around the house or helping someone build a house or something. Daddy could build anything. He always had a variety of small tables, cabinets and such around the house for sale. He also worked on clocks, filed saws and barbered on Sundays. That man was always working.

Chapter 9

After living in Redtown for several months, Mama finally relented and said she would let us get to know the locals a little bit better, as long as we stayed together.

She still said they were all crazy, but at least they weren't snooty like the folks in Hampton were.

Redtown wasn't incorporated, so there wasn't city tax on things like there was in Hampton; therefore, things were cheaper. Mama did her grocery shopping there, such as it was. She seldom bought anything but the basics, like flour, sugar, tea and coffee.

Mama always bought her groceries at Mr. Pickett's grocery. He was a kind man and seemed to respect Mama for her outspoken ways.

She'd complain to him how high the prices were on just about everything that she'd be buying.

He'd just smile and say, "Yes Ma'am, they shore is."

I was scared of Mr. Pickett at first, because he had one regular shoe and the left foot had a small leather contraption on it. The sole of the left shoe was about four inches thick, so he always walked with a limp.

Next to Mr. Pickett's store was Pig Meat Malone's billiards and café, which was frequented by young folks in the daytime. At night, it was transformed into a juke joint.

We had to cross the tracks and go into Hampton to buy our school supplies at V. J. Elmore's department store. They carried several items other than pencils, such as paper, notebooks and color crayons. They also had toys, cheap clothing, a huge variety of candies. Best of all, Elmore's had a giant glass container that popped popcorn right before your eyes. It was a nickel a bag, and smelled so good. We grew our own popcorn though, so we never bought any.

There were a few more small establishments on the left side of the road.

On the other side of the street, I especially liked going to V. J. Elmore's on Saturday evenings when we'd make our excursions to town to sell our bottle of bootleg whiskey from Daddy Jim. Things weren't as they are now, so scattered out. Everything was downtown, so every Saturday night, the town was crowded with shoppers and sightseers.

Hampton's elementary school wasn't but a block from downtown, and unlike our little rundown red school, Hampton Elementary was a huge brick building with a fine playground area. The chains on those swings must've been thirty feet long, and once we got started it seemed we could swing almost as high as the tall pecan trees that provided shade in the spring and summer months.

We'd always take our bologna, bread, and RC Colas to the playground. There was seldom anyone else there, so we could eat and "swing up a storm" before the Saturday matinee came on.

On the right side of the road at Redtown was also a huge barn that was used as a livery stable. Mr. Lester operated it. He sold and swapped mules and horses. He was a midget, but he was a shrewd business man. He wasn't but about four feet tall, and he had jet-black hair that he plastered down the middle of his head with a thick oily hair tonic.

The nearest thing to Lester's barn was a pawn shop. It was owned and operated by two brothers, Slim and Leroy Parnell. They were two huge men who must've weighed five or six hundred pounds each. If you had an extra nickel, you could see the snake man, who stayed in the back of the pawn shop.

That was one hard earned nickel that I wished I'd kept in my pocket.

Pap and I gave Slim our nickels and he wobbled toward the back of the building, motioning for us to follow him.

There, sitting at the kitchen table eating, was the snake man. Every hair on my head must've stood straight up, and I would've run out of there if Pap hadn't been holding me by my arm.

The snake man acted as though we weren't even there; he kept eating and reading his paper that was lying on the table.

He was naked from his waist up, and sure enough, his skin was like scales on a fish or a snake. I remember looking at his toenails and they were thick and pointed, as were his fingernails.

I guess he got tired of us looking at him, because in about two minutes, he turned his face toward us and his eyes were red as fire. That was bad enough, but when he stuck his forked tongue out at us, I couldn't stand it any longer. I snatched loose from Pap's grasp and I ran. We could hear the sound of hysterical laugher following us as we dashed out of there; it was coming from the direction of the snake man.

To this day, that awful noise is one of the worst things I've ever heard in my life.

Toward the middle of town was Hughes' Mercantile. Like the others, it was painted that chalky red color on the outside, but unlike the other buildings I'd seen, it was painted inside and was very nice. It had ceiling fans and just about everything you needed in the clothing line. We bought most of our school clothing and shoes there.

The mercantile also sold a variety of tools, small musical instruments, and even tap dance shoes.

Mr. Hughes was normal, but I heard his wife was so big that she couldn't get out of the bed.

Mr. Reese, who operated the gas station, was a puzzlement to me. He was a small man with dark red hair. He always kept a big cigar in his mouth but he never lit it; instead, he'd gradually chew on it all day.

No matter what question you'd ask him the answer would always be, "Two," and he'd repeat the word "two" for about five times.

For instance, if you asked him how many children he had, he'd say, "Two, two, two, two, two." If you'd clap your hands and get a rhythm going, he could sing the proper answer. It was all very strange, but they said he could sing up a storm and play the steam out of a banjo. In time to come I found it to be true, for I heard him picking and singing some nights at Pig Meat Malone's juke joint.

Mr. Bowen, on the days that he wasn't walking backward, would sit with some other older men on what was called the "liars' bench." It was located on the porch of Mr. Hugh's store. I found that Mr. Bowen wasn't too friendly, but his little dog was very nice, and loved being scratched around his ears.

Black Boy, who was never farther than a few feet away

from us, wanted to play with Mr. Bowen's dog, but the man never would turn him loose from that leash.

I found Sarge, who directed the traffic, to be nothing but a gentle giant once you got him away from that intersection. He was all business when he stood in the street, though, for he took the job of directing the cars very seriously, even though very few of them ever came along.

Sarge's main occupation was selling pork meat, for he didn't get paid a dime from doing his traffic directing. He'd butcher his own hogs and either smoke them or salt them down so the meat wouldn't spoil. He had a small covered wagon that he'd push to town on Friday and Saturdays, loaded with meat.

Mama said she wouldn't buy a damn thing he had, but a lot of other folks did.

We learned that the lady who covered her body in dirt at the intersection was very nice. I think she just wanted attention, and bananas.

I also learned that she was called "Miss Minnie," and that she claimed she suffered from the pain of arthritis and the dirt was healing to her. She sure was friendly, and seemed to love talking to us. She wanted to know everything about us, but we were too sly for that. For all we knew, she could've been a spy or something, like we saw in the movies we paid for with our moonshine money. She sure didn't talk like the other folks in Redtown.

Of course Mama said the dirt in her own back yard would be just as stimulating, but I knew no one would see her there, and she wouldn't get the bananas that she must've craved.

Fellow townsmen knew how she loved bananas. Most times people would give her one or two, but one day someone stopped at the intersection, jumped out of a big long black car, and gave her a whole bunch of them. There must've been fifteen or twenty bananas in all.

She sat straight up out of that hole, and ate one of them. Then she got up, dusted herself off and, while no one was looking, she gave the rest of the bananas to Sarge, who quickly hid them in a brown paper sack. She then went toward her house.

Evidently she'd had enough bananas for that day, but not enough of the dirt, because she was right back in that hole the very next day.

Miss Minnie was very intellectual, too. She knew all about the history of the area. I soon learned from her that most of the people who lived in Redtown were former members of different carnivals. Their strange appearance made more sense after that.

I just marveled at the things she knew! If there was something I didn't understand in school and the weather wasn't too inclement for her to be in her hole, I'd run down to the intersection and she'd explain the problem to me.

Mama found out I was going down there pretty frequently, and she told me that the woman was crazy. She insisted I ought to stay away from down there, but I still went if I needed to know something. I never had any bananas to give Miss Minnie, though, and after witnessing the scene that day with Sarge, somehow I knew she wasn't there for the bananas. Why she was really there was a mystery to me. I didn't know, but I knew she was up to something. Maybe she was just lonely, but she didn't seem to mind it, and she was always very nice to me.

I was too young to know why she was in that hole, or why she seemed to treat me so well, but it wouldn't be long before

I found out—and what I learned about Miss Minnie would change a whole lot of what I knew about people in general, and about my own family in particular.

Chapter 10

I learned pretty early on that not all of the members of my family got treated the same. For some reason Mama was stricter on us, her own children, than she was on Sunshine. I guess she figured that the little girl caught enough hell at home from Big Mama.

Sunshine stayed with us a good bit of the time, but when she and Rumby started to school in 1952, she just moved in with us.

Big Mama's excuse was that we lived closer to the school. The situation suited us fine. Sunshine was just someone else to play with, as far as we were concerned.

Sunshine wasn't as feminine as Mama would have liked.

Mama loved to comb and fix Sunshine's light blonde hair in different ways, and would've kept her in the house with Shelby, but Sunshine wouldn't have it. She loved running and romping with us boys. She was tall for her six years, and very outspoken like Mama.

Sunshine and Rumby were in the same grade. Rumby was quiet and tranquil, so Sunshine had to jump in and help him defend himself in more than one scrap.

Word soon got out that Sunshine could out-run, out-fight, and out-cuss everybody else. She could knock a softball as far as any boy in their room, so things soon settled down and the bullies in their room left Rumby alone, because they all knew it wasn't worth tangling with Sunshine.

Willie Joe and Talmer never went to school a day in their lives. The truant officer threatened to send them to reformatory school. Daddy Jim told them that would be fine with him; go ahead and take them, that day.

Big Mama feigned one of her fainting spells and fell in the floor. After that, the truant officer would make an occasional visit, but nothing was ever carried out about them.

It was a shame, too, for I later learned that Talmer was

actually very intelligent.

Of course, when Rumby started to school, he had to join in with the chores, which he hated. He was slow, and would whine a lot until Mama came out there with the belt. Then he'd pick up some, but his heart just wasn't in it.

Sunshine didn't seem to mind the hoeing and other manual labor at all. Mama didn't like the idea of it, but she finally gave up and just let her run with me and Pap.

"As long as y'all stay together," she said.

It seemed that Buddy was born with a greater knowledge of things than the rest of us. He was quiet and level-headed, while Pap and I were quick to judge and just wanted to get away from the house and experience different things. If I really wanted to know the right thing to do about something that was troubling me, I'd go see Buddy. He always told me the right thing to do, especially if it was something going on at school.

If I'd listened to Mama, I would've wound up in the penitentiary in the first grade.

She'd tell us if there was more than one of the bullies, or if they were older than us, to cut the hell out of them with our knives. We all carried pocket knives and kept them so sharp they'd shave the hair off your leg. As I've stated earlier, we walked to and from school, which gave time for the bigger boys to make us their target.

Two brothers named W.C. and Frankie walked with us every day. W.C. must've been on up in high school, and Frankie was in my room.

W.C. would goad Frankie into fighting one of us each day, and we'd take turns whipping poor old Frankie, but every day it was the same thing. W.C. dared Frankie to jump on Rumby one day, so naturally Sunshine and I jumped in and helped Rumby out, because he wouldn't even try to defend himself.

I didn't hit Frankie that day, but I grabbed his arms, giving Rumby time to hit him, but he never would.

Finally Sunshine got tired of the hassle. She popped Frankie in the mouth a good one with her fist, and drew blood. When Frankie managed to get off the ground, he ran toward his house; they didn't live too far from the school.

W.C. meant to get even, so he found a big limb lying in the ditch and struck Shelby across the back with it, knocking her down.

Pap went into action so fast that I could hardly keep up with him. He pulled that razor-sharp knife out of his pocket and swung it at W.C., cutting him across the side of his neck.

Blood flew and so did W.C., but not before Pap told him as he turned to run away, that if he mentioned what happened, he was going to get him good the next time.

From that day forward we weren't bothered with W.C. and Frankie.

I just imagine that W.C. was too ashamed to let anyone know that a fourth-grader had bested him. The embarrassment and the fear of retaliation kept him away after that, because he had learned that if you fought one of us you had all of us to fight. We never heard another word about it.

Chapter 11

The fourth grade was rough. The teacher's name was Miss Rumbling, and she was a holy terror. She dressed like women did at the turn of the century. She wore long-sleeved dresses that swept the floor, and when you could see them, she wore tight-fitting black high-topped shoes. Her shoes didn't have holes for the laces, but little metal eyelets that the laces zigzagged through.

She had a big purple wart on the end of her tongue, and she'd sit at her teacher's desk in the front of the room, just staring at all of us like she was daring us to act out. She had a nasty habit of running that warty tongue in and out of her mouth. It gave me the cold chills, and I was scared to death of her. She looked just like a witch on Hallloween to us kids, and treated us about as bad.

Pap wasn't scared of her, though. He only went to school because he had to, and I guess he figured while he was there, he might as well go ahead and make a good time of it, so he did.

I actually think Miss Rumbling was scared of his temper and strong will, so she just let him slide by as the other teachers had in the past. It was something that I never understood; Pap was very intelligent, but he just didn't like school.

The first thing we did every morning was that all the boys had to line up at a water faucet that was just outside the door. We each had to drink a full pint of water before class, then as we entered the room Miss Rumbling inspected our teeth. Of course, none of us ever passed that to her satisfaction, so we had to hold out our hands and she'd give us a rap across our knuckles with one of those big green pencils.

She separated the boys from the girls. The boys were on one side of the room, and the girls were on the other. The girls never had to drink that water and their teeth were never inspected.

Miss Rumbling was a tall, frail-looking woman, but she had a big wide rump. When she'd sit at her desk, she'd just fall into her chair, sometimes jarring the whole room.

One morning on our walk to school, we found a small box of long thin nails. They were so sharp they looked almost like needles.

Each day at play period, Miss Rumbling would pull out a sharp pocketknife from her black purse and peel an apple. She'd peel that apple so thin, and she'd never break the peeling. It always came off in one long, perfect curl, and she would stick her ugly, warty tongue out of her mouth to concentrate while she peeled that apple.

She never sat with the other teachers. She'd try to find some shade, and would hold a newspaper over her head to block the sun from her pale face.

Well, the day that we found the sharp nails, while Miss Rumbling was concentrating on peeling that apple during recess, Pap and I sneaked into our classroom and pushed about a dozen of those nails up through the cushion in her chair, making sure that the sharp points weren't sticking up high enough to be visible from the top of the seat. Then we sneaked back out and rejoined the rest of the boys on the playground.

I had mixed emotions about what we had done. I was scared, yet anxious with anticipation. Pap could hardly wait until play period was over; he wanted to see some results.

Miss Rumbling finally yelled in her shrill, high-pitched witchy voice that it was time for us to come in.

As usual, she went before us, so that she and the girls could inspect our hands and fingernails as we entered the room.

She should have known that something was up because Pap was first in line, which was very unusual.

After the hand inspection she stood by her desk until everyone was seated, then as usual she plopped down into that chair.

She shot up like a rocket, knocking the heavy oaken desk over with her knees.

When she ran out that door, the cushion was still stuck to her big old behind with those sharp nails, and she was hollering for dear life.

We all just looked at one another in bewilderment. I

know Pap was dying to laugh, but it would've been a sure giveaway, so he opened a book and put it in front of his face.

It didn't take but a few minutes before we heard Mr. Fraily, the principal, come stomping down the hall. He was a small man, but you could hear him all over that school when he walked.

He came straight to our room and snatched the door open.

He had a thunderous voice to be so little a man. He asked all the girls to leave the room and go outside until they were called back in.

Some of the girls left the room actually crying their eyeballs out, not only because of Miss Rumbling's plight, for they really didn't know what had happened, but because of the principal's loud frightening voice.

After the room was cleared of all the girls, the principal started in on us.

"Alright, I have a pretty good idea who did this . . . this . . ."

There was a long pause as if he was trying to think of the proper word to say that would be appropriate for a room full of schoolboys.

He finally said, ". . . who did this dastardly thing to poor Miss Rumbling. Why, right now the coach is taking her across the tracks to a doctor for a lock-jaw shot."

"What happened to Miss Rumbling?" Donnie Jones asked.

"Shut up, you little heathen!" the principal screamed.

"Yes Sir," Donnie said, shrinking down in his seat.

"I'll tell you how I'm going to handle this," Mr. Fraily told us. "I want each and every one of you boys to line up outside. You're going to come in this room one at a time."

Then he reached down and turned Miss Rumbling's desk back upright, and placed a piece of paper and a pencil on top of the desk.

"I'm going to give each student thirty seconds alone in here to write on this piece of paper the name of the person who stuck those nails in Miss Rumbling's chair cushion. As for the culprit, if you go ahead and own up to it, you'll just be expelled from school, but if you don't confess, when I find out later who did this thing, you will be beaten, expelled, and possibly criminally charged!"

There were two brothers in my room, Roy and Rudy Ru-

dolf. They claimed to be twins, but I always thought there
was something strange with the two, because they looked
nothing alike. Roy was a little frail blonde, very small for his
age, and the family was very poor. Roy and Rudy wore the
same clothes day after day, and never brought anything to
eat for lunch. Surprisingly, Roy was very bright and made
good grades in school. If I had any extra food left over from
my brown paper bag dinner, I'd always offer it to him, but he
never would accept it.

Rudy, on the other hand, was fully developed. He stood
as tall as a man, and was already sporting a thick black beard.
Rudy was as dumb as a rock, and stank profusely from under
his arms.

Well, we all lined up outside the classroom, and Mr. Fraily gave each of us a shove toward that piece of paper on Miss
Rumbling's desk as we entered the room.

There were sixteen of us boys, so it didn't take long.

I was toward the end of the line. When Fraily gave me
a swift shove in there, as I approached the desk, I could see
that clearly scribbled on the sheet of paper were the words
RUDY RUDOLF.

71

When I saw the name on the paper, all I could imagine was that Rudy was ready to leave school, and he must have figured this was a good opportunity for him.

Mr. Fraily's white face turned beet red when he saw the name on the paper.

He walked over to Rudy and grabbed him by one of his arms.

Rudy, who was clearly bigger in size than Mr. Fraily and much more muscular, pulled loose from him.

Fraily tried it again, and Rudy drew back his fist, causing the principal to turn him loose a second time.

"Come with me to the office, you low-life," Fraily hissed. He was so mad he was shaking.

With more intelligence than I'd ever heard him say in a sentence, Rudy spoke his answer loud and clear.

"Principal, you must be some kind of crazy. You don't want me in that office. I'm going home, where I belong."

Very slowly Rudy walked out the door, and I never saw him at school again.

Roy knew that Rudy didn't do the deed, but I think he knew that school just wasn't the thing for Rudy, and he understood his brother was glad to just be through with it.

I actually felt bad about the whole affair until the principal, who was forced to sit in for Miss Rumbling for the last couple of hours that day, sent Pap and me to the cloak room for the rest of the day for nothing at all. (I think he had a strong suspicion we were the ones that did the deed.)

Well, we started a ritual that day in retaliation.

Miss Rumbling had been saving Time Magazines for years. She'd often sit at her desk and read them while we did our work. There were just stacks and stacks of them in that cloak room.

When the principal made us go to the cloak room the day Rudy took his shot at freedom, me and Pap pulled out our "tally whackers" and peed all over those magazines. It wasn't hard to do, either, after drinking that pint of water in the morning.

I remember one of the magazines on top of the stack had a picture on the front that showed the coronation of Queen Elizabeth.

I couldn't help but laugh to myself, thinking the Queen really got coronated that day.

When the bell rang to signal the end of the day, Principal Fraily didn't even bother to let us know it was time to go home.

We could hardly wait until the next day to see if Miss Rumbling was going to show up, but we found out as soon as we entered our room. She was standing by the shelf to hand out the fruit jars to the boys so we could get our drinks as usual.

After we drank our water and had our teeth inspected, we were told to sit at our assigned desks.

I noticed that Miss Rumbling limped to her desk and turned the cushion over two or three times, inspecting it carefully before she finally seated herself gingerly in the chair.

I noticed that not only Rudy wasn't present but Roy was absent also.

And that was the last day Miss Rumbling ever plopped down in her chair so hard it shook the floorboards.

Chapter 12

While we were out of school for Christmas holidays in 1953, Mr. Reese's two oldest daughters disappeared.

Sheriff Watson came from across the tracks and snooped around a little after he'd talked to Mr. and Mrs. Reese, but nothing ever came of it.

The Sheriff had a tough time finding out any kind of information from Mr. and Mrs. Reese. Mr. Reese had his stammering problem and Mrs. Reese seemed simple minded.

It was very strange to hear of the disappearance. Two of the Reese girls were in my class, a set of twins named Sula and Zula.

All of the Reese girls were very bright. They sure were

pretty, too. Both Sula and Zula had long red hair, as did all of the sisters.

Of all the people who took the disappearance of the girls most seriously, it was Sarge that seemed bothered by it the most.

In fact, he took it so seriously that it actually pulled him away from the intersection a few hours of the day, a thing none of us had ever seen him allow before.

Unbeknownst to Mama, of course, he even took me, Pap and Sunshine with him on some of his excursions around the area to help him search for the missing girls.

We really learned a lot about the locale as we searched. We found a nice clear-water creek that would make a good swimming hole in the summertime, if we could only find time in the summer to go swimming. We had plenty of free time in the winter months, but from spring until fall, we worked.

We never found hide nor hair of the girls on any of our searches, but we did discover just about every thorn on the brambles and bushes, though.

One day Sarge even took us out to his place.

He lived in a big rambling ranch-style house that must've

been a hundred years old.

Hogs and chickens were running everywhere, except the chickens were in the yard and fields, making sure to keep their distance from the hogs, as the birds knew the hogs would make a fine snack of them if they were foolish enough to get too close.

The fat hogs of all sizes were fenced into a pen that had been constructed around two buildings. One was a big two-story barn where Sarge stored the corn for the hogs and chickens, and the other building was the slaughtering house. The slaughtering house had a huge padlock on the door, and was make of concrete blocks.

The barn had a wide breezeway that ran down the middle of it, with gates on the front to keep the hogs out. This meant it was a pretty safe place for the chickens, so they would climb the ladder of that barn and lay eggs up there in the hay.

Sarge gave us a cardboard box, and told us to help ourselves to the eggs. We stopped counting at four dozen. The problem would be explaining all those eggs to Mama, without letting on that we had gone to Sarge's house.

Along with the free eggs he gave us, Sarge even invited us into his house for some lemonade. He chiseled some of the ice from the block in his ice box, making the drinks good and cold. This was a delight to us, for ice at our house was used strictly to keep things cool in our ice box, with none to waste on luxuries like iced drinks.

I marveled at the spacious rooms in the house, all of which were just packed with old things. From the quality of the belongings, evidently his folks must've had money.

It didn't take me long to learn, though, that Sarge was a little slow and he was just a lonely old man.

To our surprise, when we carried all the eggs home and Mama questioned us about them, she didn't get mad when she found out where we had been. In fact, she told us to go to the intersection the next day and invite Sarge to Sunday dinner. However, she told us to never go back to his place, or anywhere else in town, unless we were together.

Little did we know what had made Mama change her mind about Sarge.

There was a big Chinaberry tree at the very back of the property that we rented.

Through the weeknights, Pig Meat just usually had a rockola going, but on Saturday nights he had a live band with singers and boy, could they put it on.

The piano player was a big black greasy looking man, who always smoked a cigar with a gold band on it. He could do everything but make that piano stand up and walk, while the saxophone player make his horn talk.

I don't know who the big lady was that did the singing, but she could sure belt out the songs and get the crowd on the dance floor.

I'm not sure the names of the songs are the correct titles, but I loved to hear her sing what we knew as the "Jelly Roll Blues," "Dark Town Strutter's Ball," and "Bing, Bang, Boom." Oh, she was good.

Mama and Daddy went to bed with the chickens, so on Saturday nights; me, Pap, and Sunshine would slip out the window (after we heard Daddy snoring), and down to that Chinaberry tree we'd go, to enjoy the spectacle taking place at Pig Meat Malone's juke joint.

Pig Meat had the bottom windows painted black, so we'd have to shimmy pretty high up into that tree before we could see what was going on in there.

Occasionally we could hear gunshots being fired inside. When the shooting started, we could slide down that tree a lot quicker than we went up it.

The law from Hampton never was called unless someone was killed. Redtown was its own place, all in itself, and folks from there preferred to handle their own business whenever possible.

Pap heard those musical instruments being played at Pig Meat's—the guitars and banjos and piano—and oh, how he yearned to play an instrument himself!

Daddy did his best, even though he couldn't afford much. First, he made Pap a flute from a bamboo reed, and Pap quickly mastered the few notes on it. Seeing he was serious and had some talent, Daddy then bought him a harmonica, and Pap was playing "Wabash Cannonball," "Lost John," and several other tunes in no time at all. I mean, he was good at it! He impressed all of us with his musical abilities, even on such simple instruments as the homemade flute and the harmonica.

We all knew Pap would really shine if he ever got his

hands on better instruments, but none of us suspected how soon his dream would come true—or from what unlikely source the instruments would come.

REDTOWN: A NOVEL BY L.E. GULLEY

Chapter 13

The Sunday that Sarge showed up for dinner, he was wearing a tight-fitting blue suit, and he was carrying a banjo and a Gibson guitar. He was also sporting a big toothy grin when he presented the two musical instruments to an overjoyed Pap, and said "Son, these old things was just settin' round the house, and I thought you might could get some good use out of 'em."

I thought Pap was going to faint; he was dumbfounded, and was stuttering near as badly as Mr. Reese.

Finally he managed to say "Thank you, Mr. Sarge."

Daddy, who very seldom smiled about anything, had a wide grin on his face and I could have sworn I saw a tear in his eye, something I'd never seen.

I could tell Sarge had dressed for the occasion, and Mama had put on one of her nicest dresses. She didn't have many, but what she did have was quality. She would scrimp and save to be able to afford the things she wanted, and her choices showed good taste.

Daddy wore khaki pants and shirts seven days a week, and Mama always made sure they were starched and ironed. That Sunday was no exception; he wore the same thing he always wore, on the day that Sarge came.

Mama had been cooking all morning. We had a long, wide wooden table and eight wooden chairs that Daddy had built himself, and Mama had that table loaded with food—mostly vegetables. Daddy had slaughtered a couple of chickens early that morning, and the huge platter of fried chicken was our only meat. At one end of the table was a plate of buttermilk biscuits, and at the other end was a hoecake of cornbread, made from fresh ground corn. There were two desserts: egg custard pie and a huge coconut cake, in the center of the table.

There was even chipped ice in a dish pan for sweet tea.

We never went to church. There were two kinds of people that Daddy never trusted, and that was preachers and doctors. I always thought it was strange, because he never cussed, and he was raised in church.

Mama had a big thick Bible that she read occasionally, even though she could let them cuss words fly with the best of them if you made her mad.

I remember every time I would open that Bible it would open to the same page, and it would be a frightening picture of a ragged looking man begging for something. That picture would scare the wits out of me, so I quit opening the Bible after awhile.

Anyway, Mama had a standing rule at our house: the food was always blessed on Sundays and on Christmas Day. Mama always said the blessing. She sat at one end of the table, and Daddy was at the other.

We all knew to be on our best behavior since Sarge was eating dinner with us that day, but yet and still, Mama made sure to give us all that "stare down" that only she could do. I reckon she wanted to make sure we wouldn't embarrass her, or ourselves. At any rate, we just focused on our food, and once Sarge started in on his, it was a good thing, too.

Daddy never ate much. Mama knew what he liked, so she'd always fix his plate and set it before him, but he'd always make sure we'd all start eating before he'd start.

She had Shelby putting ice in the glasses and pouring the tea for everyone, making sure to set each glass on the left side of their plate.

Sarge's hands were the size of two big hams, and he had a huge appetite to go with them. I'd never seen anyone wolf down so much food in my life!

Mama had made brown flour gravy from the fried chicken crumbs to go on the mashed potatoes. Sarge poured a generous helping of the gravy over four biscuits and a pile of creamed potatoes on his plate. He had gravy dripping off his dark blue tie, but he didn't seem to notice, or if he did, he didn't seem to mind it. He just kept on eating, and whenever he came up for air he would keep complimenting Mama on everything she cooked. Then he'd take another piece of chicken.

For supper on Sundays we usually had the leftovers from Sunday dinner, but all I saw left over when Sarge was done, was a little piece of corn bread and two old scrawny chicken necks. I swear I don't know where he put it, but he finished up with some of the egg custard and the coconut cake, both.

After dinner, Sarge stood up, let out a thunderous belch, and then wiped the gravy from his tie with the sleeve of his coat. Again, he thanked Mama for the meal.

Mama, Shelby, and Sunshine stayed in the kitchen to clear away the table, while the rest of us went into the living room.

For some reason Daddy never sat in a chair; he'd always squat and lean his back against the wall. I figured he might make an exception for company, but sure enough, when we all went into the living room he just squatted down in his usual spot.

Sarge remarked to Daddy that if he squatted like that, he'd never be able to get back up.

Daddy never was a conversationalist, so about all he did was grunt and smile at Sarge.

Pap couldn't wait to get hold of that banjo and guitar, so he started strumming on the banjo right away. He knew that Daddy wouldn't say anything to him about playing it indoors. But just as he got going pretty good on it, Mama stuck her head through the kitchen door and said, "Take that thing outside!"

We didn't have any fancy furniture in the living room. There were two big wooden rockers, some straight-backed chairs, and a couple of small tables in the corners of the room. Daddy had made them all.

There was one thing that he didn't make, though, and that was a huge, ornate wooden radio. It must've been four feet tall. It was powered by a great big battery, with an antenna outside. The radio was only turned on early in the mornings to hear the local news, and on Saturday nights to listen to the Grand Old Opry on WSM. (Daddy and Mama liked it, but I personally couldn't wait until it went off so I could climb that tree and eavesdrop on what was going on at Pig Meat's; in my opinion, the music from the juke joint was a whole lot better.)

When she was finished cleaning up, Mama joined us in the living room. Sarge had claimed one rocker, and Mama seated herself in the other one.

It didn't take long for the conversation to turn to the

missing girls.

"Them gals ain't missing; I believe they left from heah of they own accord. I've looked high and low, and if they was anywhere around heah, I would've found 'em," Sarge said.

Then he looked down in his lap and sort of mumbled, "You know them gals didn't have too good of a reputation round heah. They was pretty tough."

About that time, Sunshine and Shelby had made it into the living room. Mama cleared her throat instead of answering, even though she obviously had plenty of her own thoughts about it. She wanted to let Sarge know it wasn't a good time to say anything else on the subject in front of her girls.

I could tell that Daddy felt out of place and wished that he was in his shop working, but I also noticed that Daddy's interest perked up when Sarge mentioned he owned a hundred and twenty acres of land that adjoined his house.

Sarge told us that he rented the land out to a farmer for just enough corn to feed his hogs and chickens.

We children didn't know it at the time, but Daddy had gotten a promotion at work. He had been made a supervisor over all the people who ran the machines, saws, and so on, and he was saving money to buy a small piece of farm land and build us a house.

Now, as I've stated before, Daddy hardly ever talked to us at all unless it was pertaining to work, or occasionally reading to us. Mama had always talked to us as adults, so she wasn't used to sticking to simple subjects. Therefore, her conversation with Sarge was very limited.

In fact, I don't think he understood very much of what she talked about. It became clear pretty quickly that he was a simple-minded man, to say the least.

Finally, she just gave up, but I could tell that she liked and felt sorry for him.

About all that Sarge talked about was his short stint in the Army. He said he fired the boilers to keep the soldiers warm. The more he talked of his Army experiences, the more he'd guffaw and the harder he'd rock in that rocker.

Mama, who looked for her rocker to pop any second, and knew that Daddy wanted to go outside, excused herself and went into the kitchen.

In just a jiffy she returned with a shoe box that contained

some fried chicken, an egg custard pie, and a piece of coconut cake that she had put aside. She must've prepared it for him during the dinner, and just not said anything, because I knew there weren't any leftovers on that table when we all got done eating.

After opening the box and seeing what was inside, Sarge didn't tarry. He shot up from that rocker like a bullet, making excuses to go home before it rained; even though we all knew there wasn't a cloud in the sky.

Daddy managed to tell Sarge on his way out the door, that when Sarge had more time, he'd like to talk to him about buying a piece of his land.

Sarge only paused for a second, just long enough to say, "Sure, Mr. Charles, you and your Madame come out and pick out a piece. I'd love to have those chilrun' near. 'Course, land is high," he finished, as he pulled the door to, all the time keeping a sure grip on that shoe box full of fried chicken and sweets. It was obvious he didn't eat like that every day.

As it turned out, Mama had made another pan of corn bread earlier that day. Supper that night was slim pickings for the family, with just corn bread and a few odds and ends, but not a one of us begrudged Sarge a mouthful, and nobody ever said another word about it.

Chapter 14

There were five rooms in the old house that we rented: three bedrooms, a kitchen and a living room.

There was a large pantry in the kitchen that Mama stored her canned goods. One of Mama's prized possessions was a white china cabinet, complete with two drawers and two glass doors up top and two wooden doors on the bottom. Daddy built it and gave it to her one Christmas. She painted it white and had even painted small red roses, complete with tiny green vines, on the two glass doors.

She dared any of us to even touch that china cabinet, so we made good and sure we walked around it when she was in the kitchen.

Two beds were in each bedroom, and two of us slept in each bed. I slept with Rumby, and Buddy and Pap slept right next to us in their bed. Shelby and Sunshine slept in the next room. Mama and Daddy slept next to the kitchen in separate beds. She said she couldn't share a bed with Daddy on account of his long toenails that shredded her sheets, and she was telling the truth, because all of his sheets that were hung on the line were just cut to pieces on one end.

We survived the winter month of December. We didn't get much for Christmas, just a little fruit and some hard candy. Daddy was saving to buy that land. Of course, we never got much anyway. Sometimes, though, Daddy would get us boys firecrackers, which Black Boy hated. Whenever we set them off, he'd run and hide under the house.

You can leave it up to a bunch of kids to come up with ways to entertain themselves, and we had a special use for those firecrackers. The bottom of our outdoor toilet had a board missing in the rear, and if we caught someone in there, we'd light the fuses on the firecrackers and throw 'em in with all the waste. And whoever was unlucky enough to be inside at the time, it took more than a few pages from the Sears and Roebuck catalogue to clean their behind, once those firecrackers blew.

Maybe it was Mama that put the skids on Daddy buying us those firecrackers. Every one of us kids knew better than to go running to Mama if we got picked on, because the hell she'd raise on us would be way worse than anything we could dish out to one another, but she must have found out about it in that curious way mothers have of knowing exactly what her children are up to. Anyway, there were no firecrackers for us that year at Christmas.

Pap liked to have driven us all crazy with that guitar and banjo, especially the banjo. Mama finally took it away from him and locked it up in the cedar chifforobe.

He was also learning a few chords on that guitar, though, and that was easier for everybody to put up with.

I sent him down to see Miss Minnie, when the weather was allowable. I told him she knew a whole lot about music. She could even pick songs like "The Wild Wood Flower," and "Chicken in the Bread Pan Picking Out Dough," so she taught Pap some simple chords, and by April he was picking and I was singing.

Meanwhile, for the rest of that year, we just tried to keep up with our schoolwork, and kept on peeing on them magazines.

When school was let out that May, Pap and I found ourselves a lucrative business when we were through with the gardening and hoeing for the day.

Somehow or other, Pap found out the snake man loved to eat rattlesnakes, and that he would pay fifty cents for one that was four feet long or longer. So we found some gall berry bushes that had forks on them, with stalks would be about five feet long. We'd cut them forks down to about two inches, just high enough so the snake couldn't get his head through when we pinned it to the ground. Once we pinned the snake's head, we'd pick it up by the tail and put it in a thick burlap bag.

We scraped up a dime to buy a quart jug of gasoline from Mr. Reese.

When Pap told him what we wanted, instead of telling us how much it cost, or passing the time of day with us like most shop keepers, as usual Mr. Reese just smiled at us and said, "Two, two, two."

So we handed him the dime and the jug, and he filled it up.

It was sort of brushy looking toward Sarge's house, so we went in that direction, plundering around under the bushes until we found a likely spot. There were two pretty good-sized holes in the ground, so we poured about a pint of gasoline into each hole. Sure enough, four big rattlers came out of the same hole.

That gas must've stunned them or something, because when they came out of that hole, they didn't try to bite us. Instead, they coiled up on the ground and started rattling, giving us plenty of time to jab those forks behind their heads and separate them before we dropped them into that sack.

For some reason, the snake man didn't want the snakes dead, which would have been much less dangerous for us.

We dealt strictly with Leroy or Slim. We had no desire to see what the snake man did to those snakes once he got ahold of them, or even to see him again, for that matter.

Slim and Leroy were surprised at the number and size of the snakes. After emptying the snakes into an empty garbage can and putting the lid on quick, they told us that they couldn't handle but four snakes a week.

I quickly figured it up to be two dollars. When Leroy only gave Pap a folded dollar, he turned to walk away.

"No sir, Mr. Leroy, you owe us another dollar," I said.

"Didn't I give your brother two?" he asked.

"No sir, you gave him one folded dollar," I insisted, and Pap showed it to him.

Leroy acted all surprised. "Well, do tell! My bad, my bad," said the fat man as he reached into his pocket and peeled off another dollar from a roll of money stuffed in his front pocket.

Boy, we were stepping high when we left that pawn shop and headed toward Pickett's Store. We had never had a whole dollar of our own to spend as we liked.

"What you going to get with yo' money?" Pap asked.

"I'm gonna get me an RC cola and a moon pie, which will cost a dime. I saw that Miss Minnie was in her hole, so I'm gonna buy her a dime's worth of bananas. She's been so good to us, and the other eighty cents I'm giving to you, to start saving up for that saxophone you've been eyeballing at Mr. Hughes' store. Shoot, that thing has been setting in that showcase so long he's done marked her down to nineteen ninety-five."

"Yeah, but it's still in that box, and it still shines like gold," Pap said.

Pap just bought him a chocolate moon pie and an RC, then he gave me his ninety cents and asked me to keep up with all the money for both of us.

I agreed, and then told him the result of my mental arithmetic. "Well, the way I figure it, less moon pies, RC's, gas, a few bananas, and tax, in order to get you that horn, we're gonna need about forty-four more rattle snakes."

REDTOWN: A NOVEL BY L.E. GULLEY

Chapter 15

When we stopped by Miss Minnie's, we noticed that a strange woman had walked up and was conversing with her. The woman was wearing a colorful long dress that swept the ground, she had a scarf around her head and the bottom part of her face, and of all things, a small monkey was perched on top of her head.

It was a good thing we made Black Boy stay at home, for he would have had a field day with that monkey.

That strange-looking woman was talking in some kind of broken English, and when I handed Miss Minnie the bananas, that monkey sailed from the top of that woman's head and landed straight on top of the bananas in Miss Minnie's hands.

She jumped up out of that hole and popped that monkey a good one.

Dust was flying, and that monkey was screaming. The strange woman forgot all about her fancy accent, and was cussing up a storm.

Sarge left his post at the intersection, came over, and blew his whistle long and hard. It was so deafening the poor monkey couldn't stand the noise, and apparently the lady couldn't either, because she left with her monkey cradled in her arms like it was a baby.

Miss Minnie thanked the Sarge for his efforts, and then she thanked us for the bananas. It was getting pretty late in the evening, so she started shoving the dirt back into her hole, to go home.

We hid our snake poles and the canvas sack in some tall weeds before we got home.

Boy, did Mama raise hell when she laid eyes on us!

"Where the hell have you two been? You both smell like billy goats! Go into the kitchen and wash that stinking scent off you, and then go milk the cow.

"Your Daddy has got Buddy working in the garden, where

you two are supposed to be too. I have an order for milk in one hour, so jump to it," she snapped, as she gave us a shove toward the kitchen.

I never noticed the strong odor until Mama mentioned it, but we both washed our hands and arms and headed toward the milk shed.

"Mama's bound to find out about those rattlesnakes sooner or later," Pap said.

"Maybe not. All we have to do is find us eleven more holes like we did today, and you'll have that saxophone," I told him.

"What we going to do if she finds out about it?" Pap asked.

"We tell her the truth," I said.

We'd stretched the truth with Daddy a few times, but never with Mama. We knew she'd be sure to give us one of them Willie Joe and Talmer whoopings.

Bossy the cow was already at the stall ready to be milked and to eat the sweet feed grain that she loved so well. We didn't talk any more about our side business or the saxophone; we just got to the job at hand. Neither of us wanted to find out what would happen if Mama didn't have the milk to deliver to her customer on time.

Daddy had recently sold Bossy's calf, which was a good sized steer by the time Daddy sold him. Rumby cried as they loaded the steer up, because he loved it like a pet, but Daddy said letting it go would sure cut down on the corn we needed to feed the animals.

Daddy also built a smokehouse that summer, for the smoking of the hogs that we would slaughter when winter came.

Things went on pretty much as usual until June 15th rolled around. That was the day I turned nine years old, and a miracle happened on my birthday.

Daddy rented a wagon from Mr. Lester, and we all loaded up and went out to Sarge's place. It was on a Wednesday afternoon, but there was still plenty of daylight left.

Sarge had agreed to sell Daddy five acres of land for five hundred dollars, and Daddy had the cash.

The location was right at the corner of where Sarge's land began. The land hadn't been farmed in years, so it was overgrown with small pine saplings and underbrush.

That's just what me and Pap had been waiting for, because Slim and Leroy wanted some more rattlesnakes for the snake man.

Sarge already had the place fenced off; it was old wire, but still good, and there was even an old barn in the rear with a shed on each side, one for Pete the mule and the other for Bossy the cow.

Daddy made his way through the briars and brambles and inspected the barn. He said that with a few boards and about three pieces of tin, it would be in good shape.

Sarge waited at the wagon with Mama. When Daddy and us boys came back, he told Sarge that he'd knock off early from work the next day and meet him at the courthouse at three o'clock to sign the paperwork. They shook hands, and we left to go home.

Us children didn't realize the significance of the transaction. We'd never seen Mama or Daddy show any kind of emotion toward one another. Lord knows we would have fainted and fell out if we saw them hug or kiss.

They each were devoted to their job. Mama's work was the running of the household, and Daddy's responsibility was providing a living.

All me and Pap could think about was all them rattle-snakes that were probably hidden under those bushes.

I punched Pap in the ribs as I saw Mama slide her arm around Daddy on our ride back to Redtown. The sight of Daddy actually being able to buy his own land was a wonderment enough, but seeing Mama show him open affection like that just put it over the top. It was a special day, for sure, and a good one.

The ever faithful old Bossy was waiting by the milking stable when we made it home.

Daddy sent Buddy back to Mr. Lester's to return the wagon and, of course, Pap got on one side of Bossy and me the other. It made the process a whole lot quicker if we milked her together.

Black Boy's biggest treat of the day was when we milked Bossy. We'd always turn a teat his way so he got a good squirt of fresh milk, and boy did he love it. He always showed right up at milking time, and he made sure not to miss a drop, because he always licked his muzzle clean.

We hadn't made it in the house too long with the milk

before Buddy walked in.

Sunshine, who was all legs and arms, was useless in the kitchen, so she was sitting on the floor worrying Daddy as he was trying to read something by lamplight.

Surprisingly, Daddy was a man of few words but he had the patience of Job. If it was raining outside and we couldn't work, he would sometimes sit and read to us for hours.

Daddy was a well-read man; what idle few minutes he had, you could always find him reading.

I loved to hear him read aloud, particularly from Robinson Crusoe and Treasure Island. I think his favorites were Moby Dick and Gone With the Wind.

I think Mama liked to hear him read, too, for she'd always sit in her rocker and start mending clothes while he read.

It didn't take long for Mama and Shelby to whip up a quick supper. She had most of what we ate canned in quart jars in the big pantry. The fish man came by once in a while, and she'd spend some of her milk money and would even preserve fish.

The canned fish sure was good, poured over rice or to

just eat with biscuits.

That night Mama was so happy about the land, that she served us both.

Chapter 16

Sarge met Daddy at the courthouse and signed the deed. Daddy paid him off in hundred-dollar bills. They didn't linger once the deed was done, for Sarge was in a hurry to get back to the intersection.

He told Daddy he'd spotted a strange green car that morning that kept driving up and down the muddy road. What with the missing girls and all, Sarge's normal suspicious nature was on high alert. He didn't want to miss any evidence, so as soon as they walked back outside, he was on his way.

Daddy had the deed recorded while he was in the court-house, and when he came back to the house he seemed to have a spring in his step. For the first time in our lives, we saw Mama hug his neck, and I'll swear I believe to this day I saw a tear in her eye, which she quickly wiped away with her apron. Mama wasn't the sort to ever shed a tear, no matter what.

I actually didn't faint and fall out as I had predicted; instead, I felt a warm glow in my heart that I still remember to this day.

Of course us children didn't realize the extent of the big deal about the whole affair, but it was the first piece of land they had ever owned, and until their dying day it was home to us children, a place of refuge to come home to.

That night over the dinner table, everything about the coming move to the new land was planned to the last detail. Buddy was to stay home and finish laying the crops by, and keep an eye on things around the old house. Pap and I were to take two bush axes and start clearing away the land.

Daddy told us to wear our rubber boots in case of snakes. Pap and I looked at each other when he said it, and we were both trying not to let on that we were hoping to find the snakes on purpose instead of trying not to run into any. Daddy didn't notice a thing, though. He just went on and told us to pile the brush in heaps, but not to dare burn it until he was there.

We both just murmured, "Yes, sir" and went on with our eating, trying our best to act normal. Even Mama was so caught up in the excitement over the move to the new land that she didn't seem to catch on that we were up to anything; on a normal day, she didn't miss a trick.

Sunshine put in wanting to go with me and Pap.

"Don't be foolish!" Mama told her sharply. "Whoever heard of a little girl your age out there that far out of town? You can stay here and cut out paper dolls."

"Paper dolls? I'd just as soon gag myself," Sunshine scoffed.

"Well then, Miss Prissy, you can do the churning for me," Mama answered her right back.

Sunshine sulked and ran over to Daddy, hoping to get solace from him, but all he did was just pat her on the back. Then he looked up at her and said, "You know something, Sunshine, you're the prettiest little girl I've ever seen, to have such a mean old gruff-looking face on you."

That was all it took for her. She couldn't help but slowly grin, even though it made her mad to do so.

Daddy just had that knack with children.

Nobody had to run me and Pap from home the next morning. Daddy had those bush axes razor sharp, and before the dew dried we got our jug, snake poles and sack, then hit the road.

Mr. Reese was just opening up. He started clapping his hands and stomping his feet, and to the tune of "Mary Had a Little lamb," he sang "Where you boys going with them axes?"

I never understood why he couldn't talk like normal folks, but was clear as a bell when he sang the same words he couldn't seem to say. I almost sang the answer back to him, but instead I told him what we were doing, then gave him the dime we'd been hoarding.

He filled the quart jug again, then said "Two" by way of wishing us a good day, and we left. Somehow we knew from the way he said that one word, that he was warning us to be careful also, and that he would keep his mouth shut about our business.

We had just started cutting down some sagebrush at the front of the property when we heard the familiar sound of Sarge pushing his meat wagon toward town.

He saw us and stopped, but only briefly.

"What you boys got in that jug?" he asked.

"Gasoline," I answered.

"Don't you boys start a fire out here; it'll get away from you."

Pap spoke up.

"No sir, Mr. Sarge. It's to pour on fire ant beds," he fibbed.

Sarge saluted us and said, "Carry on, carry on, and watch for rattlers." Then he continued his half-mile trek toward town.

"Yes sir, Mr. Sarge, we sure will," Pap agreed, and it was all we could do to keep from busting out laughing until he was far enough away not to hear us.

By the time that Buddy, Shelby and Sunshine brought us our lunch that day, we'd chopped the heads off of thirteen small rattlers, and we had hidden six big ones in a wooden barrel that we had found in the old barn.

The place was a pure haven for rattlesnakes! Thank goodness our five acres was the only acreage Sarge had that was overgrown. The rest of it was farmed or fenced in for cattle that Sarge rented out. It even had about a three-acre pond on it, and as soon as we were through with the rattlesnake business we were dying to get to that pond for some fishing and swimming.

After we chopped the heads off the smaller snakes, we had thrown them in a heap next to the road.

Sunshine saw them first. She yelped out loud and jumped back, which caused Shelby to do the same.

"Where's the big 'uns?" Buddy asked, knowing that where there were that many little snakes, the larger ones had to be nearby.

Not wanting to lie, I just said "They're out there," and waved in the general direction of the barn. Then, quickly changing the subject, I asked Buddy, "Why didn't Black Boy come?"

"Since Sarge's chickens are running loose, Mama was afraid that dog would have a field day."

"Aww, the devil! All we'll have to do is scold him one time, and he won't fool with them chickens again," I replied.

We found some shade under a huge sweet gum tree and opened our lunch bags.

Mama had us each a sandwich made from homemade bread and homemade souse, two tomatoes straight from the garden, a bell pepper and one of her delicious peach tarts. Shelby was toting a half gallon of ice tea. Mama even chipped some of the precious ice from the block stored in the ice box. Most of the ice had melted, but you could hear an occasional tinkle as we turned the refreshing sweet tea to our lips. We didn't bother with cups, just passed the jug back and forth while we ate.

Sunshine came over and sat back to back with me for a few minutes. She didn't stay there long before she jumped up, fanning her nose. "Boy, you stink," she said.

"It's those rattlesnakes," Buddy said. "They smell just like a stinking billy goat."

Buddy got our gas jug and poured a little on top of the snakes, then threw some straw on top of them, lit a match and threw it in.

We told him what Daddy had said about not burning without him there, and warned him what Sarge had said about a fire. But Buddy went on ahead anyway, saying the Sarge wouldn't mind since it was on gravel.

We knew what would happen, so we took cover, leaving Shelby and Sunshine right in the danger zone.

When those snakes got hot, they started swelling up and popping like firecrackers, slinging guts and foul smells all over the two girls.

They left running toward the house, not waiting on Buddy.

When the snakes stopped popping, Buddy took off in a trot, heading home too.

We worked hard that day. I'm sure we wouldn't have worked as hard if we weren't searching for snakes, but we killed six more little ones, caught two more big ones, and two real good ones that were each almost four feet long. We threw them in the barrel with the others.

Then we came up with a plan. Right before we got to Slim and LeRoy's, we planned to grab each snake by the tail and spin it in the air until we stretched every one of them to four feet long, so that made us a total of ten snakes for one day, if they fell for the trick.

We didn't even have to use any of our gas, so we stored it along with the bush axes in the barn.

Pap came up with an ingenious plan to snare those snakes out of that barrel. He rigged up a pole with a loop on the end made from wire. We'd get the snake's head in that loop, then pull one end in our hand until that snake couldn't do anything. We'd lift him out of there and drop him in the sack.

We put three big ones and one of the smaller ones in the sack, and headed toward the pawn shop.

Right before we got there we eased the sack open and snared the smaller one around the tail and started spinning him.

Sure enough, that sucker must've stretched six inches or more.

Pap knocked on the door and went in. I stood outside, still holding that snake by the tail.

Slim finally waddled to the door.

"Damn, he's a skinny son of a bitch."

"You said four feet long," I retorted.

"Yeah, well, drop his skinny ass into the garbage can."

Slim was well satisfied with the other three, though.

I'd calculated the time, and they had to start buying more snakes than four a day before school started, or else Pap wouldn't have enough money to get that saxophone he wanted.

I waited until Slim gave me the two dollars, then I sprang it on him.

"Slim," I said, "we're either going to have to go up to seventy-five cents a snake, or the snake man is going to have to improve his appetite on them."

"Oh, that son of a bitch would eat a dozen a day, but he's not bringing in that much money," Slim said.

"What about six a week, still fifty cents each," I said.

Slim thought for a few seconds, then said, "Deal."

After we bought our RC's, we leaned back on the post of Mr. Pickett's store and rested our backs. I remember thinking it was the best cola I'd ever drunk. Off in the distance I could hear the lonesome sound of a whippoorwill calling its mate. I remember thinking, "Make yourself always remember this peaceful moment." And I have.

Afterwards, we dove into Mr. Lester's watering trough and washed ourselves off.

It was a Friday, so things were beginning to stir at Pig Meat's. We noticed a few members of the band arriving.

There'd be no sitting in the Chinaberry tree for me tonight, though. I was too tired.

On our walk home, we noticed that Miss Minnie had left her hole, and Sarge had abandoned his post for another day. We knew that all was well in Redtown, as we threw our snake sack into the tall weeds before we reached home.

Chapter 17

To our amazement Buddy, who hated milking the cow (for he thought it was women's work), was bringing the milk in from the stall as we walked up the door steps.

"What in the world are you two doing dripping wet?" Mama asked.

Without lying, I told her we smelled so bad that we bathed ourselves off in Mr. Lester's watering trough.

"Lordy Mercy, Mama said, you two boys are going to be the death of me. Shelby and little Sunshine came back here with snake guts blown all over them. I've about decided to not let you two boys go back out there with all them rattle-snakes crawling everywhere."

"I'd send Buddy instead, but for some reason Charles don't want him to leave the place, with just us three females here."

This was Mama's way of reminding us about the missing girls, without directly bringing it up in front of Shelby and Sunshine. I wasn't worried for them or our Mama, though; whoever had made off with the Reese girls would surely be in a lot more danger than they were. Our Mama was tough.

"Who knows, maybe we killed all them rattlers today and there won't be any more," I said, which really wasn't a lie since I didn't know for sure.

"Well, go on in there and put on some dry clothes. Charles will be in directly, and we'll talk about it over supper."

Daddy was late coming in. Mama had supper on the table, but she covered it with a clean tablecloth. We wouldn't think of eating until he got home.

Mama was getting worried; it was very unusual for Daddy not to be right on time with anything. She went to the porch and looked out a couple of times.

Finally, we heard Daddy whistling coming up the road, and I could tell without her breathing a word that she was one happy woman. I reckon everybody's nerves were on edge, not knowing who was around and whether something would happen to make someone else go missing.

Mama uncovered everything on the table and had Sunshine and Shelby shooing the flies away, when Daddy walked into the kitchen and took his place at the table after washing his hands.

We knew not to help ourselves to the food until Mama had prepared Daddy's plate and set it before him.

He never ate over about three tablespoons of anything, and whatever it was we would drink with our meals, Daddy would never drink anything until he'd finished eating. Then he'd turn up his glass and drink the entire amount. He always ate with a teaspoon, while the rest of us used a fork. I don't know why; he just liked it better that way, I guess.

That night we had fresh butter beans and sliced tomatoes from the garden, corn bread, and potatoes with a thick milk and flour sauce.

While we were eating, Daddy spoke up and said that he had walked out to the land when he got off work, and was amazed at the amount of work that me and Pap had done.

Mama spoke up and said, "I don't know, Charles. You know how rambunctious them two are, and that place has rattlesnakes on it."

"You two just go at it a little slower and be more careful. They'll be all right, old lady," he said.

"Yes sir," we answered in unison. Neither of us let on how relieved we were that Daddy had come down on our side of things.

So, it was settled.

I never understood how two people so different could get along without an argument or fussing, but Daddy and Mama did. If they ever did disagree, we never knew it.

Usually Mama's word was the law where us children were concerned, but for some unknown reason she went along with Daddy that night.

After we had all eaten, the table was cleared. Mama told us not to leave the table.

In just a few minutes, Mama opened one of the bottom doors of her white cabinet and brought out a beautiful seven-layer chocolate cake with nine candles on it.

"A day late and a dollar short," Mama said, as she lit the

candles on the cake.

She knew chocolate was my favorite cake.

"I had time to stop at Mr. Hughes' store to get you this for your birthday, Lew," Daddy said, as he reached into his lunch bag and brought out a scabbard knife, complete with the scabbard that looped through your belt.

"Oh my God, Charles, that boy will be cut his whole hand off with that thing."

I couldn't believe it!! The shiny blade had "Jim Bowie" stamped on the side. While they were all singing "Happy Birthday," it was irresistible. I grabbed that knife by the point and slung it across the room, and dang if it didn't stick perfectly into the wall.

"Give me that damn thing!" Mama hollered. "You are bound and determined to be in the penitentiary before you get grown. If it wasn't your birthday, I'd slap some sense into that head of yours."

Boy, Mama was pissed, but I didn't see any danger in it. I wasn't aiming it at anyone.

As much as I liked chocolate cake, I pushed my plate away from me and went into my bedroom.

Sunshine followed me and sat down on the bed beside of where I was lying. Slowly she started stroking my black hair.

"Honey, try not to be mad with your Mama. When we came in with those snake guts blown all over us, I saw her hand trembling as she was trying to layer your cake.

"She thought about going down there and getting you two, 'cause she was so worried you'd get snake bit. At least you know she loves you, or she wouldn't care enough to fuss like that.

"I know she's hard, but I don't know what I'd do without my sister. You could've had my Mama. That woman has hated me from day one. Willie Joe and Talmer can do no harm as far as she's concerned, though.

"I've never even told your Mama this but one day, I must've been about four years old, and Talmer asked me to get him a piece of bologna. I told him to go get it himself. Daddy was gone, and when he wasn't within eyeshot or hearing range, my Mama was even meaner to me.

"Well, Talmer wailed like a hyena and told Mama I had pinched him. She took me into the bedroom made me pull my panties down and whipped me with a hairbrush so hard until it felt like my butt cheeks were gonna grow together. She said if I told Daddy about it that she would whip me harder next time.

"From then on, unless Daddy was there, I'd just crawl under the house and stay under there until he came home. She's mean as a snake, but honey, she can quote you that Bible from scripture to scripture."

"Boy, was I a proud little girl when Bessie rescued me and brought me up here! So you'll never hear me say anything bad about my sister. She probably caught just as much hell from that old woman as I did, I don't know, so why don't you come back in the kitchen and eat your piece of birthday cake? She worked so hard to make it, and liked to have burned up in that kitchen baking those layers."

I turned over in the bed.

"You know, for a seven-year-old, you have wisdom beyond your years, Sunshine," I said.

"Well, I've had to, in order to survive," she said.

I returned to the kitchen and did something I hadn't done in years. I leaned over and hugged my Mama's neck.

I noticed that she hadn't been eating her piece of cake

but just pushing pieces of it around in her saucer.

She was still seated in her chair. Mama looped her arms around me and patting me saying, "There, there, Lewty boy, you might just make something of yourself yet." Then she added, ". . . if you don't get killed first."

While I was out of the kitchen she and Daddy had made an agreement that I could wear the knife as long as I was outside, but the minute I came through that door I was to have it off my belt.

Chapter 18

We had to rush in order to get through with that five acres before cotton picking time, for a lot of the days we couldn't work for the rain, but on August 14th we finished it up.

We had captured fifty-six snakes at least four feet long.

There was only one problem. We'd just sold Leroy his quota for the week the day before. We sacked up the six snakes and took them to the pawn shop anyway.

Slim told us we could put them in the garbage can for two dollars, so we took him up on the offer. Thus ended our rattlesnake business, or so we thought.

I knew we'd finish up that day, so I'd brought our precious hoard of money from the house. After paying for the gas and saving out the money for our RCs and moon pies, and including today's two dollars, we had twenty-four dollars and eighty cents, well over the amount we needed to reach our goal.

I was hot and thirsty, and wanted to stop by Pickett's for those RCs, but Pap couldn't wait to get his hands on that saxophone, so we went straight to Hughes' Mercantile.

With the tax, it came to twenty dollars and fifty-five cents. Pap told me I could keep the remainder of the money.

He barely got out of the store before he opened the box up.

"Oh boy, just look how pretty and shiny! It's even got some instructions to it," he said.

He was blowing on that thing as we went past Miss Minnie in her hole.

By this time she knew our names, of course.

"Pap, come over here and let me show you how to blow "The Tennessee Waltz" on that thing.

"No thank you, Miss Minnie. It's got the instructions to it," Pap answered.

Sarge had a big wide grin on his face as he blew his whistle at a nonexistent vehicle to come on through. That was his way of saying he was happy for Pap.

We had stored Daddy's bush axes in the old barn, and were going back to get them. After we got the axes, Pap decided to sit in the doorway of the barn and blow that saxophone.

I told him to come on; I was ready to go home.

He had the instruction paper unfolded on his lap, and was already doing a Gene Autry song that was recognizable.

"See there," he smiled, "no hurry getting home, because we're gonna have to explain this sax to Mama." Then he started tooting again.

He didn't see it because of the paper covering his lap, but the biggest rattlesnake I'd ever seen came crawling from under that barn and headed straight for me.

I guess that saxophone got him stirred up. I was so scared I couldn't move or think; I just froze right there in my tracks.

Then that big old rattlesnake turned and went back toward Pap. By then I could move, but I wasn't fast enough.

Pap finally saw the snake when I cut it half in two with

that bush axe, but it was too late. With its dying act, the rattler struck Pap right on top of his big toe.

Its rattlers were still rattling as I raked the snake away from my brother.

Pap snatched his boot off, and sure enough, right on top of the first knuckle of his toe were two big purple fang marks. That big old snake must have been full of poison, for Pap's toe had already swelled up to twice its size by the time he got his boot off.

I picked up my brother and threw him across my shoulder. He didn't holler out in pain or anything; all he said was, "Get my saxophone."

I bent down, and with him still on my shoulder, I managed to throw the saxophone and instruction booklet in the black case, snap it to, and pick the whole thing up. Then I headed for the closest person I knew who could help.

To this day I don't know where the strength came from, but I ran all the way back to the intersection, without dropping Pap or his precious instrument. As soon as I spotted Sarge, I screamed out to him what had happened.

By this time Pap had passed out; he was as limp as a dish

rag draped over my shoulder, with his arms dangling down my back.

Sarge didn't say a word; he just snatched Pap up in his arms.

I didn't know a big man could move so fast, but it took all I could do to keep up with him as he ran for our house.

Buddy was in the yard. His mouth dropped open when he saw us coming.

"Pap got bit by a snake," I gasped. "Run to the mill and get Daddy!"

Buddy didn't tarry. He took off running as fast as he could go.

Sarge found a patch of shade on the porch and gently laid Pap down. Then he quickly pulled out his pocketknife, cut a long piece of cloth off Pap's pants leg, and tied a tourniquet tightly around his leg at the knee.

By this time, my brother's whole leg was swelling up; the sight of it was horrifying, to say the least.

I was sweating profusely, and my heart was pounding away in my chest from the fear and effort. Not knowing what else to do with it, I stuck the saxophone case under the end of the porch before going inside to break the news to Mama. I knew how emotional she could be, so I did my best to try and act calm as I went into the house.

I found her in the kitchen as usual.

"Oh my God, Lew, what have you been up to now? And why do you have that confounded knife on inside my house?"

"Mama, Pap's been bit by a rattlesnake and he's out yonder on the porch with Sarge," I blurted.

I didn't have a chance to say another word; she was already making a beeline for the porch.

After seeing Pap's condition, she told Sarge, "Bring my baby inside the house!" Then she added, "Please."

She directed Sarge to Pap's bed, where it was a little cooler.

"Lew, run get your Daddy."

I was just about to tell her that I'd already sent Buddy, when he came bursting through the front door.

He stuck his head in and said that Daddy decided to just run straight to Dr. Redding's office to get him.

Shelby and Sunshine were out in the hallway sobbing. Mama called them into the room.

"If y'all don't hush up that commotion I'm gonna slap you both! Now go chip some big pieces of ice off into a dish pan, and bring it here with a towel, right quick," she told them.

They knew better than to argue, so they did what they were told.

"Ma'am, is there anything else I can do?" asked Sarge.

"No, Sarge, you did the best thing you could do, just by bringing him here."

"Only from the intersection, Ma'am," he corrected her. "Your boy Lew had him till there."

The Sarge looked at me then with a puzzled look on his face. "Speaking of that, son, how did you manage to carry Pap all that way from the new land? Seems to me, he'd be too heavy for you to carry!"

"He's my brother, Sarge," I said.

Mama just looked at me, then back at Sarge, then at me again, and shook her head. Finally she said, "Well, Sarge, there is one thing if you don't mind. Could you stay here with me until my husband gets back with the doctor? I don't know what I'd do if . . . if something else happened, and me here alone with these young'uns."

We all knew what she meant, without her saying it out loud.

Bless old Sarge, he might not have been the brightest fellow but he knew enough to try and take Mama's mind off things.

"Yes Ma'am, be glad to stay. Your Pap's a good boy; he plays music like nobody's business! The last time I seen him, he sure was a happy little fellow. He was a-blowing away on that horn outfit."

"What? What horn outfit?" Mama asked.

"I don't know what you call them thangs, but he and Lew here, they bought it brand new from Mr. Hughes' store today, because I seen 'em come out of there," he told her.

I could tell Mama either had no idea what Sarge was talking about, or she was too worried about my brother to discuss it right then. Either way I was relieved when all she said was,

"Sarge, sometimes I think them two are plumb crazy, but they're my boys and I love them."

"The both of them boys are going to make you so proud

of them one day," Sarge said.

I didn't want to say what I was thinking, that it seemed like it was taking Daddy forever to bring the doctor. And I knew there was nothing else I could do to help my brother. I didn't know what to do with myself, so I went outside and started throwing my knife at the trunk of a big oak tree just to have something to do while we waited.

Daddy must have paid a good price for that knife, because it had perfect balance. I learned very quickly that the further you were away from the tree trunk, the slower you had to put the spin on the knife. Soon I was right on target every time.

As I pulled the knife from the tree for another throw, I saw Black Boy walk up onto the front porch where the Sarge had laid Pap down. The dog sniffed and snuffled at that part of the porch floor, over and over. Finally he started slobbering from his mouth. I knew he could smell that old rattlesnake, and that he could tell something was bad wrong.

I got some water from the pump and washed the porch off, so he'd be satisfied, and he was.

I threw that knife until Daddy came running through the

gate about dusk dark. He was alone; there wasn't a doctor with him.

Black Boy went under the house, and I followed Daddy inside.

"Where's the doctor?" Mama asked.

"His wife said he was at the north end of the county delivering a baby, and the people there didn't have a telephone."

"What about that old drunkard, Dr. Muhl? He'd be better than nothing," Mama said.

"I went by his house and he was so drunk he couldn't even get out of the bed. He said if Pap was just rattlesnake bit, that Pap was in better shape than he was," Daddy told her.

It was getting full dark out. Sarge said he'd pray for Pap, and then went on home, but not before Mama thanked him profusely for his kindness.

Daddy's Indian instinct kicked in by this time.

"Lew, go get two lamps and put one on each side of the bed," he told me. "And get that jug of kerosene oil by the stove."

As I left the room to get the kerosene and the lamps, I

heard him ask Mama to bring him two onions and a plug of his chewing tobacco.

"And some of your old towels," he added.

Mama was taking Daddy's orders for a change, and she went into action.

While she was in the kitchen she told Shelby and Sunshine to make a baker of biscuits, boil a half package of rice, then fry two eggs for everyone.

"The young'uns have got to eat," she told them as she reached for the onions.

By the time Mama and I made it back to the bedroom, Daddy had gotten rubbing alcohol and sterile gauze. He chopped up the tobacco and onions and mixed them together into a thick paste.

Me and Buddy stood at the foot of the bed and watched every move, mostly trying to stay out of Daddy's way. Every now and then he'd tell one or the other of us to run the wick up on one of the lamps, or move it closer in order for Daddy to see better.

We could tell from the smells drifting in from the kitchen that Sunshine and Shelby were doing their best to make supper. Mostly it smelled like something burning, but Mama didn't go and check. She didn't even seem to notice; she stayed right with Pap, sitting beside him on one side of the bed.

Pap was breathing, but that was about it. He lay there still as a stone.

When he had that tobacco and onion paste made up, Daddy took out his pocket knife that was sharpened to a perfect hone. Then he cut the remainder of Pap's pants leg off.

Next, he held the sharp blade of the knife over the flame of one of the lamps. After the knife was hot enough to suit him, he poured some alcohol over it. Then he commenced to cutting on Pap's foot.

He started at each bite mark, and cut upward about three inches.

Very little blood came out. What little bit that did ooze out, was sort of like a ropey thick syrup and had an awful odor to it.

Daddy then turned Pap over and found the big vein right behind my brother's knee. He cut about a five-inch strip there, until he reached the vein.

I'd always thought your veins were purple, but they're not; they're red.

Daddy then told Mama to go get him the smallest needle that she could find and thread it with at least a foot of white thread.

While she was out of the room, Daddy started cutting the top of that vein, but nothing came out. He cut the vein the entire five inches. Still nothing but that stinking ropey substance oozed out.

Mama returned with the needle and thread. Daddy stitched the top of the vein back, but left the lower part open.

By this time his pocketknife had lost its keen edge, so Daddy took the little whetstone from his pocket and re-sharpened the small bloody blade. He did the same procedure to sterilize it.

Then he commenced to cutting again.

Mama started crying, which set off a chain reaction out in the kitchen with Rumby, Shelby, and Sunshine.

"Shhh, shhh," Daddy said.

Mama put her hands over her mouth, trying not to make a sound while Daddy continued his cutting with steady hands. He came up a short distance from his last stitches, made about a two-inch cut, and blood started flying.

Mama held the dish pan beside Pap, and Daddy let him bleed until the blood looked normal. Then he corded the vein with his thumb and forefinger, and began to stitch it up. He left it open at the bottom until he cleared the whole vein, massaging it and pressing downward until all the stinking rotten mess stopped coming out and the blood looked normal again. He did this all the way down Pap's leg, pressing the poison down to the open cuts in the top of his toe until he got as much out of there as he could. After that, he stitched everything up.

Finally, Daddy put a poultice of the onion and tobacco on Pap's toe and on the cut behind the knee, wrapped both of the wounds tightly with the gauze, and soaked them good with the kerosene.

He looked up at Mama and said, "Sweet Pea, it's left up to the good Lord now."

Mama looked at Daddy square in the eyes.

They both got up from their sitting position on the bed, one on each side of Pap's still body.

"Charles, I want you to know something, come what may. I've never loved you more than I do tonight," Mama said.

Daddy didn't answer her with words. He'd already talked more that night while telling us what he needed us to bring him in order to help Pap, than he usually did in a whole week. But as he walked past Mama toward the kitchen, out of the corner of my eye I saw him pinch her on her behind.

She jumped like she'd been shot, but didn't say anything.

"Come on in heah and let's get some of Shebby's burnt up stuff," Daddy said.

"No, y'all go ahead, I've got to clean up all this bloody mess," Mama said.

I looked over at my brother in the bed and wondered how he'd survived the bite from that big snake. I noticed his whole leg would convulse now and then, too, I knew that I had just witnessed a miracle from a common man—a skillful craft performed by an untrained person.

Maybe that's why he was all the time reading, I thought. Or maybe it was because it seemed as if he was always in deep thought on something other than his surroundings, I didn't know.

I was pretty sure of one thing, though; if any of us took any of Daddy's qualities, it would be Buddy. He never complained, and was an expert at anything he tackled.

Chapter 19

Daddy was right; everything was burned or scorched but the biscuits.

We all just poured some syrup over our biscuits and ate them and drank lukewarm tea with our meager meal, for all of the ice was being used to keep Pap's fever down.

It was hard for me to fall asleep that night. Mama was sitting in the chair beside me and the lamp was on. We were all accustomed to sleeping in the dark.

Mama was reading her Bible. I was scared to look that way. Just as sure as I did, she'd have it opened on that page with that smoked up horribly ugly man, so I put my head under the covers and prayed for Pap. I'd learned how to pray during devotion at school.

Before long I drifted off to sleep with Mama reading out of the book of Luke.

At four o'clock in the morning Black Boy awakened the whole household. He was barking to beat the band, running around and around the house.

Daddy was the first one to get up and try to quiet him but he wouldn't stop.

He came into our bedroom and asked us to see if we could do anything with him.

We boys just slept in our underwear, so we got up and got Daddy's flashlight. Mama was still reading her Bible. She'd worked herself down to Revelations. That's the one that Big Mama would always pop you on your arm with that big fingernail file and read to you when she could hem you up at her house.

We got the flash lights and went outside. Sure enough Black Boy was having the time of his life running around the house and barking, almost as if he were laughing. He finally let Buddy catch him and we petted him for a short while until he settled down, but when we went in the back door he did something that he'd never done before. He followed us inside and made a B-line to Pap's bed. Mama didn't say a word when Black Boy put both his front feet on Pap's bed and started licking him in the face.

Pap opened his eyes.

"Hey Buddy what you doing in here?" And then he added, "Mama's gonna get you," then he fell back to sleep.

Mama knew the crisis had passed. She lay her Bible down, blew the lamp out and crept out of the darkened room.

I soon went back to sleep with my hand on the old sentinels head. Every now and then he'd lick me on the hand as he had Pap's face.

Even though we all didn't get much sleep, we were still up at the usual time, 6:00 o'clock.

Pap woke me up, moaning and groaning.

I looked for Black Boy and he wasn't in the room.

Pap reached his hand out toward mine, as our beds were only separated by about two feet.

We clasped hands.

"What happened," he asked?

"You were bit by that big rattler and Daddy had to operate on your leg."

"Daddy," he asked?

"Yep, Dr. Redding was out of town and Dr. Muhl was too drunk to come."

"I wish you could have seen Daddy, Pap! He was as cool as a cucumber, and acted as though he did it for a living."

"Yeah, well, my leg feels like it weighs a hundred pounds and hurts like hell,"

"Humph, you should have seen it earlier," I said.

"My saxophone, what did Mama say about it," Pap asked?

"She doesn't know about it, not exactly," I told him, without letting him know Sarge had pretty nearly let the cat out of the bag. I stuck it under the porch when I brought you home, and now it's hid over yonder in the back of our closet. I snuck it in there when she wasn't looking."

"Good, today is Saturday, you go on down yonder and help Daddy Jim, I'll tell her about it while I'm down with this snake bite, it won't go so bad now I don't think.

We could smell the bacon frying and the aroma of Mama's coffee. So it wasn't too long before she called us all for breakfast.

I don't see how she managed to accomplish anything that morning. She was constantly coming in there and shewing Sunshine out of our room and every time she did, she'd gently pat Pap on his cheek and check for a fever.

Daddy never came into the room

We were all sitting at the table eating breakfast when we heard a commotion at the door. It sounded as though Black Boy had hold of something and we could hear someone cursing.

Mama left the table and ran to the door to find Dr. Reddings kicking at Black Boy, who had snared him by one of his trouser legs.

Mama called Black Boy off and apologized to the doctor, while thanking him for coming.

Dr. Reddings smiled. "I had a dog like that when I was a boy. Isn't it strange how protective they are over children."

"Ok, to get to the gist. Did the child make it over night?"

"By the grace of God he did and seems to be fine," Mama said.

Dr. Reddings followed her into the bedroom.

Pap was sitting in bed.

Mama had concocted him some of that milk mixture that she had given me when I had the pneumonia.

He took a long drink of it as they entered the room causing an awful scowl on his face.

Dr. Reddings pulled up the chair and sat down.

"What's your name young man," he asked?

"Pap."

"Well, Pap first of all I promise I'm not going to hurt you, okay?"

Pap shook his head in acknowledgement.

First thing, he took out his stethoscope and listened to Pap's chest and back.

He scribbled in his book.

He then started unwrapping the gauze from Pap's leg.

He asked Mama to bring him a pan of warm water.

By the time Mama returned with the water from the stove reservoir Dr. Reddings had finished unwrapping Pap's leg.

The doctor smiled and said to himself, "An old Indian treatment."

He washed Pap's leg with a green bar of soap then greased

everywhere that Daddy had cut with something that smelled like rotten eggs. Then he gave Pap a shot in the rump before rewrapping his leg.

Dr. Reddings scribbled down something on a small envelope and dropped some pills in it, then told Mama to give as directed.

Dr. Reddings seemed to relax for a minute.

"I must say I feel compelled to tell you this."

"As you probably know, I have been into almost every home in this area, and I've yet to see one as well maintained and clean as this one. With all these children, it's unbelievable! The children all look well fed and clean. You should see some of the places I go into. My, my, my," he said.

The doctor continued, "And that operation your husband performed, it took me six years of medical school to do that. If that poison would've gotten a little bit stronger in the iliac artery it'd be a different story to tell this morning, and it was only inches from there."

"Tell your husband he is to be commended. The stitches are so fine that within time and at his age he might not even have a scar."

The doctor got up to leave.

"See to it that the bandages are changed twice a day for three days, then you can narrow it down to once daily until the swelling goes down and the leg stops draining. Take the antibiotic tablets in the envelope as directed and he'll be up and about this time next week."

"Oh Doctor that's such good news," Mama said.

I stayed in the room with Pap, but I heard Mama invite the doctor for breakfast and he took her up on the offer.

We could already hear Daddy banging on something in his shop and I knew that Buddy would be with him.

Chapter 20

After The doctor left, Mama went out to the shop and brought a protesting Buddy inside the house.

"I want you and Lew to go down to Daddy's and help him with his whiskey today," she said.

"Mama, do I have to? That old woman down there is the pure devil itself and she hates us."

"We have to go inside to syphon that whiskey into the bottles and that's when she starts in with her Bible."

"If she hasn't just flown in from New York City, she's just written another song for Hank Williams, and him being dead for years. The truth's not in her and that Willie Joe and Talmer either."

"Now Daddy Jim's a different case, he's a good old man. I don't see how or why he stays there," Buddy said.

"Honey, as you know I married your Daddy when I was 14 years old to get away from that woman. Even though your Daddy's 15 years older than me he was just what I needed and I thank the Lord several times a day for getting me away from there."

"The fact remains though, it is what it is and Daddy can't handle them big five gallon jugs by himself him being all drawn over like he is. I know how you hate it but Pap's down with that snake bite and he can't go, so it's you and Lew today."

Talmer and Willie Joe had a big old brown dog named Rat. They never fed him much, because there was very little cooking that went on down there. Black Boy liked to go with us to Daddy Jim's so he could jump on Rat and whip him but he didn't want to leave Pap, so me and Buddy soon left running the mile to Daddy Jim's house.

Daddy Jim would have been a tall man if he wasn't so drawn over with arthritis. He had black hair and sharp blue eyes and was very knowledgeable about things. I'm sure he would have accomplished a lot more if it wasn't for his physical condition and Big Mama.

He had an adult sized high chair that was on his front porch he'd sit in, making it easy for him to get up and down and he'd sit there all day long, weather permitting and smoke "Bull Durham" cigarettes that he'd roll himself.

He was quick tempered but he loved us to death and I felt that Big Mama was jealous about it.

Big Mama was a pretty woman. Since she never cooked or did much around the house she was dressed seven days a week in her "Sunday" clothes, even though they didn't go to Church.

She had black hair and just sat on the couch, read the bible and dipped snuff.

Mama and Sunshine were the only natural blondes in her family, inheriting their looks from Daddy Jim's Mama.

Sure enough, as soon as we'd picked up the first five gallon and had it on the table. Daddy Jim had his hose ready.

I sucked on the hose until the white liquor started pouring out.

Daddy Jim started filling his pints and half pints.

Big Mama started reading out of Revelations. The more she read, the louder she got.

Finally, Daddy Jim stuck his finger over the end of the hose to stop the flow of whiskey and with his other hand he shook his stick at Big Mama and told her to shut up.

Big Mama was taken aback to say the least so she sat down on the arm of the couch.

"Well, I was just trying to get a little bit of the bible into these heathen grandchildren of yours."

"You take my Willie Joe and Talmer, if they weren't so sickly they'd be in Church every time the doors were open and I can't go and leave them here with you, cause there's no telling what you'd do with my darlings if I left them alone with you, cause they don't know what sin is.

I looked over at Talmer and Willie Joe, who were sitting on the couch behind Big Mama looking at the pictures out of some comic books, because neither one of them could read.

They both flicked me the finger and grinned.

I jumped toward them, and they both whined and grabbed Big Mama.

"My babies haven't done a thing to you. You know how

sick they are, so leave them alone," Big Mama said.

We got through syphoning the whiskey and hiding it across the road so that Talmer and Willie Joe couldn't find most of it and after Daddy Jim gave us our pint to sell, we told him about Pap being bit by the big rattle snake.

"I'd wondered why he and Black Boy didn't show up," he said

"Well tell your Mama if she needs me to let me know," then he did something that he'd never done. He gave Buddy $40.00 and told him to tell Mama that was for her taking care of Sunshine and that he appreciated her getting her away from there.

I was surprised for the roll of green backs that he'd peeled the $40.00 from was quite substantial, undoubtedly moonshining could be quite lucrative.

Buddy decided he didn't want to go to the Courthouse, so I went by myself.

It didn't take but a few minutes before I spotted a regular customer named Virgil. I didn't even bother to go down into the basement. I just slipped it from underneath my shirt, received my two dollars and headed back toward home. I didn't want to go to the movie, I wanted to go home and check on Pap.

I remember someone stopping and asking me if I wanted a ride but I turned them down. I wanted some time to think.

It was little wonder that Mama and my oldest aunts had left home at such an early age. It was because of Big Mama.

Yeah, I thought, Redtown was definitely the town for Big Mama she fit right in.

I'd seen pictures of all Mama's sisters and they were all beautiful.

Margie had coal black hair and owned a grocery store in Pensacola, Florida. She had one Son, named Wayne.

Joyce had Auburn colored hair. Her husband owned a car lot in Camden, Alabama.

They were forever trying to give Mama a vehicle, but Daddy wouldn't accept it unless he could pay for it and he felt like the house and land came first.

Chapter 21

Dr. Reddings was right. In about a week Pap was up and about. Daddy took some needle nose scissors, clipped the stitches loose and he didn't have any trouble with it.

Me and Buddy had to strip the fodder from the corn and store it by ourselves, while Pap tooted on that saxophone, but come cotton-picking time, Pap was out in the fields with us, along with Rumby.

You know, Mama never did ask the story behind the saxophone, I guess she was just too scared to ask.

We three boys could pick nigh two bales of cotton a day in good cotton. Rumby had picked up, after a couple of wallops across the behind with a cotton stalk by Mama and had really improved his picking.

Word soon got out and farmers were offering us up to three cents a pound to pick for them, which really pleased Mama.

The summer of 1955 according to the news it looked like hurricane Brenda was going to come up through the gulf coast and through our area. We were picking cotton for Mr. Gardner. He wanted that cotton out of his field in case the hurricane came through our area, so he went up to 5 cents a pound. Me. Pap, and Buddy carried three rows each and Rumby picked two.

I remember being proud of Rumby for he kept up with me.

Pap would get far out in the lead and he'd whirl around and pick on each one of our rows so that we could catch up with him.

At the end of that first day we weighed in. Pap had picked 475 pounds, me 360, Buddy 340 and Rumby 225.

Mr. Gardner paid that price for three days, then when he picked us up on the fourth day he said the hurricane wasn't going to come our way and he had to drop the price back down to three cents a pound, which was still a half cent more than most the other farmers were paying.

The one I hated picking cotton for was Mr. Goddins. He never paid over two and a half cents a pound, even though he ran a store and it seemed to me like he could have paid more. He charged twice the going price for everything at his store. At around noon, two big three-quarter-ton trucks would come to the fields and pick us up. We never would get anything but RC colas, making it impossible for him to over-charge us because we'd get them out of the box.

It was nigh impossible to bring anything to eat because by dinner, we'd be picked our way a far piece from where we had been put off that morning.

Just as soon as the poor pickers had purchased their food, which was usually sardines and crackers with a large belly washer soda, we were hurried into the back of the truck and hit the bumpy road getting back to the field, making it a stinking mess by the time we arrived back ready to work, for he expected you to have it eaten by the time we arrived back at the field.

He'd hurry and prod us like we were dumb beasts, just

because we were poor and had to work for a living.

I had already left home when Mr. Goddins' died, but I heard he stayed sick for ten years before he died, lost everything he had and was having to live in his chicken house at the time that he expired.

Luke 16: 19-31.

Chapter 22

School year started in 1955 on Sept. 9th.

We really had some nice clothes that year, due in part to Mr. Gardner.

Rumby and Sunshine were in the third, me and Pap in the fifth, Buddy was in the sixth and Shelby was in the seventh.

Shelby looked older though, for she was physically matured in the fifth grade.

Lately I'd noticed Buddy going through the same transition. His voice was getting deeper and the hair on his legs and arms were getting courser. He spent more and more time with Daddy or out in the shop alone when he didn't have chores to do.

When school did start it was unusually hot for September, and boy we could smell Mrs. Rumbling's cloak room clean down to our room, which was next door. Those magazines sure were stinking.

On the fourth day of school that day, as we were going to play period, we saw the janitor and the coach with two huge wheel barrels stacked high with those maggot eaten magazines. They were gaging and rolling them down the hall to the nearest exit.

Our teacher for the fifth grade was Mrs. Sessions, and I would grow to love her.

Mrs. Sessions saw what was going on and told us to go out the door down the hall in the other direction.

I noticed that the Principal had all the fourth grade boys in the hall and some of them were crying.

The next day we heard that the Principal paddled every one of those boys. Also two of the boys' fathers came to the school the next day and knocked Mr. Fraily out. They said he cried like a baby and begged for them to not hit him again.

He never came back and he was replaced with the football coach until they could find another one.

Around the time that the Principal was knocked out, another young girl turned up missing in Redtown.

I knew her very well. Sometimes she'd walk with us to and from school.

She was a beautiful black haired girl that lived on the other end of town.

She was in the ninth grade.

Mama didn't like her family, she said they were lazy and shiftless and she would scold Shelby if she saw the girl walking with us.

Her name was Willa Dean Lee. She smoked ready rolled camel cigarettes and she cussed worse than Mama, I mean words that I'd never heard before.

She kept those cigarettes stuck down in her bosom.

She acted very lonely to me, as no one seemed to have anything to do with her but the boys. And boy could she strut when she'd catch the boys watching her, I mean she walked completely different. She jiggled and shook all over.

Mama wasn't the only one that didn't like Willie Dean. Faithful old Black Boy still walked with us every day and he made it a point to stay ahead of Willie Dean. I think it was her strong perfume. I don't know, but something made him sneeze if he got near her.

One day after school started that year, she had both her hands full of books and asked Buddy to reach down in there and get her cigarettes out for her. Buddy shook his head "No".

Pap went down one side and me the other. Pap brought out the cigarettes and I had a small cardboard of matches.

"Gee, thank you darlings," she said and then she added, "You two may tote my books."

We already had a load of them but we gladly made room for Willa Dean's until we made it to our house.

That day as we parted ways and Willa Dean headed on down the road toward her house Shelby said, "I'm ashamed of you two! What if Sunshine had looked back and saw you sticking your hands down in her bra? Now wouldn't that be a fine sight? You boys are supposed to set an example, and here you are doing right opposite of that."

"Yeah, but she wasn't," I said.

"Well you'd better not be doing such a thing as that again, or I'll tell Mama myself," Shelby said.

"Ah bologna, a feller can't have any fun," I said, as I looked over at Pap who had kept a smile on his face for quite a while.

Mama usually had some kind of small snack or something waiting on us when we came in from school, but me and Pap headed straight to our room.

"Did you feel em," I asked?

"Uh huh, as soft and warm as it could be," Pap said.

"Boy that nipple was sticking straight out," I said.

"I didn't get to feel the nipple because I had that pack of cigarettes," Pap said.

"If she asks me to get them cigarettes again, I'm gonna do it. It'll be worth an ass whooping from Mama to feel of them babies again," Pap said.

"Uh Huh," I responded.

Chapter 23

As it turned out we never got to see Willa Dean again because she disappeared a couple days later.

The day that Willie Dean turned up missing me and Pap decided to walk out to the land. Daddy was beginning to move building material to the site.

We'd talked to Miss Minnie for a few minutes and we learned that Slim and LeRoy were trying to teach the snake man how to do tricks on a bicycle, and the Snake man was thinking about hitting the road again in the spring.

We could see from a distance the two fat men really had the snake man fixed up. What small amount of hair the Snake man did have LeRoy and Slim had it dyed a fiery red and he was dressed in stripped red and white pants, clown style. He was still naked from his waist up.

We saw the Sheriff's car as it flew across the railroad tracks barely missing a train and skidded to a stop at Mr. Reese's service station.

Mr. Bowen was standing there with his poodle on the leash so we knew it was his day to walk backwards.

Black Boy was with us and started running around and around Mr. Bowen wanting to play with his toy poodle, but as usual Mr. Bowen wouldn't have nothing to do with it.

The Sheriff must've had a girth on him of at least 60 inches. He walked straight to Mr. Bowen and Mr. Bowen started stepping backwards. The faster the Sheriff ran, the faster Mr. Bowen stepped backward holding to the leash of the poodle dog.

After he was completely out of breath he made his way to Sarge and asked him if he knew anything about those girls disappearing. After directing a couple of nonexistent vehicles through and blowing his whistle Sarge snapped to attention and saluted then said "Sir, I cannot tell you anything until you go through the chain of command Sir." Then he saluted again and blew a long deafening whistle.

"My God," said the Sheriff, sticking his fingers in his ears and walking over to Miss Minnie.

"What are you doing in a hole in the dirt," asked the Sheriff?

"Am I breaking a law, or is it any of your business" answered Miss Minnie?

"Do you know anything about these girls that are disappearing around here," the Sheriff asked?

"How in the name of Jesus can someone just disappear? Do you mean like in thin air? You must be crazy," said Miss Minnie.

About that time Sarge started blowing his whistle profusely. It seemed that the snake man had that bicycle going and he couldn't stop it. He zoomed right past everyone with that forked tongue sticking straight out. And I noticed that Slim and LeRoy had those long, pointed toe nails painted beet red.

"What in the name of Jesus was that?" demanded Sheriff Watson as he grabbed his chest and Sarge assisted him over to Mr. Reese's, where we were standing.

(We didn't know it at the time, but we learned later that

the thought running through Miss Minnie's head was, How stupid, to be a sheriff! My disguise must be really working. As it turned out, there was a whole lot Miss Minnie was keeping to herself.)

After drinking a Nehi orange drink and resting himself for a few minutes Sheriff Watson asked the frightened Mr. Reese.

"Mr. Reese, I know you have trouble with your speech but try real hard."

"Do you have any idea where your daughters are and now this other girl that's missing," Sheriff Watson asked.

Me and Pap started stomping our feet, clapping our hands and humming the tune to "The Wabash Cannon Ball,"

"Now the Sheriff thought we were crazy as well," I thought.

Instead of Mr. Reese telling him he didn't know to the tune of the song, he was so nervous he started singing "The Wabash Cannon Ball,"

"She came down from Birmingham one cold December day," in perfect pitch.

It was a Friday, Sarge had his meat wagon with him so

the Sheriff bought him five lbs. of pickled pig feet and told Sarge he'd better catch that crazy son of a bitch on the bicycle before dark or somebody would shoot him.

He fired up that 55 Ford and he couldn't get back across those tracks fast enough.

We decided we'd better walk on out to the land so that we could get back in time to milk the cow.

We were surprised at the amount of lumber and nails that were already there and covered with a thick tarpaulin.

What we couldn't understand was when we were going to find time to build it. We found out however that we were going to discover that the very next morning.

Black Boy was going to love living at the new place. We could already tell that we were going to have to get us a shot gun because he treed one squirrel right behind the other.

He ran down two rabbits and caught them that day, when we went home we gave them to Mama and we had fried rabbit smothered in gravy for breakfast the next morning.

After breakfast Mama told me and Pap to run down to Daddy Jim's and tell Big Mama that we wouldn't have time for her foolishness. Work as fast as we could, sell the whiskey but instead of going to the movie, go directly to the house site. Charles and Buddy would already be there.

I'll swear I believe Black Boy understood every word she said, laying under that house because when we got ready to leave, as much as he loved to jump on old Rat (Talmer's dog), he wouldn't go with us. He'd rather go with Daddy and Buddy.

When we reached Daddy Jim's he had Big Mama and them two no good boys hemmed up in the small kitchen with his walking stick, and was cussing up a blue streak.

Besides being a pathological liar, Big Mama was also a kleptomaniac. That woman could steal the sweeten out of gingerbread and never break the crust.

All the store keepers around town knew to keep a sharp eye on her when she entered their establishment.

They knew that Daddy Jim would pick up the tab if she was caught, but Willie Joe and Talmer were forbidden inside any of the nearby stores.

Anyway, it seemed that someone had stolen a hundred dollars out of Daddy Jim's bill fold while he was sleeping the night before.

We all knew it was Big Mama.

"Now you three stay in that kitchen and I'll swear Mama if you go to quoting bad things from the Bible to these young'uns, I'm coming in there with this walking stick."

"I've read some things out of that Bible too, and everything in there ain't as doom and gloom as you say it is."

Without Big Mama's interruptions, we were through by dinner.

We crossed the tracks, sold our pint and came on back to the house. We'd decided to start saving our money for a shotgun and we would have it too by the time that hunting season came in.

When we arrived at the building site, we found that Sarge had given Daddy two 12x12 60' long tarred beams and four 40' long beams.

Daddy and Buddy had laid them down across some cemented concrete blocks and they were already working on nailing in the floor joists.

It was going to be a slow tedious task, for Daddy was used to sawing everything with a hand saw.

But that was about to change.

Me and Pap jumped in and followed Daddy's orders. We were still on the floor joist and those suckers were heavy. I really think that Daddy was surprised at how strong we actually were, but from all the running and exercising we did there wasn't an ounce of fat on us.

I always will believe Daddy thought that me and Pap to be a little off center, because about all we did was hold lumber and do some markings with some flat lead pencils.

I did learn to use a square and a level though and after a while I really felt as though I was of some use.

It was getting pretty late in the evening, the saws were getting dull, but we had managed to nail all the sub flooring down.

Daddy and Buddy gathered up the handsaws, so that he and Buddy could put them in the vice and sharpen them when they got home.

We told Daddy that we were going to run down to the pond and go swimming.

Daddy told us that he wished that we wouldn't. He said there were probably moccasins in that water.

We told him that we'd send Black Boy in first, he'd run

them all off.

"Ok then, but don't tell the old lady I agreed to it," Daddy said.

Black Boy had treed squirrels all evening. He'd really had a good time.

We called him off the squirrels and he followed us to the pond.

There was no coaxing Black Boy in, he looked around, waded off into the water and started swimming.

We stripped off butt naked and dove in. Boy was it refreshing after a hot September day!

The water must've been spring fed too, because the water was ice cold in spots and there wasn't a snake in sight.

Black Boy even caught a good sized bass that was swimming near the shore and he got out of the water to eat him.

We swam and played in the water for about twenty minutes and then a whole herd of cows came toward the pond from one direction, followed by a great big red bull with long horns.

I'll swear that bull had eyes that looked just like the snake man's, red as fire.

Our clothes were right beside the pond and every time we'd snatch up our clothes and run naked toward our house site that bull would get too close on us and we'd have just enough time to make it back to the pond and jump in before the long horned, red eyed devil got us.

Finally, after about the fourth attempt of running across that pasture naked, Black Boy caught on to what was going on. As we were running back toward the pond again as fast as we could, Black Boy jumped up and grabbed that big bull by the nose and threw him to the ground and held him there until we could get back across the fence and get our clothes on.

From that day forward we could swim, fish, do anything we wanted to at that pond and we weren't bothered with that bull again.

By the time we made it to our house Mama and the girls had supper on the table, we ate and it was bath time.

Mama and the girls always went out to the bath house first, which was nothing but two tubs of water surrounded on all four sides. You bathed in one and rinsed in the other.

Pap and I just went through the motions that night. We

felt that we were pretty well clean, even though we did smell a little fishy.

The next day was Sunday, by the time me and Pap woke up Daddy and Buddy were already gone.

Me, Pap, and Sunshine had stayed in the chinaberry tree pretty late the night before. So there was no doubt we were sleeping a little late the next morning.

Mama could make the best fig preserves. She had to watch me or I would eat a whole pint of them.

That morning that's what we had for breakfast, fig preserves, fried salt pork and homemade biscuits. We ate hurriedly, wanting to get back to the building site to explore, and to also help Daddy.

After we ate I split two of Mama's buttermilk biscuits, put some figs between the layers and wrapped them up in a brown paper sack.

I thought about Black Boy saving our lives the day before, so I quickly unfolded the bag and placed him a biscuit and a piece of the salt meat in there also.

I could hear Mama peddling away on her old Sanger sewing machine. She was a wiz at that thing. About all of Shelby,

Sunshine's, and her clothes, Mama sewed them on the sewing machine.

As we walked by her we told her where we were going.

"Uh, uh, uh, Bossy is waiting on you boys."

"Damn, can't Buddy milk that cow," Pap said.

"Where did you learn that word," Mama asked.

"What word, Pap said?

"You know what word! And if I ever hear you say it again, I'm going to give you something you've been needing since that rattlesnake bite!"

"Yes Ma'am," Pap said, so we returned to the kitchen to get the scalded metal bucket.

On our way to the milking stall and making sure we were out of the distance of Mama's hearing range Pap said. "What in the hell does she do with all this damn milk around here? I don't ever see anybody drink it."

For some unknown reason I defended Mama. "She makes butter, buttermilk, so that we can have those delicious buttermilk biscuits. She makes that horrible cheese that the blow flies swarm if she leaves it out and she sells some of it so that we can buy school supplies when our cotton picking money runs out."

I noticed that Pap quit pulling on poor Bossy's teats so hard and I know she was relieved.

I could just see him grinning, "Yeah, that damn cheese would gag a maggot," he said laughing.

Chapter 24

I thought that Sarge's place was the only thing on that side of town past Redtown, but I'd been noticing a little dim dirt path to the left and I always just thought it led to a field or a cow pasture.

We saw fresh tire tracks so we decided to investigate.

We didn't have to walk too far before we came around a bend in the road and saw a house similar to ours, painted red and everything.

There was about a four foot wooden fence around the place and a little stout gray haired lady outside hoeing around some flowers that she had planted around the fence. In fact there were flowering shrubs and flowers everywhere in the yard.

Of course the first thing that Black Boy did was cock up one of his back legs and pee all over some of her flowers.

The lady shook her hoe at our dog and hollered at him, but that didn't deter him. He leaped over the fence and walked up the steps toward a little red haired girl that was sitting in a swing holding her hands out to him.

We walked hurriedly toward the house and told the frightened lady that our dog wouldn't hurt the little girl, who in fact was already patting Black Boy on the head.

The short little lady sat down on the door steps and put one of her hands to her breathless chest.

We introduced ourselves and told them we were building a house up the road.

The cute little redhead blurted out that her name was Myrtice, that the other lady was her Big Mama and that she, Myrtice, could run a hundred miles an hour.

The old lady laughed and said her name was Sara Watson, the little girl that could run a hundred miles an hour was her granddaughter. She lived there with her son and his wife.

Miss Watson made her way into the kitchen and brought us all some homemade peanut butter cookies and some ice cold lemonade.

The first thing I did was look up and I noticed electric wires coming to the house and I thought how wonderful it must be to have cold lemonade without the ice.

We told them a little something about our family, leaving out our Big Mama of course, for there seemed to be a world of difference in the two Big Mamas. That difference definitely wouldn't have come out in favor of ours.

We learned that Myrtice was in the fifth grade too, but she went to school across the tracks. Her Daddy Joe put her off on his way to work at the sawmill.

We didn't stay too much longer, because Black Boy ran one of her cats up a tree.

Myrtice said she'd race us to the main road.

We counted to three and lit out. Of course, Pap was in the lead because he was a year older and taller, and before we reached that main road, I didn't have much doubt that the red-headed Myrtice couldn't run a hundred miles an hour. We came in at the same time. I found out later on that she was a few months older than me.

It was a lot more work, but Daddy tied the studs into the foundation, meaning as we nailed the main flooring down, we had to leave a gap every sixteen inches so we could drive the nails into the sturdy foundation, instead of the modern way of just nailing everything down directly on top of the flooring.

We learned a lot building that house, and I really enjoyed being around Daddy. He seemed to never run out of energy; he stayed steady at it, and the main thing he seemed as though he knew exactly what he was doing.

I remember him telling us a hip roof was a lot stronger than a gable roof, so our house was going to have a hip roof and an eight-foot back porch on the back as well as a front porch.

We were about through putting the studs for the walls to be put up, when a big black four-door car came driving up. Daddy Jim and Sunshine were sitting in the passenger's seat. We took a good look before we ran over to the car, to make sure Big Mama wasn't in there. Mama and Shelby were in the back.

Daddy got everything nailed down so that he'd be able to walk over to the car, because Daddy Jim never got out of the vehicle.

Daddy Jim couldn't turn his neck due to the arthritis, so he just opened the door to the car and threw a brand-new Skill saw down on the ground, still in its box.

Mama and Shelby were already outside, walking on the foundation of the house and being amazed at the work that had gotten done in just two days.

"That skill saw won't do any good out here, Jimmy; there's no electricity," my Daddy said to Daddy Jim.

"Charlie, let me do this for my daughters and grand-children," Daddy Jim insisted. "Allow me to run the electric wires out here, and buy at least a refrigerator and a stove.

"I'm not going to live much longer, and Mama keeps stealing about everything I have," he went on. "Not to mention Willie Joe and Talmer. I shore have to keep a close eye on it, or them three sorry things wouldn't be eating."

"I don't know. I'll talk to the old lady about it," said Daddy.

"You're too late on that," Daddy Jim answered. "I've already talked to her, and she's fine with it."

"Jimmy, I'll be lucky if I have enough to finish this house. It might take me a long time to pay you back."

"You don't understand. You don't owe me a damn thing. Now, you're making me mad. Take the money and don't skimp on your house, either. If you need any more to finish it, get word to me, okay?

"I paid my place off years ago. I've been lucky with a few other things that no one knows about, so let me do this. I owe it to you.

"Another thing, you build a bathroom in there somewhere. I'll buy the damn hot water heater, bath tub and commode."

"All right, then," Daddy reluctantly answered.

"Okay, I'll get Sam here to drive me to the power company tomorrow morning and they'll start running the lines, and oh! Charlie, don't you attempt to wire that house for electricity yourself."

"I know how," Daddy said.

And that was the end of it.

"Let's go, Sam," Daddy Jim said as he set out a six-pack of

Coca-Colas and package of chocolate cookies for us children.

Daddy Jim was true to his word. We had an electric pole and a long electric wire to hook that Skill saw to, Wednesday afternoon when we got out of school.

We worked on the house every afternoon until the time changed, and then we only could work on it on Saturdays and Sundays.

Daddy intended to just put down another hand water pump closer to the house, but Daddy Jim sent a well driller out there, and we had an electric pump and running water that same day. There was even a brand new wringer-type washing machine sitting on the back porch. All in all, it was a big change for the better, for our family.

Chapter 25

Pap had mastered that guitar; he could bend those strings and pick that thing. He could play the saxophone, too, but he hadn't quite mastered it. Mama kept it and the banjo under lock and key in the cedar robe. She said those two instruments made the dogs in the neighborhood howl, and got old Pete braying, and they were just down right nerve-wracking.

Right before the Christmas holidays of 1955, there was going to be a talent contest at school, and the winner would get twenty-five dollars. Pap and I entered. He was to do the picking on the guitar, and I was going to do the singing.

We had already priced the new shotguns down at Mr.

Hughes' store, behind Mama's back, of course. A new Remington breech loader with a box of shells was forty-five dollars. With the whiskey and the rattlesnake money I'd been saving, we'd only need eleven more dollars to buy the guns if we won the contest. We planned on putting it on, big time.

Surprisingly, Mama brought Shelby and Sunshine to the event. They paid their quarters and were sitting on the front row.

I remember looking at my Mama and thinking how pretty she was. For some reason or other, it seemed as though I was looking at her from a different perspective. I also noticed how she turned the heads of some of the men folks there, but she paid them no attention; she came to see her children perform.

Shelby was pretty, too, with her long shiny black hair and black eyes like Daddy.

Sunshine was Mama made all over again.

We were number twenty-five to perform, and like I said, we really put it on. Instead of doing just one song or routine like the others, we did two.

We did "Lovesick Blues" and "I Saw the Light." Both selections were from Hank Williams.

We had the crowd on their feet, and I encouraged them to join in on "I Saw the Light."

When they heard us sing and saw that the crowd was with us, some of the other contestants that had already paid their dollar entrance fee left and went home.

Sure enough, when the judges named the winner, they called out our names. I looked at Mama, and she was one happy woman.

I think Mama realized we had a stash of cash somewhere. Maybe she'd found it, I don't know, but she never asked us for that talent contest money to spend on school supplies.

The next night, we were to cross the tracks and perform at Hampton High School auditorium. The winner there was to receive a fifty-dollar cash prize, plus a trip on to state competitions after the holidays.

Mama had us all slicked down, and those clothes had so much starch in them you could've shot us with a .22 caliber rifle and the bullet would have ricocheted right off us.

Contestant number one had the same color hair as Mama's, a golden blonde. She had it swirled and styled and pasted into place with so much hair spray it never moved through her whole performance.

As the master of ceremonies announced, "Contestant number one is Miss Linda Gail Snell!" I couldn't take my eyes off the spectacle the girl made.

I'd never seen a lady dress in public as she was dressed that night. She had on a tight, shimmering gold bathing-suit looking outfit, and she started twirling a stick with fire on each end of it. I would later learn it was called a baton—and also that Linda Gail was the Hampton mayor's daughter.

She was dancing, twirling and carrying on to the music of "Shake, Rattle, and Roll." The crowd was really paying attention. Linda Gail danced around, and would throw that burning baton up into the air and catch it with the next hand, then twirl some more.

Finally, she let the baton get too close to her head, and it set her hair on fire.

Linda Gail was so caught up in her own performance that she didn't even notice; she just kept on twirling, even though the crowd was yelling that her hair was on fire. She thought they were just amazed at her twirling abilities, so she threw the next one even higher in the air, and missed it.

I'd already seen the tub of water on stage, so me and Pap ran out there and stuck her head into the tub of water.

No one else would do anything.

Linda Gail cussed a blue streak and ran off stage, and I don't think she realized even then that her hair had caught on fire. She must have thought it was pure meanness on our part, even though by the time we stuck her head in the water, most of her hair was burned off.

It was about 9:30 p.m. before the other children were through performing, and we were the last to perform.

We did the two by ol' Hank again, and I really put it on. They had a microphone and I could throw my voice just like Hank.

When we finished, the crowd stood up and applauded.

Mama motioned for us to bow and to just stay on the stage.

The judges passed around a few notes, and then a man practically snatched the microphone out of my hand and announced the winner.

"Ladies and Gentlemen, once again Hampton has toed

the mark and beaten Redtown in the talent competition!"

Some of the audience members started booing and throwing their crumpled paper cups toward the master of ceremonies.

He fought through it, though, and said, "This year's winner is our very own mayor's daughter, little Linda Gail Snell."

The girl with the hair burned off came out of nowhere and said, "I'm only accepting this so that I can donate it to the needy at Christmas time." Then she bowed and ran off the stage with a death's grip on that fifty bucks.

Everyone was booing.

Somehow or other Mama climbed up on that stage and cussed out every judge up there, and then told us to follow her home.

In a way I was ashamed of my Mama that night, and then in another way, I was proud of her. We could always count on Mama to look out for us. There was one thing about her: she was rough around the edges, and domineering, but we knew she loved us.

I never thought about Mama's situation much until I was on up in age, but she married at fourteen, to a man fifteen years older than her. She birthed five children by the time she was twenty-one years old, and raised six, counting Sunshine. She had no one to turn to in order to learn how to cook and tend to all of us, but she somehow did it anyway.

That household was run like a well-oiled machine. She made sure that we kept our bodies clean, and that we had food on the table.

In order to keep up with everything, she was constantly on her feet. About the only time Mama sat was to shell beans or peas or do a thing she dearly loved, sit at her old pedal sewing machine and just hum away, sewing something for Shelby or Sunshine to wear.

I often wondered why she never sewed us boys anything, but as far as I remember, she never did.

Early the next morning after the talent show in Hampton, we'd just gotten through with the milking when a new pickup truck drove into the yard, and the driver blew the horn.

Black Boy automatically ran under the doorsteps to snare him if the man tried to come up onto the porch.

Mama walked out on the porch, drying her hands with

her apron.

"Yes sir, may I help you?" Mama asked.

"I take it you're the mother of these two talented young men here," the man said.

"Oh, that," Mama laughed. "Yes, I am."

"Ma'am, I'm George Snell, owner of Snell Hardware and lumber company. Your husband has bought a great deal of material from me, and I just want you to know I appreciate it.

"I also want you to know that I had nothing to do with the judge's decisions last night. You know, and everyone else that was there knows, your boys won that contest hands down."

He then reached in his pocket and pulled out a crisp new fifty-dollar bill and handed it to Mama.

"Mr. Snell, we don't accept charity, but as you said, I know those boys won that thing last night and I will gladly accept the money on their behalf. You are truly a good man," she told him, taking the bill from his hand.

Mr. Snell smiled and said, "I am very pleased at your re-action this morning."

Mama laughed, showing her perfect white teeth. "After

the show I put on myself last night, I'm the one that really deserves the fifty dollars."

Mr. Snell laughed and slapped himself on the thighs, and said, "That's just fine—they deserved it." Then he added, "I'm going out to the building site now to deliver some light fixtures. Does anyone need a ride?"

"Yes, these two," Mama answered, "as soon as they put the milk in the kitchen."

"Do you mind if our dog rides with us?" I asked, then added, "We'll ride in the back."

"Sure," Mr. Snell agreed.

Mama followed us into the house, and of all things, she stuffed that fifty dollars into my shirt pocket!

"Now, I want you to half it with Pap. That's quite a sum for boys y'all's age! Use it wisely."

"Mama, are you sure?" I asked.

"I don't know, but to me, money made this way is sort of like the money you get for helping Daddy. I feel that you should do with it as you please. Now hurry. Mr. Snell is waiting on you."

I ran back outside to the cow stall, where I knew no one

would be prying, and I got our stash of thirty-four dollars and ninety-five cents.

We called Black Boy and sailed onto the back of Mayor Snell's truck. It was a short ride to Sarge's intersection, and we tapped on the back of the cab to tell him to stop and let us out there.

Miss Minnie hadn't even had time to cover herself in dirt when we spoke to her.

"Good morning gentlemen," she said.

"Good morning, Miss Minnie. Hope your rheumatiz ain't bothering you much today," I said, as we walked by.

"Oh it's always bothering me, boys," we heard from a distance as we walked by.

Mr. Hughes hadn't opened yet, so we walked over to Mr. Pickett's and bought Miss Minnie some bananas and took them back to her.

She had about dug all the dirt out of her hole when Pap asked her something that had been on his mind.

"Miss Minnie, if I was to bring my banjo and saxophone to you, could you teach me some tunes? Mama won't let me practice them much around the house."

"Yes, Pap, I could, and I will. If not played properly, each instrument can be quite annoying. In fact, I'd be glad to; it will be my Christmas present to you, and we could certainly liven this old corner up for the holiday," she said.

I loved to hear Miss Minnie talk. The words just seemed to flow out of her mouth, and she always spoke with perfect grammar. She seemed much too refined to be the kind of crazy woman who would dig a hole in the dirt and sit in it all day. I also noticed that despite her "rheumatiz," there didn't look to be anything wrong with the way she walked or moved.

Miss Minnie was hiding something; I sensed it. In my nine-year-old mind that had been fed on adventure books and movies, I thought that maybe she was a Russian spy or something in that order, but she was too sweet for that. I did know that she was destined for greater things than to lie in a hole covered in dirt, eat bananas and read books all day.

Even as simple-minded as Sarge was, I believe he sensed it too.

Mr. Hughes opened about the time that Miss Minnie got her umbrella set up and was conversing with her first visitor, so we told her goodbye, and we left.

As it turned out, we were too young to buy the shotguns ourselves, but that didn't deter us. We walked up to the pawn shop and Slim and Leroy had just what we wanted. The shotguns they had were barely used, and we got both of them for fifty dollars, plus two boxes of bird shells—just what we wanted. Neither Slim nor Leroy gave a hoot how old we were, just as long as our money was green.

Before I put the cash in Leroy's hands I told him, "We'll have to see both the guns shoot, first."

We walked through the snake man's room. We had learned his real name was Romalis, or something like that. Anyway, he was from overseas, and we couldn't pronounce that last name.

Slim and Leroy held each gun in the air and shot them at a post in back of the place.

The guns looked all right to me and Pap, so we paid them the fifty dollars and left with thirty-four dollars and seventy cents in our pockets, less the guns, shells and bananas.

Black Boy had already run four squirrels up the trees, and we killed them before we got to the lane that went to

Myrtice's house.

We shot two more by the time we reached where she lived.

She and her Big Mama were standing on the front porch to see what all the shooting was about.

Black Boy was about to pee on Miz Watson's pretty flowers again, when I called him off.

We were holding the squirrels by the tails.

"Oh my, do I love me some fried squirrels and gravy. I haven't had squirrel since I left home in Franklin," Mrs. Watson said.

"You gave us the lemonade and cookies, so you can have them," I told her.

She had a black plastic belt with a knotted handkerchief tied around it. She untied the many knots and asked us to come to the porch with the squirrels. She counted out six quarters, one for each squirrel.

I remember looking at the little plump lady's short red shoes, and thinking that she had the shortest feet I'd ever seen.

Myrtice wanted to race to the road again, but I told her

that we had our new guns and we'd better not run.

"That's okay, I'll just walk that far with you, then," she said, and so she did.

On that short little walk, Black Boy treed some more squirrels. I wanted to shoot them so Myrtice could see us handle our new guns, but we didn't have time for that. We had to go on to the building site and help Buddy because Daddy was working. But I found a friend in Myrtice that day, one that would last me the rest of my life... and boy, would we have some adventures on that dirt road, until she moved across town.

We decided to hide our shotguns and shells in the loft of the new house that afternoon.

We'd tell Mama in due time; we had already told Buddy how we'd gotten the money, and he swore not to tell Mama unless she asked him about it.

Chapter 26

We had swiped some of that horrible smelling cheese of Mama's a few days before school was out. We figured it would be perfect catfish bait. On the way to our place was a small stream with a clay bottom. We dug up a little of that clay, mixed it with that stinking cheese, and set it out in the sun for it to harden.

Miss Minnie noticed us going through Mr. Reese's garbage cans and asked us what we were about.

We told her we were looking for gallon jugs to tie fishing lines to, so that we could throw them in the pond and we could be fishing while we'd be working.

She laughed and pulled the lid off a shoe polish can and

brought out a shiny quarter.

"Go over to Mr. Pickett's store and buy some balloons, and tell him I sent you or he'll push some cheap thin ones off on you. That should do the trick for you, better than the gallon jugs."

"Miss Minnie, do you like catfish?" Pap asked.

"Oh, heavens, no! Nothing but scale fish for me, and I wouldn't scale and clean one for anything."

"What do you eat, Miss Minnie?" Pap wanted to know.

"Oh, besides the bananas, I eat mostly out of cans. Nothing that I must cook, and I do very well with it. I eat no meat whatsoever," she said.

We didn't want to hurt her feelings, so we took her quarter and bought the balloons.

We told Buddy he would just have to wait on us until we got those hooks baited and in the water. When we got them all set, we could see the bright red balloons from the roof, for we were tacking down the shingles just like Daddy had shown Buddy.

Sure enough, in about fifteen minutes those balloons started to bob up and down in that pond.

Buddy told us only one of us could go check our lines, and since Pap was the faster worker, he chose him to stay.

Me and Black Boy dove off into that pond, and I started pulling the lines, making sure to grab the line right below the balloons, one at a time.

I pulled out five long wiggling catfish at least a foot long. Then I rebaited my hooks with that stinking cheese and slang them back out there.

Boy, would Mama and Daddy be pleased! And I sure wasn't going to tell her what I had used for bait.

I tied a stick about a foot long on a piece of fishing line, then threaded the other end through the gills of the obstinate, grunting fishes and put them all back into the water near the pond's edge so they would stay cool. I tied the other end of my stringer to a small sapling, securing my catch.

No one must've never fished that pond, because I'd caught twelve big, squealing, grunting catfish within an hour.

Every time I got one, I put it on the stringer so it would stay alive and fresh, then I would throw them back into the water and secure my line to the sapling again.

I could see Pap looking at me from the roof, and I knew

he wished Buddy had picked him to go fishing instead of me, but for once in my life it came in handy for me that Pap could out-work me.

I let all the air out of the balloons and brought everything but the fish to the new house so the cows couldn't get into anything.

Pap's job was mostly just toting shingles up the ladder, and I think just for punishment about the fishing, he and Buddy gave me that job instead.

Those suckers were heavy. I couldn't carry but twelve shingles at a time up that ladder, and I'll swear both my brothers picked up speed on the nailing when I started bring those shingles up that ladder, just to make me work that much harder.

Thank goodness, Mama had sent us a small lunch by Buddy, so about the middle of the evening we knocked off to eat our peanut butter and jelly sandwiches. She'd fried us some apple tarts again, wrapped in brown paper to absorb the grease, and a half gallon of lukewarm water. I know I drank my part of that water and then some, because I was so exhausted.

Pap and I wanted to go jump into the pond and get cooled off, but Buddy wouldn't let us, reminding us that it was December and it would probably kill us.

"My Lord, I've been without a shirt and shoes all day," I protested.

"If I'd known you were going to be swimming around in that water to get the catfish, I would've told you not to. Don't you tell Mama. Thank God you'll be dried off by the time we get home."

"Then how am I going to explain the fish?" I asked.

"Just tell her you caught them, and let that be it," Buddy said.

If only the good Lord had made me like Buddy, I thought. He was only a couple of years older than me, yet so much wiser about things. He definitely has a level head on his shoulders, and I can never remember Mama whipping him.

I sure remembered one day when Mama whipped me, though. That day, it seemed as though everything I did, I got a whipping for it. She'd already whipped me five times that day and it wasn't even dinner, so I'd just decided to climb under the house and stay under there with Black Boy.

My thing was, I'd always get two whippings for the same offense. Right before Mama would start in on me, I'd run. She'd have to send Buddy after me to catch me, and she'd whip me for the thing I did and then she'd whip me for running.

Out of all my whippings, though, I never got one of them "Willie Joe and Talmer whippings," and I sure thanked the Lord for that.

One thing about it though, I thought before Buddy told us it was time to start back to roofing that house, Daddy loves catfish, and I know he'll be pleased when I bring that long string of fish in.

We'd been putting shingles on that house for three days, using awkward hands and child sweat, but at about four o'clock that evening Buddy nailed the last shingle onto the front porch roof.

We didn't take the time to go back down that ladder. We just jumped off the porch.

Buddy stood off from the house on both sides and looked at the roof and porches. On the side facing Sarge's house, he found a small sag that was down a short row of shingles.

He told us we had to go back up there and straighten that part out.

Our fingers were already as sore as a risen from that hammer. In fact, Pap had even thrown his hammer away several times, just to have to go down the ladder and hunt for it, slowing us down.

When Buddy told us we were going to have to climb back up on top of that house again, we both cussed like sailors and drew back our hammers at Buddy.

Black Boy had been mighty patient just to lay around in the shade all day, sensing we didn't have time to squirrel hunt, but now he growled at us, thinking we were serious about those hammers.

Pap winked at me and we threw down our hammers and rushed Buddy, throwing him on the ground.

Black Boy even joined in on the fun. We rolled around and around on the ground playing, but we never could get the best of Buddy, who seemed to be enjoying the roughhousing too.

Black Boy got carried away and got a good hold of Pap's britches' leg and kept pulling at them until he finally pulled them completely off and ran across the yard with them.

Black Boy kept tripping over the britches, so Pap soon caught up with him and slipped his pants back on.

We were all tired and hungry that day, but we did get a laugh out of the usually solemn Buddy.

He told me and Pap to just clean up the pieces of trimmings and scraps left over from the shingles, and he believed he could straighten the sagging row of shingles by himself.

And so we did.

Chapter 27

That string of fish was too heavy for me to tote by myself, so Buddy rigged up a short pole and tied the string of fish in the middle. That way, Pap carried one end of the pole and me the other. The only thing that was so taxing was that the string of fish was so long we had to hold them shoulder high to keep them from dragging on the ground.

I was sure hoping Miss Minnie would be in her hole so that she could see the results of her balloon trick, but she was already gone.

Sarge was still in town, though, selling his hog meat, and he said he was mighty pleased we had caught so many.

He also said that he'd never allowed anyone else to fish

in the pond, not even the man that rented the pasture for his cows.

"Of course, he's old as the dickens and has never asked me anyway," Sarge added.

Of course, Mama already had supper on the table by the time we arrived, but she was thrilled with the catfish.

There was a big nail sticking out of the barn wall, and it was just right to hang the gills of those catfish on. It was messy work to clean them, but easy enough. All we had to do was cut around the bottom of the head of each fish, then strip the thick skin straight down, making sure to avoid the long barb-like dorsal fins on each side of the head. Both me and Pap had been "finned" before, and we knew they were poisonous if you got stuck. (We also knew that even though Mama would say to use antiseptic, the best thing for the swelling was to rub the puncture with belly slime from the fish that got you. Daddy taught it to us; he said in all his life he never once got infected from it.)

Using our pocketknives and a pair of pliers, we had those fish skinned and in Mama's ice box within thirty minutes. We had to hurry, as it was December and darkness came pretty quickly in the winter months. We were pretty good at it by now, so neither of us were finned.

Mama covered the fish so they wouldn't stink up everything else in the little ice box, then she made me and Pap wash our hands with some of that strong lye soap of hers. As an extra precautionary act she had us to rinse our hands, using baking soda to make sure all the stench was gone.

I didn't see the need, because we'd all be traipsing out to that cold bath house right after supper.

It was very late when Daddy came in from work that night, so Mama decided that we'd better go ahead and eat our supper while it was still hot. She fixed Daddy a plate and put it on back of the wooden stove so it would stay warm.

Mama decided it wasn't quite cold enough to build a fire in the bath house, so we all made our baths as quick as possible.

Every night, it was the same routine: Mama always made sure Shelby's and Sunshine's hair was clean and brushed after their baths. Shelby's hair wasn't hard to brush, because her hair wasn't as curly as Sunshine's.

If Mama ever loved a child, she dearly loved Sunshine—

and Daddy did too.

Mama would be as gentle as possible as she tried to brush the tangles out of Sunshine's hair after each washing and before she left for school, but at times you could still hear yelps and whines coming from the tender-headed girl.

Mama always made sure it was brushed completely dry, though, taking as much time as needed to get it just right before Sunshine was sent off to bed.

I told Mama about Myrtice that night and what a nice little girl she seemed to be.

Mama said that Sunshine did need a little girl to play with.

"Why don't you ask and see if her parents will allow her to come over and spend the day with Sunshine tomorrow? Lord knows, Shelby and I need to pack everything that we can to make the move, since we'll be going to the new house in a few days. Maybe Myrtice can help keep Sunshine out of our way while we work."

"Ok, I'll ask Miz Watson tomorrow," I said.

We had all gone to bed by the time Daddy came in. I heard the muffled sounds as he told Mama the good news from his long day.

"Even though everything is being rushed up at the mill so they can be shut down until after the holidays, the boss man just gave me, without any charge, enough windows and all solid matching wooden doors for the entire house!

"It's just too good to be true," Daddy told Mama, and then he added, "All brand new."

I also heard him tell her that he'd be getting a Christmas bonus this year, now that he was in management.

That's all I could remember hearing before I fell off to sleep, knowing that everything was all right now that Daddy was in the house.

Chapter 28

The next morning, as soon as we ate breakfast and milked the cow, we headed out for the new place. There wasn't much left to do but to clean up the yards and set out a few camellia shrubs that Mama had dug up at the old house.

She placed the three shrubs in a cotton sack so they wouldn't be so awkward for us to carry.

Pap had talked Mama into letting him have the banjo and saxophone, "Just through the Christmas holidays for Miss Minnie to play," he said.

"Well, as long as it's down there! Heaven knows that Pig Meat's place is bad enough on the weekends," she said. Mama then did something I thought was unusual for her, as she had already classified Miss Minnie as being crazy. She gave me a small tin of Christmas cookies that she had baked, and told me to give them to Miss Minnie and wish her a Merry Christmas.

She also told us not to take too long, since there was a lot to do at the new place that day.

Boy, Pap was thrilled to get back ahold of that sax and banjo! As soon as Mama said we could, we walked straight to Miss Minnie's hole, with the instruments and the tin of cookies.

When she saw us, Miss Minnie pulled herself to a sitting position. I handed her the cookies first and told her Mama sent them.

She must have heard by my voice that I was surprised by Mama's gesture, because she said, "Yes, we've become friends. I like spending time together—when the poor woman has a spare moment, that is; she works so hard.

"Tell your dear mother thank you for me, and on your way back from your new house, be sure to stop by. I have something for her as well."

With that, Miss Minnie turned to the instruments, seeing that Pap was more than ready for her to get started. She picked up the saxophone first and played impeccably, never missing a note.

I recognized some of the tunes, and some I didn't. I do remember one of them was "Up a Lazy River."

People started gathering. Pap and me were not the only ones who could tell that Miss Minnie had real talent with her musical abilities.

When she began to play, Sarge looked over and grinned. I could tell he liked the music as much as anybody, since almost nothing was important enough to distract him from his duties at the intersection.

After playing a few songs, Miss Minnie handed Pap the sax, and he gave her the banjo. It took quite a bit of turning, but she started out with "Foggy Mountain Breakdown," and her next selection was "The Alabama Jubilee."

Even though Mama had told us not to take long, we stayed right there and listened to her play till she was done. We knew we would have to work that much faster to catch up, but it was well worth it to hear that music.

She played for at least an hour before she took a long

breath and said, "Whew! You boys couldn't have given me a finer gift than to allow me to play for Christmas time."

"Just keep the sax and banjo with you through Christmas Eve," Pap said generously. "That's not but two more days," he added.

"Tell you what, I'll play them for the folks, but you can pick the instruments up each afternoon," she answered. "I don't know whether you realize it or not, Pap, but that banjo is a Buckbee, very old and expensive. I'd take good care of it if I were you."

"Yes, Ma'am, I will, and I'll be sure to tell Mama what you said, too," Pap promised.

Miss Minnie had drawn quite a crowd by the time she was finished for the session. A few people even threw coins her way.

After they left, she asked us if we'd pick the coins up for her; after we did, she told us to just keep them.

We tried to give the money back to her, but she wouldn't take it. She insisted we keep it, so we did.

Right as Miss Minnie was finishing up, the Snake Man came whizzing by on a pair of roller skates with the toes of

the skates cut off, showing his pointed red toenails. I believe he'd pretty well mastered the roller skates, though, even though it was hard for him to come to a sudden stop with the toes of the shoes cut off.

As we were leaving, we saw a new sign outside one of the old empty buildings near the pawn shop, so we walked up there to investigate. Even though we were late to the new house already, we had to stop by. We wanted to know who had hung the sign, and why.

As it turned out, it was the lady that had the monkey on her head, who had cussed Miss Minnie so.

Come to find out, the monkey woman claimed to be a palm reader; she already had two or three ignorant folks in there. We could see her through the glass, and we stood there staring at the goings-on until she came to the door and ran us off.

Between hearing Miss Minnie playing world-class music from her dirt hole, seeing Sarge directing non-existent traffic at his intersection and blowing his whistle at the Snake Man whose red toenails flashed in the sun as he zipped by on his roller skates, and watching the monkey woman reading palms and acting mean as ever (and all of that before noon), we were pretty sure Redtown had to be the strangest place on the planet.

It had turned out to be a decent enough morning, even though we hadn't seen the backward-walking man with his little dog, or heard "Two, two, two," that day. There was plenty more crazy left over for another day.

Chapter 29

After all that, we decided we'd better get on toward the house and help Buddy, but first we had to stop by and see Mrs. Watson about Myrtice spending the afternoon and night with Sunshine.

Black Boy had decided to go with Buddy, so for once we didn't have to worry about him peeing on Mrs. Watson's flowers when we walked into her yard that morning.

Myrtice was sitting on the porch coloring in a coloring book, and Mrs. Watson had brought the ironing board out and was ironing clothes on the porch, where it was cooler than inside the house.

Mrs. Watson noticed us first.

"What you boys up to this morning?" she asked, causing Myrtice to lay down her coloring book and look up.

"We told Mama about Myrtice, and she asked us to stop by here and see if Myrtice would like to come up and play with Sunshine and maybe spend the night," I said.

"You know, I've been thinking about that very thing. I know your Mama and Mr. Jim. I've even heard the story about why that pretty little girl came to live with y'all."

"I feel sure it will be all right with Joe and her Mama. I'll walk up there with her after dinner today," she said.

Of course, Myrtice put in to wanting to go right then instead, but her Big Mama gave her a stern look and told her she had to finish with the ironing before she could bring Myrtice over to our house.

By the time we hit the main dirt road, a truck and trailer passed us, headed toward our new house. On back of the trailer was a big gas tank, and right behind the truck and trailer was a propane gas truck that had a picture of a telephone on the driver's side door.

We sped up, and sure enough the trucks backed into our yard.

Just as soon as the man from the first truck lowered the gas tank down on some concrete blocks near the house, the man in the gas truck started filling the tank with propane. When the tank was full, the man driving the gas truck left, and the other fellow started digging ditches and laying down pipes in them to hook everything up.

The man introduced himself as Mr. Hooks. He seemed to be such a nice young man. I remember he had coal black hair, and said he had a little boy, too.

It didn't take Mr. Hooks but about an hour and a half to do everything. Before he was done, he brought out a gas heater for our dining room and a hot water heater for the bathroom. He even finished running the short distance of water line and checked everything out for gas leaks.

Mr. Hooks waited around a few minutes, then he turned the water on at the kitchen and bathroom sinks as well as the bathtub. He told us to hold our hands under the water so we could see that it was already getting warm.

The first thing I thought of was Mama, and how much easier life would be for her. Right after that, it dawned on me how nice it would be not to have to go out to the bath house for a cold bath anymore.

Hooks was quick to get all that done in such a short time, but he did a thorough job. He double-checked for gas leaks before he covered the gas lines back up with dirt, and then he showed us how the gauge worked on the gas tank.

We knew this wasn't the doings of Daddy; it had to have been Daddy Jim.

After Mr. Hooks left, we went ahead and plugged up the refrigerator and stove, making sure to put some water in the four aluminum ice trays that came with the refrigerator. The little ice trays had handles on them that you pulled up to release the ice.

We could hardly wait for the water to freeze into ice, because we wanted to try out those handles.

Readymade ice, right from our own refrigerator's freezer! It was hard to believe, after so long of using the big blocks of ice that you had to chip pieces off of with an ice pick. We could hardly believe our good fortune.

Next, we went to work setting out the camellias at Mama's designated areas.

Just about the time we had the camellias planted and the

yard spotless, we saw Myrtice and her Big Mama coming up the road. Mrs. Watson was pushing an old rickety wheelbarrow that was loaded down with a bunch more flowers and shrubs to set out, and Myrtice was trotting along beside her.

The old lady could tell what we were thinking from seeing the looks on our faces.

"Don't worry, boys," she grinned. "It won't be much work a'tall. About all we'll have to put in the ground today are these two sweet shrubs; they smell so heavenly! The rest are an assortment of roses and periwinkles. With those, we can just cover the roots in dirt, and your Mama will have all winter to set them out. I have the roses tagged as to whether they're running roses or not."

That suited us fine, because we didn't want to be worried with setting out flowers. The camellias and sweet shrubs were bad enough.

Me and Pap wanted to go hunting, and Buddy was ready to go back to work on the shop that he and Daddy were building.

"Sure is a nice house," Mrs. Watson said, giving the house a good going over.

"Yessum, and I heard Daddy say there wasn't a penny owed on it," Pap spoke up.

"Would you like to see inside?" Buddy asked.

"No, I'll wait until y'all move in, and I'll come visit with your Mama then," she said.

"I'd like to go in," said Myrtice, who hadn't gotten a word in edgewise while her Big Mama was going on about the plants.

"Shush, child," Mrs. Watson said, causing Myrtice to stomp the ground with one of her feet and say, "I don't ever get to do anything but color!"

Hearing this, Mrs. Watson gave Myrtice a soft slap on her backside. "If you can't behave yourself any better than that, you won't be spending the night with Sunshine, young lady."

At that, Myrtice just dawdled her shoes in the ground, knowing better than to say anything else. "Tell your Mama the plants are a Christmas gift, and I hope she enjoys them," Mrs. Watson said, and she and Myrtice left.

Chapter 30

Even though we wanted to hunt, and squirrels were abundant, we knew Mama didn't have time to fool with any squirrels today, with her packing and everything. Also, me and Pap were already behind time on our other work, so we decided not to crawl up unto the ladder and get our guns out after all. Instead, we got to work on cleaning out the barn so it would be ready for the animals when they arrived.

Sarge, good friend that he was, had talked to the fellow that farmed his land and he was going to get his crew of men to move our corn and sweet potatoes into the cribs that we had hurriedly thrown together.

Sarge's man was even going to move ol' Pete, Bossy and

the new calf, the sow, shoats and piglets, and even the chickens. Then, on the final day, he was going to move all our household items for us.

When we were almost finished cleaning out the barn, here came the big truck on its first run. It was loaded with corn, the braying Pete (who seemed to be enjoying the ride), and the faithful old Bossy and her calf.

Daddy had already made sure there weren't any more rattlesnakes. He'd sprayed inside and under the barn with a poison that was guaranteed to kill snakes. All that was left in there was an old safe and an oval-top trunk, which we quickly dragged to the rear of the barn next to the big back door.

The crew had the small crib in the front part of the barn filled with the corn in no time. Me and Pap climbed up to the loft and opened the door; they threw us the bundles of fodder and we stacked them neatly enough so that Daddy would be proud of us.

The next thing was our hoard of sweet potatoes, which they had in three big cotton sacks on top of the rear of the truck.

Very gently, the crew lowered them to the ground, and us

boys began storing them in the potato shed near the house.

"We'll be back in a small while with the hogs," one of the men said.

We had built a fence straight down our land, almost splitting it in half. The hog lot was in the very back, and it was made from boards. It even had a wooden bottom so the hogs couldn't root out from under the small building, and as for the other animals, there was a shed for them to get out of the rain.

The farm animals were on the right side. Daddy planned to use the remainder on the left for a garden. He said most of it would have to be planted in corn to be able to feed the animals, but Mama didn't like the idea. I heard her tell Daddy one night that it was mighty bad times when a damn mule and other critters were put before her young'uns.

The reason I can honestly say I never heard them argue is because Daddy never did say anything back to her.

I wasn't but nine a half, but I could tell this would be a smaller plot than the amount of land that we were accustomed to farming, which suited me just fine.

While the men were gone back after the hogs, the three

of us boys decided to go through the old trunk and the safe.

Ordinarily we'd have already gone through them both, but we were still wary of those snakes. Besides, we'd just been too busy.

As soon as we reached the back of the barn, Buddy took hold of one side of the rear doors while Pap took the other. (The doors were cut in half sideways, so that either the top or bottom parts could be opened independently.) I stood a little off to the side as Buddy snatched open the door on his side while Pap opened the other one.

I remember thinking it was lucky I wasn't up close like my brothers were, because as soon as those doors came open, a bunch of big long-tailed wood rats ran everywhere!

We all sprang back.

Those rats must have been as shocked as we were, because every one of them headed straight for the scrap wood pile.

We didn't have time to search for anything to kill those devils with before they reached that wood pile, so we started to stomp them with our shoes.

It took about thirty seconds for me to realize my good

luck had just run out. About the third rat I stomped got loose, and ran up the inside of one of my britches legs.

I bucked all over that yard, screaming for Buddy.

That rat would run up my leg squealing, and I would slap him down. I could feel his claws scratching my leg. I kept slapping him down but he kept running up; I never could slap him all the way out.

Finally the old thing made it between my knee and straddle, so I knew I had to do something fast.

I grabbed the huge lump and started to twist it round and around until I could see blood seeping through my britches leg.

Buddy, laughing, walked over and tied a string around the leg of my pants, right above my hand and the bloody spot just above my knee.

"Stop hollering, Lew," my brother said. "Just turn the rat loose and he'll fall out," and so I did.

Brrr! I get cold chills to this day thinking about that rat!

I couldn't wait to get those pants off. There may have been a cold December wind blowing but I didn't care. I had that rat's blood running down my leg, and the feeling made my skin crawl. I couldn't stand it, so I dashed down to the pond and sailed in. Buddy could tell Mama if he wanted to; at that time I didn't care.

I did take the time to shuck my drawers and shirt off before I hit the water.

The water was warmer than it was outside, so I was no hurry to get out.

Every time my head would bob above the water, I could hear Black Boy. It sounded as if he was wrestling with something.

I followed the sound with my eyes, and off in the distance, I could see my dog wrestling with the big red bull.

Now, most kids in that situation would have been worried about their dog, but I knew Black Boy enough to be more concerned for the bull. Every time the bull would stagger to his feet, Black Boy would grab that bull by the nose with his teeth and throw him to the ground again.

I would have to scold Black Boy for that. I'm sure the owner of that bull wouldn't appreciate my dog's actions at all, especially since we were about to be living here permanently.

I cupped my hands and called him while I was still in the water; I knew once I got out, I was going to be cold.

Fine time for him to be messing with that ol' bull, I thought as I saw him come a running. He should've had his rump up there with me catching those rats.

About the time Black Boy jumped in the pond, I jumped out, for I could hear the big truck coming with our pigs.

I threw on what few dry clothes I had, making sure to bring the wet pants with me, and ran toward the house, hurdling fences as I went.

I didn't stop until I got inside the house, struck a match and turned that new gas heater on. Boy, does that beat a fireplace, I thought as I stood there, shivering in the heater's sudden warmth.

I could hear the pigs squealing as I looked out the window and saw the men picking them up by their ears to put them in the pen.

I remember thinking Daddy wouldn't like that, for he didn't like to see any animal tortured.

I looked around the house for something to put on.

All I could find by way of clothing was a pair of Shelby's

pink and blue flannel pajamas that she and Mama had been using to clean the window panes with. I felt sure that Mama had sewn them herself, for no one would have bought something that looked so strange.

Like I said, they were of a flannel material, but one leg was blue and the other was pink. They must've been "one size fits all," because with the elastic in the waist and ankles, they fit. I might have looked like a jester, but at least I was warm. It also helped my feelings that even though the pajama pants were ugly as sin, at least they didn't have rat blood or guts on them.

Chapter 31

I waited until the men were through with the hogs and their truck was pulling out of the driveway, before I went back outside.

Buddy and Pap laughed like the dickens at my get-up, but I just slung the "rat britches" across the fence to dry, and tried not to pay them any more attention. To take their mind off me, I reminded them we hadn't yet looked in the old safe.

That did the trick, and we all three went back to what we had been doing before the rats interrupted us. Not wanting any more animal interruptions, we threw the still-upset hogs a few ears of corn to eat, thinking maybe it would settle them down some.

There wasn't much left in the old safe that we didn't break as we yanked it out of the old barn. There was just a bunch of old platters, dishes and such as that.

Next came the old trunk, and we made real sure we were prepared when we opened it. We each got a stick, and put Black Boy on alert.

The old trunk was in mint condition except for some rust on the clasps on each side at the top of the lid. We had to use the hammer to quickly pull the rusted locks open, then we sprang back in case of more rats or possibly snakes, but nothing jumped out.

My favorite subject in school was history, so when I saw the old sword lying right on top, I knew it was a Confederate sword from the Civil War. Beneath it was a Confederate cavalry uniform; I could tell by the insignias.

Snakes or not, I grabbed for that sword and pulled it out of its sheath.

I quickly inspected it, and engraved at the hilt of the sabre I could see "Boyle and Gamble, Virginia, CSA."

I don't think Buddy and Pap were as excited about the sword as I was; they just kept jabbing around in the trunk with their sticks.

Nothing rattled or ran out squealing, so we slowly began removing the remainder of the contents with the end of our sticks until we saw there was nothing dangerous inside.

I could tell that the old uniform had been folded with care. Probably by female hands, I thought as I folded the woolen coat and trousers back like they were and laid them gently on the ground.

Ain't nobody getting that stuff but me! I thought, as I begun to plunder around in the remainder of the trunk's contents.

I think Buddy and Pap grew disinterested in the treasure hunt as soon as they didn't find any money, and too, they knew how I had always liked old things.

Along with the sword and uniform, inside the trunk were a few old tintype pictures.

They were small, but a few were encased in beautiful frames.

There were all sorts of needles and threads, some little tiny medicine bottles, old brass buttons and an old newspaper that had "The Claiborne Southerner" boldly printed at the top, even though the lettering was a little lopsided.

About all else I could read was the date, February 1865, because when I picked it up, the old newspaper crumbled back into the dust to which it belonged.

Buddy and Pap had already started down the road back toward our old place. I ran back into the new house to double-check the gas heater, to make sure I had turned it off.

I carefully put everything back into the trunk except for one of the tiny bottles that had a glass stopper on top. I closed the lid, and then me and the waiting Black Boy ran down the road to catch up with my brothers.

We heard the music long before we got to town, and by the time we reached Mr. Reese's gas station we saw that Miss Minnie had drawn quite a crowd.

Miss Minnie had crawled out of her hole, and she was sitting in a chair. Coins and bananas were stacked or thrown everywhere around her chair.

We noticed that Pig Meat's guitar and saxophone players had joined her, and what a time they were having!

Of course, most of the selections were Christmas songs, but I'm here to tell you, it took all Pig Meat's boys could do to keep up with Miss Minnie, when she picked up that banjo and started playing. She left them behind with "Jingle Bells," and "Deck the Halls."

The guitar player was known as "Fat Boy Fats," and I believe he would've burned the strings off that guitar in order to keep up with Miss Minnie. She played with a fast, hard, striking rhythm, and everyone around marveled at her style.

I noticed that Pap couldn't keep his eyes off her hands, and he had moved within a couple of feet of her.

After she had finished her selections, she handed the instruments to Pap.

"No, Pap said, "this Banjo and sax don't belong with me, not after what I just heard."

"Oh, nonsense! I'll tell you what let's do," said Miss Minnie. "I'll take them home with me, since your Mother won't let you play them at home. You can come around my house when you get the chance, and I'll give you free lessons."

"But your hole, Miss Minnie. I don't want to take you away from that and all them free bananas."

Miss Minnie smiled, showing a perfect set of teeth.

"Ah, the dickens with the bananas. Besides, winter's

coming on, and even I am not crazy enough to be out here in the cold rainy weather."

Pap smiled and stuck out his hand for Miss Minnie to shake.

She clasped his hand and shook it one time and said, "Deal."

Chapter 32

A fter being shown up so badly by a supposedly crazy person, Pig Meat's boys wasted little time hurrying back toward the juke joint, for it was Friday, and things would soon be getting lively there.

Buddy went on to the house with Black Boy. Me and Pap gathered up the coins for Miss Minnie and helped her carry all those bananas.

I loved Miss Minnie's house. It was set back off the road so it was barely visible. There was an eight-foot fence that surrounded the whole property, and a locked gate.

Unlike the other places in Redtown, the grass wasn't hoed up, but mowed.

It was getting pretty late in the afternoon, but it was still light enough for me to be able to see a fruit orchard that peeked from behind the house.

The steps leading to Miss Minnie's house were made of cement, and they were at least twelve feet wide. They were painted red, as was the house. There was a swing on each ends of the long front porch, which covered the entire width of the house. Several rocking chairs were scattered about the porch, along with small handmade tables.

Miss Minnie laid her load of bananas down long enough to unlock the door and invite us in.

I was carrying the rest of the bananas, and Pap had the banjo and saxophone.

When we got inside, she directed us to a beautiful table with a lace tablecloth on it and a crystal chandelier hanging above it. Miss Minnie flicked on the lights, and the crystal chandelier lit up, with brilliant flashes of different colors coming from the sparkling prisms that hung down from it.

I felt as though we were out of our element when I saw how nice Miss Minnie's things were, but Pap didn't seem to feel that way at all. He just casually pulled a chair from the table and sat down, crossed his legs and started swinging his free foot.

Miss Minnie left the room for a couple of minutes. When she returned, she brought each of us three very small little bland-tasting cookies and a cold drink.

We drank our drinks, and told her we had to go because it was so late.

Before we left, I went over to her and said, "Miss Minnie, I brought you something for Christmas." Then I handed her the small bottle with the glass stopper. I'd cleaned it with the tail of my shirt, until it sparkled almost as brightly as the chandelier above our heads.

She took the small bottle, pulled the glass stopper from it, and held it to her nose.

"Why Lew, a swoon bottle! It's just what I always wanted, and it still has a faint scent to it," she said. "Thank you so much."

She followed us to the door, hugged both our necks briefly, and asked us if we could, to try to come and see her on Christmas Eve.

Then she added, "Oh, and Lew . . . I just love your decorative trousers."

I looked down and saw that I was, indeed, still wearing Shelby's pajamas. I had been so caught up in things that I had forgotten all about them. At first I was embarrassed, but then I thought, Ah, it doesn't really matter to me anyway, because I know Miss Minnie likes me, and that means a lot to me.

It didn't dawn on me until much later that if Miss Minnie had seen me wearing my sister's home-made pajamas, it meant most of the residents of Redtown had seen me in them, too.

Chapter 33

I won't ever forget our walk home early that evening from
Miss Minnie's. Not because of what I was wearing, however.
And not because I was consciously thinking about how I had
survived the battle with the rat that climbed up my britches,
or about Black Boy wrestling the red bull, or about the sword
and uniform I had found, or even about Miss Minnie's music,
although there must have been elements of each of these
in my mind as I made my way home with my brothers that
evening. I remember it so well because it was one of those
special moments that comes so rarely in a person's life, the
kind of times where everything just seems right.

In those days, everyone in the neighborhood used wood

to heat or to cook with. I looked toward our house, and it may have simply been a trick of the light, but I could see a halo around it from all the white wood smoke from our chimney and all the others. Floating toward me on the crisp, cool evening air were the scents of supper cooking in the different houses. I could make out the separate and delicious smells of fried chicken, fried pork, and the occasional scent of fish frying, so I knew the fish man had made his rounds that day.

I can smell the scent of burning wood to this day, so many years later, and in an instant my mind flashes back to Redtown, a place and time now of just majestic memories.

Chapter 34

Myrtice was older than Sunshine by a couple of years, but she had very little over her. Sunshine was as fleet as a deer and they both were of about the same height.

Myrtice was just a couple of grades ahead of Sunshine in school but in time as they played together that didn't matter.

Myrtice would grow to be a good influence on Sunshine, as we were all boys except Shelby, and Mama kept her pretty busy.

As we walked into the yard that day from Miss Minnie's, Mama was frying the catfish and had Shelby grating a head of cabbage, for slaw.

Me and Pap headed straight to the kitchen for the milk

pal, forgetting that Bossy was over at the new place.

Mama took her eyes off the frying fish long to look at us and ask us what was going on. Of course the first thing she noticed was the Jester pj's of Shelby's.

"What in the Hell," she asked, then added, "No I don't want to know. I'm scared to ask. You two frighten me at times. I guess you already know that though."

"We don't mean to be bad though Mama," I said.

She laid the long wooden handled fork down on the table and drew us to her side then she whispered in my ear. "Don't tell any of the others I said this, but you are special to me and the joy of my life."

She hugged Pap's neck and whispered something to him too. I never asked him what she whispered to him and he never asked me, but after that she gave us both a pop on the butt and told us to go outside and watch after Myrtice and Sunshine.

For some unexplained reason I have failed to mention a few people that meant so much to my childhood.

First of all, there was "Little Bessie," "Guyniy," and "Tina."

Guyniy and Tina were more Shelby's age, and if they showed up Mama would usually find them something to do.

Little Bessie was my age. She was very black, and had the gentlest nature about her. Whereas Guyniy and Tina had broad noses and big lips, Little Bessie didn't possess these features.

She'd play with Sunshine, me and Pap, and was not allowed by her parents to roam the streets like Guyniy and Tina.

I never understood why there weren't any little Black Boys in Redtown for us to play with, only girls.

If there was any racism going on in Redtown, I never saw it. We were all just a bunch of either poor misfits or disables that needed a roof over our heads.

No one seemed to know who owned the red clapboard buildings in Redtown. Everyone just paid their rent at the same mailbox number in Hampton.

I believed that Mama dearly loved Little Bessie. She was forever sewing her little shifts, pajamas, blouses and such.

That afternoon as Mama sent us out to watch over Myrtice and Sunshine, Pap walked behind the house to help Buddy finish packing up some tools in the shop.

.Sunshine and Myrtice were throwing spears made from corn stalks at each other.

The back of the house was high enough that you could actually sit under the house, so that's what I decided to do.

I sat there, not over five minutes before I heard someone whimpering, toward the middle of the house next to the base of the fireplace. I turned to see that it was Little Bessie.

I crawled over to her, as the overhead space was more limited, and about all we could do was lie down.

Black Boy was trying his best to lick her tears away, and it did make her smile.

"What's the matter," I asked?

Bessie didn't hesitate.

"My Grandma, I'm afraid she won't let me come over anymore if she finds out Sunshine has another little girl to play with."

"Maybe she won't find out," I said.

"Yes, she will. She just sits on that front porch, dips that snuff and makes them quilts. Folks comes around and tells her everything."

"Well, just cross that bridge when you get to it," I said"

The pretty little girl looked me in the eyes and said.

"Lew the reason I'm really crying is because you're moving and Grandma won't ever let me walk down that long dirt road to see you, like she does here."

As I've stated before, we were both about the same age but I'd been noticing the pretty "Little Bessie" began to blossom right before my eyes.

It was beginning to get dark under the house when Little Bessie and I kissed. It was mutual.

The last time I saw Little Bessie that night she was stealing away through our corn patch, "I'm sure trying to hide her shadowy figure from Mama, in case Mama looked out the back door."

That night after a fine meal of fried catfish, French fries and cole slaw, we all helped Mama pack for the big move the following morning. We all stayed up a little later than usual, but Mama finally told us we could skip our baths and just go to bed.

We waited until we heard Daddy snoring. Pap and I slipped out the window.

Myrtice and Sunshine were already on the ground waiting for us.

The night had turned off to be chilly, but not too cold when we four shimmied up that chinaberry tree.

"Just wait until you hear that big lady sing "Bing, Bang Boom" when she says "Boom" the men they come up to her and sticks money in her bosom, she rubs his head in her bosom," Sunshine said.

"Oh my Lord," Myrtice said.

We had to sit perched in that tree for about an hour before the big lady started to perform.

She was like Miss Minnie. There was something she possessed that only few had. When she walked out onto that stage, she owned it.

She sang a couple of (What I would later find out to be Billie Holiday medleys,) then she knew the audience was waiting on it, so she started in with "Bing, Bang, Boom!"

The audience went wild. I'd never seen such a big woman shake and shimmy so.

The men rushed up to the stage with their hard earned dollar bills and began to stuff them down into her oversized bosom.

One thing about her she never missed a word singing while she was rubbing the men's faces on her bust, one at a time.

"Oh my Lord," Myrtice kept saying.

Finally she said "I'll bet the poor dear's feet hurt. I know Big Mama's does, 'cause she's heavy up there, too."

Everyone seemed to be enjoying the show but me. My heart just wasn't in it. All I could think about was the sweet little "Little Bessie."

After the performance of "Bing Bang Boom, "Pap and I told the girls it was time to go, besides it was a full moon and I could imagine that everyone within a mile could see four black silhouettes up that bare tree and wonder what was going on.

It was hard for me to fall asleep that night I wondered if Little Bessie was thinking of me as I was her. I did know one thing though. I fell in love with that pretty little girl that night.

I learned something in a few days too. Little Bessie was right about not seeing each other so regular anymore. We weren't the only ones that would be moving the next day.

After not seeing Little Bessie around in a few days I walked to her house and there was a sign on the door that read "Moved to New Jersey."

I was devastated about it but I never told anyone, not even Pap, as we were still at the age of supposing to hate girls. It was all so confusing to me.

Chapter 35

We all had everything packed and ready to go early that morning when the big truck backed up to our house on the 23rd of December to make the move.

Thank Goodness Mama had sent me, Pap and Rumby on ahead to milk ol' Bossy.

She sure was looking at us with mournful eyes when we arrived. She was ready to be milked. I don't believe I'd ever seen her bag as big as it was.

We had milked two gallons of milk from Bossy before the first truck load arrived.

Mama stayed behind to make sure that everything was loaded properly. She sent Shelby with the first truck load to make sure things were put in the proper places and or put together.

I noticed them take the old wood burning stove to Daddy's new incomplete shop and I was glad. I knew Daddy would stay warm when he'd be out there working.

The second truck load finished it up.

Instead of carrying the mattresses into the house Mama had them to lay them on some tin that was placed on the ground so they could sun for the rest of the day

I don't know how much Daddy was paying them poor fellows moving that stuff, but by the time they got through with Mama's wrath, they earned every penny of it.

Every chair had to be set in the exact spot she insisted. She moved everything from the old place into our new home and there was still plenty more room, because the house was bigger.

The house had three bedrooms and a small room in the back that Mama had no idea what to put in there. Finally she said she could use it for an extra bedroom for unexpected company.

The kitchen was small but it had a separate dining room.

Mama liked the big walk in pantry room lined with shelves that was next to the kitchen. Then of course the huge living room that covered the entire width of the house.

She looked at the gas heater in the dining room and was glad that it was at that location, for on cold wintry nights if someone was sick the door could be left open to their bedroom and they could get some heat.

Mama opened the doors to her new stove and refrigerator.

I knew Daddy Jim hadn't spared any money on it either because it was a big one.

She walked from room to room flipping the electric lights on and off.

After the moving men left, she told me to walk Myrtice home and that Sunshine could go with me. "Make sure to take Black Boy," she added.

Black Boy treed one squirrel behind the other on our walk to Myrtice's house.

Mrs. Watson was sitting in her rocking chair on the front porch and she spied us as soon as we turned the bend in the road.

As soon as she laid eyes on her, you could certainly feel the enthusiasm and love the old lady felt for Myrtice.

She had a handkerchief in her hand and she looked over her glasses and waved at us before we reached the house.

I remember wondering what all those little keys fit that she always wore on a ring pinned to the bosom of her dress.

Of course, she invited us in, but we didn't hang around long, for both Sunshine and I wanted to get back home. We didn't want to miss out on anything.

I guess that was her Mama and Daddy's voices that we could hear coming from the inside of the house.

All I know is Myrtice seemed to have changed from a happy little girl to a sad camper within a matter of seconds.

As we were walking up the lane going home I saw that she had crawled into her Big Mama's awaiting lap.

I also noticed that Myrtice's gangly legs were longer than her little ole' short Big Mama's.

We could hear Mama raising hell about something before we even reached the house.

We soon found out.

As the day began to warm up, the hog pen got to stinking

and of course as soon as Mama tried her new oven out with a quick baker of biscuits, Pete came to the very edge of the wire fence separating his domain from ours and started his braying for some of those biscuits.

He was getting serious about it too, for once in a while he'd throw both his back feet into the air, in mocked pretense of kicking the fence down.

She had us all to bring the mattresses into the house to get them away from the stench of the hog pen.

She personally threw a half pan of blazing hot biscuits over the fence to Pete, who certainly didn't seem to mind the heat, for he swallowed them right down.

After Mama got the mule settled down she came back into the house and dusted all the mattresses' with baking soda before she put the sheets on.

After that she gathered us all into the living room for a family meeting, making sure to close every door between there and the hog pen.

When we had all found a place to either sit or squat, she started.

"First off I don't know why in the world Charles had that

hog pen built so close to the house."

I raised my hand, and Mama nodded at me to speak.

"We built it as far away as we could. It's right on the edge of our property," I said.

"Shut up, that is not a sensible answer," she said.

"Yes Mam," I said.

The others laughed.

"Another thing, Daddy and Mama have been invited for Christmas dinner. Now you know how Mama is, so just try to stay away from her."

"I know that we've never had electricity, running water, nor gas before. You're to use it only long enough to do what's necessary. I'd better not go into a room and find the bulb burning and no one in the room."

"No one is to fool with that gas heater but me, your Daddy or Buddy."

"Let's all enjoy our new home. It's the nicest house we've ever lived in. We might not have rugs on the floors or paint on the walls yet, but I do thank the good Lord for it."

Then at the last thing she sort of said under her breath, "He's just going to have to find a place to put them damn hogs and that's all there is to it."

After her little speech she instructed me, Pap, and Buddy to get some long pieces of tin that Daddy had stacked in the back yard, and she had us to nail it along the side of the hog pin facing the house.

After we'd finished our task, we sat on the back porch. I'll have to admit, I think the stench was subdued somewhat.

Every once in a while Mama would walk out onto the back porch and just look around, and as if we were in oblivion she'd say, "I hate that damn biscuit eating mule."

We knew Mama and we knew it was just a ruse, for without ol' Pete she wouldn't have her canned vegetables she had lined up in rows in her pantry.

It was just something for her to fuss about.

After Mama went back into the house, Buddy couldn't wait until he and Daddy got the shop finished so he went out there and started banging away.

Mama soon returned to the back porch with a big cloth bag and Rumby.

"Well, do you two think you're better than the rest of us? I see two big Pecan trees in the yard, I just checked underneath them and the ground is covered with them. Y'all take Rumby with you and start picking up those pecans and if he gives you any trouble you come let me know."

Things had been so busy, we'd failed to mention Mrs. Watson had brought the shrubs and flowers.

Mama decided to come down the back steps, now that the smell from the hog pen was somewhat quelled and she began to walk around the house.

I knew that she had to be thrilled about her house and all the modern conveniences.

That's when she noticed the flowers. It had been a mild winter thus far so some of them still were in bloom.

"What in the world, she asked?

We told her how they came about being there.

"How sweet of her, I'll have you to drop off a letter of thanks tomorrow, but first bring me a shovel and you three go ahead with those pecans. I want a fruit cake and pecan pies for Christmas."

Mama was having a good time setting out those flowers at just the right places, and by the middle of the evening we had about fifty pounds of pecans picked up.

We didn't waste any time, Mama found a thick board, not wanting to scar her back porch, and we all got hammers and started cracking those pecans.

Me, Pap, and Rumby cracked them, and Mama, Shelby and Sunshine finished hulling them out.

We all had a good time that afternoon. Mama even laughed and told us a few things that she and her sisters Joyce and Margie Ree had gotten into. She also told us of Big Mama's Mother, who she had never spoken of before.

She said her Grandmother could play a piano and write songs, that she was a midwife and she too carried her Bible with her everywhere she went, but she didn't use it in the wrong way as Big Mama did.

She said the lying part came in from her husband, her Granddaddy, and Big Mama's Daddy.

Mama told us that day the reason she married Daddy was to get away from home, but it had turned out to be the wisest decision she'd ever made.

She said Daddy Jim had an old mantle clock that had quit working and he had asked Daddy to see if he could fix it for him.

Daddy was standing on the outside of the house and had the clock sitting on the window sill working on it when Big Mama started beating Mama with a broom.

Daddy Jim was sitting on the front porch and him being in the physical condition that he was, it took him a long time to get in there and break the two up.

"Well," she said, "Mama walked to the back of the house and Daddy made his way back to the front porch."

"That's when your Daddy asked me to marry him, it was on a Thursday. I never will forget the day. Your Daddy was twenty nine years old and still lived at home with his Daddy and brothers. They had a big farm and were quite well off, so I told him Ok."

"We were renting a little house from his Daddy at the time, so I'd been to their house several times, and I knew the territory pretty well."

"He told me to meet him under a certain oak tree at 5 o'clock the next morning with my clothes. I did my best to just stay out of Mama's way for the rest of that day, but I'll bet you I didn't sleep a wink that night, afraid I wouldn't wake up and get away from there."

"Well, your Daddy fixed that clock and at exactly 4:45 I slipped out that window with all my worldly belongings, which was one more dress and another pair of panties. I didn't even own a pair of shoes.

"I'd already scribbled a note to Daddy. It simply said, 'Left home to marry Charles.' I crept up the front steps and laid the note on his high chair and placed a big rock on top of it."

"It was still dark but when I felt my way to that gravel road. I ran as fast as I could toward that oak tree and to freedom."

"Y'all's Daddy was waiting there with a flashlight. We'd never hugged, kissed or anything until a few days after we were married."

"Anyway, we walked fifteen miles to the County Court house. Your Daddy had just enough money on him to buy me a package of chewing gum a pair of white lace socks, a pair of shoes, and the marriage license."

"The Judge married us to avoid us paying a preacher."

Mama seldom had the time or the notion to tell us stories of her past, but when she did, she really captivated us.

Whereas Daddy's stories were read to us from a book, Mama's was always more interesting to me, or maybe it was just because I enjoyed hearing stories about the family, which I felt were all just tidbits of us, all sewn together to make such a crazy pattern.

I always just thanked my lucky stars I wasn't as sorry as Willie Joe and Talmer.

There wasn't too much day light left so Mama gave Rumby a garden rake to make sure there wasn't a speck of anything out of place in the front yard and of course Pap and I headed to the milk shed.

Chapter 36

Wasn't much to supper that night, as Mama and the girls planned on staying up late cooking Christmas dinner, so she just made her canned fish and gravy with biscuits, making sure to make three extra ones for Pete so he wouldn't start his braying and kicking.

It was late and we were all gathered around our new fireplace and the big radio listening to "The Amos & Andy Show" when Daddy came in from work.

It had turned cold outside, so Daddy had his fur lined collar turned up on his jacket.

He walked straight into the kitchen, with Mama following him,, of course we all tagged along until Mama shooed us all back into the living room and closed the door.

Didn't much filter through that door, but I picked up enough to learn Daddy got a $560.00 Christmas Bonus and his check for two weeks to live on while the mill was shut down for the Holidays.

Mama said, "Charles, I want you to invite Sarge for Christmas dinner. While he's here talk to him about buying five more acres of land, that damn hog and mule pin has got to go. It's too close to the house," she said.

I already knew what the outcome would be.

We heard Mama as she got up from the kitchen table.

We all ran back to "Amos & Andy.

"Come with me Buddy," she said, as she switched on the brand new porch light.

In just a few minutes Buddy brought in a little cedar tree that was about four feet long, there was also a brown paper bag, that we soon learned contained two strings of Christmas lights with a variety of colors.

As far as I could remember we'd never had a Christmas tree, but as I would learn it would just be the first of a tradition that I think Mama enjoyed decorating as much as we did.

Fearing the heat from the fireplace might dry the tree out, she set the butt end of the tree that Daddy had cut into a small container of water then tied the tree to the wall, so it wouldn't fall over.

She sent all us to our rooms to draw Christmas bells then color them different colors.

After about three or four bells Pap started drawing an electric guitar and I drew and colored a bright red cardinal.

We didn't know what Rum was coloring, but whatever it was it was black, and he stayed steady at it.

When we were through we all stuck holes in the top of our colorings then ran short pieces of thread through the holes so we could tie them to the tree.

Sunshine was in our room too and I remember her three bells were yellow, green, and red. She had also made an attempt at a star, which she colored bright orange. It was a little lopsided but we ran a string through it too.

We all ran back into the living room anxious to see the tree.

Mama had pulled up a chair by the tree and was sitting

down drinking a cup of coffee.

They were through stringing the flashing lights and in my opinion they were about the prettiest things I'd ever seen.

The lights would flash off and on as though they were set by a timer.

Mama parted the curtains and set her cup of coffee on the windowsill.

"Alright, come here dim-wits, and let's see what you have to hang on the tree," she said. Of course, the dim-wits part applied to just me and Pap, because she gave Sunshine a pat on her head as she reached Mama her drawings for Mama to "ooh" and "aah" about. Mama even let Sunshine stand on the chair long enough to tie the lopsided star to the very top of the tree.

She almost snatched me and Pap's colorings out of our hands. She then closed her eyes and said. "I want you two boys to know something. I've been waiting on you two to mention the shotguns to me but you haven't. Now I've talked with your Daddy about this thing and I did tell you to spend the money as you wished. I was expecting a bicycle or something."

"Of course your Daddy takes y'all's sides, but I wish you would have just told me. It makes me feel as though you're scared of me or something," she said.

I started to tell her we were, but I didn't dare because I was scared of her reactions.

"Mrs. Watson told me about the squirrels that you two brought her, so just leave your guns in the loft until you get ready to hunt and never load the things until you see something," she said.

"Lord you two," she said, as she smiled and hastily hung our exhibits onto the branches.

"What's keeping you Rum," she yelled. She then mumbled under her breath. "Lord that boy is as slow as molasses in winter."

Rum soon entered the room and I could tell that Mama was really touched with Rum's one simple coloring.

It was a black Bible and printed in the center in gold colored letters was the one simple word "Bible."

Mama pulled her baby son into her lap and wiping the corners of her eyes, she said, "It's rare, but sometimes you amaze me," then she hugged his neck.

The local radio station was playing nothing but Christmas songs. Mama whipped up a batch of pecan divinity and brought us all one small piece each before she returned to the kitchen to finish up with her fruit cake and pecan pies.

We could hear Daddy and Buddy nailing in the direction of the shop.

Mama baked her pecan pies first and she was really bragging on her new stove when she shoved her fruit cake in and turned the temperature down, so that it would bake.

I remember she opened the side window and brought in a piece of oak wood, for Daddy had built a small shed right outside the window to store firewood in, and she threw it onto the smoldering fire in the fireplace.

She then got the Bible, found a passage, turned the radio down so low until it was barely audible.

I remember looking on the page and seeing if that ugly man was on there and he wasn't.

I remember she started reading from Luke Chapter 2. It was about the night that baby Jesus was born.

She read as far as when the shepherds saw the star shining above the city of Bethlehem from out of the east and they knew that's where baby Jesus was.

I looked up at Sunshine's lopsided star on our tree, and after Mama read out of that Bible that night, I was no longer scared to open it. I would also occasionally read it, as long as I stayed out of Revelations, (Big Mama's ever relenting preaching out of that book still scared me.)

Before Mama left the room to check on her fruit cake Mama told Shelby and Sunshine to take their baths together, then let the water out of the tub. After they were finished Me, Pap, and Rum could use the same water to take our baths, then we could empty the tub for Buddy.

We never brushed our teeth with toothpaste, we used baking soda, and all our teeth stayed sparkling white. Mama saw to that. Ms. Rumbling never did have to get on to us about that.

I remember how strange it felt that night lying in the bed beside Rum because we were in a totally different surroundings than what we were accustomed.

The odor of the new wood from our new house and Mama's fruit cake was most intoxicating, but it was a weekend night and I missed the drumming beat coming from Pig

Meat's place, the occasional blast of gunfire, and the fleeting lights of vehicles as the lights shone through our window as they chugged by.

All that could be heard here was the shallow breathing of my brothers and they slept, and the crickets as they chirped outside.

The next morning was Christmas Eve and we did something that was very unusual, we all sat at the table and ate breakfast together.

While we were eating Mama said that she had made a decision. She said that she had slept on it and she wanted the outside of the house painted white and trimmed in green. She also said that she had decided not to paint or varnish the inside of her home, every lead mark from a pencil that was left with untrained hands on the lumber was a labor of love and each time she looked at it, the markings would remind her of that and she didn't want to cover it up.

"Why to me it would be about like covering up a piece of my babies' pasts and I wouldn't do that," she said.

Chapter 37

After breakfast and the milking of Bossy, Pap and I asked Mama if we could go squirrel hunting, then walk on up to town. We told her that we'd leave our guns at Mrs. Watson's while we were in town.

Mama took a deep breath.

"Do you think you two can do this and not shoot each other," she asked?

"We been doing it," I responded.

"Well go ahead then but don't load but one of those guns at a time and you two had better be back here by 1 o'clock,"

We shimmed up the ladder to the loft of the house and were back down in no time with our guns and shells.

We were dressed warm because it had finally turned cold. Sunshine heard us and fired into to going too.

"Squirrel hunting is not the place for pretty little girls, sweetie," Mama said, patting Sunshine on her face.

"Well then, I can stay with Myrtice until they come back."

"You haven't been invited. Now run along and find something to do before I find something for you," Mama said.

Sunshine left the room with her bottom lip poked out.

"Just a minute, boys," she said, and went quickly into her bedroom. She returned shortly with three sealed envelopes.

"The names are written on the outside, see they get them in town."

"Yes Mam," we said, as I poked them inside my fur lined coat pocket, that was a hand me down from Pap.

As soon as Black Boy saw those guns he was ready. He just didn't know which direction we'd be going in until he saw us walk up the road.

That dog had treed twelve times before we reached Mrs. Watson's. We didn't have to fire but six times to kill eight squirrels.

Three was up one tree and were pretty close together.

Pap kept walking around that tree until he could get all three of them with one shot. He pulled the trigger and all three fell out.

As soon as they hit the ground Black Boy always crushed their skull with his powerful jaws.

We took the squirrels to Mrs. Watson's and we got to meet Myrtice's Mama and Daddy.

I was shocked when I saw her Daddy, I'd seen pictures of Hanks Williams Sr. and to me he looked just like him, He was a tall skinny man and smiled a lot.

Her Mama was a tall rawboned, red haired woman with freckles and didn't say much.

They'd just bought a brand new Studebaker car and were outside looking at it. It was yellow and brown, a real sports model. Her Daddy's name was Joe, and her Mama's name was Minnie May, or something like that.

I gave the envelope to Mrs. Watson. I figured it was to thank her for the flowers.

Mrs. Watson's Son paid us two dollars for the squirrels, then catching his wife's back turned he gave us each another quarter.

We asked him if we could leave our guns inside his pump house until we returned from town and he obliged us.

Our first stop in town was at Sarge's meat wagon, for he had left his intersection and had customers lined up at his meat wagon.

I was so proud for him. I knew how hard the Sarge worked on smoking all that meat and especially making all those stinking chitterlings.

We'd never eaten chitterlings but one day while we were hunting for those rattle snakes we saw the Sarge preparing them in his back yard.

First he turned the hog's intestines wrong side outward, and spent a long time soaping and washing them on a wooden table he'd dragged next to his pump. Then he stuffed the intestines with seasoned, spiced meat, tying a string tightly around the whole affair about every six inches. Finally, he smoked them over an open pit.

I remember they smelled so delicious, but I don't believe I could ever bring myself to eating any of them.

They were selling that morning though, along with everything else he had in his box

Sarge sure was grinning when I walked up to him, then I reached inside my jacket and gave him the envelope Mama had sent me to give him.

I reached over the open box and gave him the envelope. He never looked at it, but just stuck it in his zipper bag along with his cash.

The whole street was alive with folks, either spending or selling for the Christmas Holidays.

Miss Minnie wasn't in her hole, so we went straight to her house. She was expecting us because the gate was unlocked.

We knocked on her door only once before she opened it. I guess she knew the cold, raw wind was blowing hard on her front porch.

"Come in boys," she said, as she quickly ushered us into the warm room and began to help us pull off our coats.

She saw some of Mama's blonde curly hair trapped in the fur lining of my coat.

"My, my, what a pretty shade of blonde! You know, my hair was once that color, but never had that natural curl in it. Your Mother is a very pretty woman."

"Come over by the heater boys and I'll prepare you a cup of hot cocoa and some cookies to help get you on your way," she said.

I gave her the last sealed envelope Mama had given me.

When she left the room we whispered that we hoped those cookies wouldn't be from the same box as those from yesterday.

When she returned, we found the cookies to be home-made and they were delicious.

She called them "Fruit Rocks," and said a friend had brought them by.

Miss Minnie then reached from beneath the table and brought out three wrapped gifts.

"This is for you, and this is for you," she said, as she handed us our gifts.

We hastily tore open the paper to see what was inside.

"It was a year's supply to the matinee movie in town."

"I hear you boys like to go there and watch the westerns," she said.

"Oh yes mam! This is the best presents we ever got," Pap said, and then he blurted out.

"Miss Minnie, why do you stay in that hole all the time?"

She smiled, and gave him an answer.

"Now if I hadn't have stayed in that hole, I'd never got to have met you boys or The Sarge and your darling Mother, who is so much like her Father,. Why, there's several things I would have missed out on if I'd just stayed cooped up in this house all the time!"

"There's nothing so special about me and Lew," Pap said.

"More than you know," she said.

The she handed us the third gift and told us to give it to our Mother.

The last thing she told us was the clincher though, she said to get word to our Daddy Jim that the new deputy sheriff was watching him and he'd better be careful.

"Yes, we sure will," I said.

"I understand he's a good Granddaddy to you boys," she said,

"The best," I answered.

"And your grandmother?"

"Ah, she's meaner than a damn snake," Pap said and he didn't bother to correct himself either.

Pap's statement brought a smile to her face.

"You know Miss Minnie there's something about you that reminds me of our Mama," I said.

"That's quite a Christmas gift," she said, as she rubbed her hands across the tops of our head.

We wished Miss Minnie a Merry Christmas, and even though it was awkward, she made an attempt at hugging our necks, and returned the greeting as we went out the door.

We didn't know till later that as we walked out onto the porch, she watched our every move, smiling to herself and thinking, Finally. Slowly but surely, my dream of having a family will come true. I might have had to lie in a hole, Lord, and look and act crazy to get their attention long enough to do it, but I'm tired of being in this old world alone.

Before we even reached the gate Pap said "Boy Miss Minnie is a sweet Lady, you reckon how she knew we liked going to the movies," he asked?

"I told you she knows everything," I said, as we lit out running toward Daddy Jim's and not letting our shirt tails hit our legs until we got there.

Of course Black Boy was running ahead and had already

given old Rat a good whipping by the time we got there.

Daddy Jim was sitting in his high chair on the porch, wrapped in a quilt when we arrived and he didn't seem too surprised when we told him what Miss Minnie had told us.

"Yeah, well, I've been waiting on the official word, but it's pretty hard for them to charge me as long as they don't see me touch it, and I'm not going to do anything but sit here on my front porch and point to where it's at."

"Yes sir," I said.

Daddy Jim laughed, long and hard.

"Poor fools," he said, then he added, "If they only knew. This is just a side line hobby of mine, a way I got my start. I enjoy seeing the people coming and going, and the way your Grandma is, why I'd never get to see my own Grandchildren if it weren't for the whiskey."

"I have other businesses out there, some of them pretty lucrative too, so I'm not worried."

"Won't you boys go inside and be lied to and insulted by your Grandma before you go. I speck it's pretty warm in there and there's a little something I want you to do," he said.

It took Daddy Jim a long time to get out of his tall chair

but he finally made it and we followed him inside.

Big Mama had Willie Joe and Talmer all dressed for Christmas. They were dressed as twins, each wearing red satin shirts, red dress pants and tan shoes with red shoe laces, and they each were wearing black string ties in their collars.

They were sitting on the couch watching "Captain Kangaroo" on their new Television and Big Mama, as usual was reading out of the back of the Bible and dipping her snuff.

We seemed oblivious to everyone but Daddy Jim.

He went into the kitchen and at the bottom of an old kitchen cabinet, covered in front with just a pleated curtain was a five gallon demi john with what looked like barely a pint of shine in the bottom.

"If you boys will, pour this up into a quart jar and give it to the two numb skulls in there. They swill it like hogs, when they can find it, then come on back in here and wash this jug until there's not a scent in it. There's four more on the back porch you can roll in here and clean them the same way; then you can roll em all back outside.

Daddy Jim then reached in his jumper pocket and gave us two silver dollars each for Christmas presents and asked us not to spend them for they were very rare.

"No sir," we both said, as he patted us on our heads.

Willie Joe practically snatched the quart jar out of my hands as I passed it beneath Big Mama's nose.

"Oh how nice, you brought my lambs spirits for Christmas," she said, patting them on their frail skinny legs.

We had to work in a hurry to meet Mama's deadline, we still had a little shopping to do in town too, but we did Daddy Jim a good job. "You couldn't smell nothing in them jugs but Ajax when we got through with them."

As we passed by the couch Willie Joe and Talmer's faces had a little color in them which was very unusual from the usual pale, sickly projection.

Big Mama said, "Behold I come quickly. Blessed is he that keeps the prophecy of this book."

Even though Daddy Jim didn't have whiskey to sell, he'd wrapped himself back up in his quilt and resumed his place on the porch.

"I'm looking for a delivery just any time. They're sure gonna be disappointed when I send them on down the road. Sitting out here in the cold beats staying in there with that bunch," he said.

Pap just plain out asked him

"Daddy Jim, why do you stay down here? We have a big enough house now you could come and live with us."

When any of us were around him, Daddy Jim's usual jovial expression on his face seemed to change all of a sudden.

"Because my boys, I guess anything beats prison," then he laughed and told us to run along.

Chapter 38

By the time we'd ran back to town the whole place was in full swing.

Pig Meat must've taken a lesson from Miss Minnie, for he had moved his entire band, including the big lady out onto the packed red clay patch in front of his establishment.

I wasn't looking for the lady to sing "Bing, Bang, Boom," though for all she was singing was Christmas songs, and no professional singer could beat her.

I don't know how much she collected in that tin coffee can that day, but it surprised me when Pap asked me for a quarter of his squirrel money to throw in her can.

He, along with most everyone else, was completely mesmerized by her deep gravelly voice. Boy she could belt out "Oh Holy Night," I was surprised she could hit those high notes but she did!

We heard the court house clock strike 12 o'clock, so we knew we had to go.

We went straight to Hughes store and bought Mama a dainty coffee cup, and a silver spoon to stir her cream with.

"You could see clear through that little cup, it had blue dragons painted on the outside of it and stamped on the bottom was fine china."

We got Daddy a leather coin purse, who was forever dropping money out of his pocket.

For Sunshine and Shelby, we got them each a charm bracelet, each one already having three tiny charms on them.

Mr. Hughes' busy clerk was kind enough to gift wrap each gift separately, warning us to be careful with the cup, and he made sure he put extra stuffing around it.

The total came to $8.75, so I had to dig into my hoard to pay for it all.

We noticed something unusual going on at Mr. Reese's garage. They were installing a drink box that stayed out in the open 24 hours a day. You just dropped your nickel in, pushed down on a lever and you could pull your selection out.

He even demonstrated it for us, but we told him we'd already spent too much money. We did tell him that we would be regular customers if he would get him a variety of moon pies.

Mayor Snell was even across the tracks buying from the Sarge. We spoke to them both as we hurried toward Mrs. Watson's.

We arrived home a little early and placed all our gifts under the tree except the one that Miss Minnie had sent Mama.

She was in the kitchen and told us our dinner plates were in the cupboard.

I handed her Miss Minnie's gift. Pap climbed the ladder to the lot and I gave him our guns and shells.

"Oh how sweet," Mama said, and these things are stamped sterling silver. They look so old yet they're brand new," she said.

"And all I did was send her a simple Holiday note. She paid a fortune for these," she said, as she sat down at the table and opened the small envelope attached to the mirror. It simply read, "Thanks for sharing your children with me."

I didn't know Mama's reasoning but she was about to stroke her hair with the elaborate brush until she read the note, but she stopped suddenly and asked me if I would put the two items in the bottom drawer of her dresser before I ate my dinner.

While we were eating Mama told us Daddy and Buddy needed our help in the shop, and then she told us to never go into Miss Minnie's alone.

"There's something fishy about that woman and I can just smell it. Someone that can pick and play instruments like she does, and you can tell from her speech she's very well educated. I don't know; I just haven't figured her out yet."

"I do believe she's a sweet lady though, but right now, I'm just not ready to share my children with anyone," she said.

I was really surprised at how far along Daddy and Buddy had come along on the shop. They had the bellows up and going and the old wooden stove had it warm and toasty inside.

The skill saw had really come in handy, as they were about to drag the lumber and material out to the pump house to build a small building to go over it to prevent it from freezing.

Daddy had enough insulation, from our old clothing and such until I believe it would have held up to almost any kind of freezing conditions.

The four of us had that thing put together in no time at all; you could barely reach the faucet due to all the insulation, so Daddy was satisfied.

After that we insulated the water pipes leading into the house and under it, making sure they wouldn't freeze, then for extra precaution Daddy blocked off the north end beneath the house, so the north wind would be blocked.

I loved working with my Daddy, even though I was inadequate with almost everything he did. He was always cheerful and was patient with me, but he never did have much free time to spend with us.

Due to his age, by the time we came along he was on up in years and didn't play baseball, football or any of the things that other boys fathers did.

What I did see was my Daddy took the time to stand for hours on Sundays and cut little boys hair, both black and white boys. He gladly did it, with a smile on his face using a pair of those old hair hand clippers that you had to use manually and never charged them anything or complained.

As Mama had stated in her summation of Daddy's people, they had land, money and affluence in the adjoining county.

Daddy's Mama, who had long been dead, they said, was natured like my Daddy, quiet and gentle.

My Paternal Grandpa remarried very quickly to a much younger woman than Daddy's Mother.

Daddy and three of his brothers were farming my Grandpa's land and trying to make a go of it and all of them were still living in the house with my Grandpa.

All they knew was to work and go to Church on Sunday.

My Paternal Grandpa had been a deacon in the Baptist Church for many years, so I can only imagine his reaction when Daddy brought home a bootlegger's daughter for a wife, and a feisty one too.

Mama and the new wife didn't get along. Mama wound up giving her a good beating and that's when we moved to

Redtown, with hardly anything but the clothes on our backs, but miraculously as soon as we moved to Redtown things seemed to fall into place.

I know one thing I sure liked it better living in Redtown than I did out there on that big ol' farm.

As far as I knew, we'd been living in Redtown for four years and we'd never heard a word from my Daddy's people. I guess Mama must've really put a whooping on my step-grand mama that day.

REDTOWN: A NOVEL BY L.E. GULLEY

Chapter 39

Christmas arrived about 6:00 A.M. that morning. We heard the squeals of Sunshine as she awoke and saw the Christmas tree with all its shining lights and the wrapped presents scattered about.

The rest of us bathed our faces quickly and walked into the aromatic kitchen and to the warmth.

Daddy had already milked Bossy, so we didn't have that chore.

On Christmas mornings Mama would always bake candied spiced pears, and I loved them with good hot biscuits and fried ham.

She wouldn't cook the pears but just that one time a

year. She said it was too much sugar. And it would cause us to be diabetics (whatever that was, but she made the ailment sound awful).

Christmas morning was the only morning she'd allow us to drink coffee. Of course, I'd just soon not drink it because it was so diluted with cream.

Until this day I will never forget the story of Uncle Dave (Whoever he was), who had the 28' long tape worm.

The reason Mama said she made sure all her pork was cooked extra done was Uncle Dave had eaten a piece of ham that was under cooked, which subsequently caused him to get a tape worm.

The worm grew and grew and Uncle Dave got skinnier and skinnier. Well it wound up he was going from house to house begging for food to eat and that tape worm was getting all his nourishment.

Finally, Uncle Dave died along the roadside and they said when they cut him open they found a 28' long tape worm in his stomach.

She would make sure that we had always eaten before she told us the story and I was thankful she didn't tell the story on that Christmas Morning.

Maybe that's why she refused to buy meat from the Sarge, I didn't know, because I knew she liked the Sarge.

Daddy had built a roaring fire in the living room, making it warm and toasty, so by seven o'clock we started opening our few gifts, with Shelby handing them out.

After unwrapping the gifts, we discovered that we got pretty much the same.

We boys got the usual, two pairs of dungarees and two new flannel shirts, then a new pair of U.S. Keds.

Shelby dropped a heavy square box while handing it to me and Pap, I noticed Mama flinch. We opened it up together and it was a box of number four shotgun shells.

"Sarge said he's been seeing an old fox hanging around and those bird shot you boys got won't do the trick Daddy said.

Due to our gifts being put under the tree first, they were shoved to the back.

Shelby gave Mama her gift from Pap and I, and dumb us forgot to put who any of our gifts were from, but Mama knew and we never told any of the rest who gave them the gifts.

Mama held the ornate little cup to the light and said, "Oh look Charles you can see all the way through it, and the dainty little spoon is sterling silver."

She then jumped up, went to the kitchen and returned quickly with a steaming cup of coffee in her pretty cup.

Of course Daddy didn't have a clue who gave him the coin purse, he just said, "Thank you," as he held up the small leather zippered bag for everyone to see.

Shelby and Sunshine received two new outfits each, with lace sweaters and of course the charm bracelets

Sunshine also received a baby doll, which she promptly threw in the corner and took turns with Rum spinning his giant spinning top that danced around on the wooden floor when you'd mash down on a screw type handle in the middle.

The day was turning out to be cold and bitter with a strong north wind blowing.

Pap and I were dying to try out them number 4's but Mama told us it was just too cold to go outside and to stay in the living room out of the way while she finished up dinner.

Well at least the Jack Benny show was playing on the radio, which was very unusual for the day time.

Daddy dearly loved that program. He liked Rochester's character on the program.

We were all laughing more at Daddy's unusual laughter than we were the program when Sarge knocked on the door.

We could see his huge hunched figure through the door panes.

Buddy Jumped up to open the door and in a rush Sarge entered with a big grocery bag of assorted fruits.

Daddy thanked him for the fruit and asked Buddy to take the bag into the kitchen to his Mama, then he invited Sarge to have a seat next to the fireplace.

Sarge didn't have to sit there long before he started shedding his long woolen brown coat.

Daddy let him get relaxed, for he had started showing us how he could run four quarters between his fingers at once and they'd never touch each other.

Of course his hands were enormous and probably wasn't much of a problem to him.

Daddy told him that he had come across $500.00 more and would like to buy 5 more acres from him.

"Well, as long as it doesn't interfere with my rented

land," Sarge said.

"No, It's the five acres that's fallow and lies between my house and yours," Daddy said.

"Why shore, I thank it's about fifteen acres there. I just don't know what I'm gonna do with all this money all of a sudden, and Mr. Charles, I been a thanking, since you're wanting farm land I might have something in my barn that you can just have," Sarge said.

"We'll have a look see this very afternoon. Maybe this wind will die down some by then."

We couldn't imagine what The Sarge was talking about being in the barn, but we were dying to find out when we heard a car as it pulled into the front.

Pap looked through the glass and yelled "It's Daddy Jim and Big Mama."

"Oh it's Mr. Jim," Sarge said as he threw his woolen coat over his shoulders and ran out to the vehicle to assist Daddy Jim into the house, so did Daddy and all the rest of us, including Mama who came running out of the house with just a long sleeve dress and drying her hands with her apron.

Everyone flocked to Daddy Jim except Sam, the taxi driver who opened the back door and assisted Big Mama and the two almost helpless young men out of the back seat (They were putting it on thick today I thought, probably hung over from drinking all that whiskey yesterday.)

All four were impeccably dressed, including Daddy Jim, even though he was all drawn over he was respected and loved by all, and still cut quite a figure when he was dressed up. So did Big Mama, she was a pretty woman, with her dark hair, blue eyes and pale complexion.

Lord have mercy on Willie Joe and Talmer though, they were as ugly as homemade sin.

Everyone was rushed inside.

Even Willie Joe and Talmer forgot their infirmities when that cold wind hit them as they got out of the vehicle.

After everyone was inside Big Mama handed Sunshine a Doll that looked like it had been shut up in the box for years, Sunshine just stacked it on top of the other one.

Mama offered to give everyone a quick glimpse of the new house but no one seemed interested but Sarge and Daddy showed him around while everyone congregated in the dining room where there was a large amount of chairs.

Daddy had even rigged Daddy Jim a temporary high chair at the head of the table.

Mama had everything on the table after Sarge and Daddy made their rounds in the house. Mama asked Big Mama if she would like to give thanks while we were all gathered around the table.

Big Mama made a lunge for that table and went all the way around it gagging over the food.

Mama grabbed her by the arm and told her, "Mama get your ass in that living room and sit down. I should have known better!"

"Honey, it's this old hiatus hernia in my throat, that's what it is."

"Hernia my ass, you're just wanting attention and trying to ruin my day," Mama said.

After doing what she'd set out to do, Big Mama walked back into the living room with her head held high and no more hernia symptoms.

Her darling twins followed her.

Sarge grabbed his stomach and looked as though he might throw up until Daddy Jim reared back in his chair and laughed, showing every tooth in his mouth.

"Lord that Woman," he said.

"Thank goodness everything was still wrapped," Mama said.

Mama gave a few minutes for things to settle down then she gave a short blessing of the food.

Boy after unwrapping everything and bringing things out of the oven and cupboard, the table was loaded.

There was chicken and dressing, a smoked ham, fruit salad, baked sweet potatoes, an assortment of canned vegetables from our garden. The fruit cake, pecan pies, a huge banana pudding, and homemade yeast rolls, still hot from the oven.

First she prepared Sunshine a plate and she sat beside her Daddy at the table, then she prepared Rum's. He was contented on just finding him a place in the corner.

Next she prepared Big Mama a plate and the dimwits a platter and sent it into the living room by Shelby.

Sarge forgot all about his weak stomach when Mama gave him a platter, he stacked it up and returned to his chair against the wall, holding the platter in his lap.

Daddy Jim Just asked for a little chicken dressing, a small piece of ham and a baked sweet potato.

Mama as usual prepared Daddy's plate and the rest of us just helped ourselves.

Daddy Jim and Sarge just kept bragging on the house and couldn't get over what a nice job we had all done; then he noticed the markings Daddy had made with a lead pencil on the wall beside the refrigerator and inquired about it.

Daddy told him that as he went along while buying material for the house he marked the price of everything down on the wall, so that he wouldn't run out of money.

"It looks like your total came to $1,835.00. Not bad, Charlie boy, not bad at all."

"Of course that fellow giving you all your doors and windows cut down on expenses quite a bit," Daddy Jim said.

"Yes it did, how did you know about that," Daddy asked?

Daddy Jim squirmed, "Why my daughter told me of course," he said."

As many years as Mama had known her Daddy she had never caught him tell an outright lie for she'd never mentioned it to him, so believing he must've had a good reason, she just cleared her throat and didn't say anything.

Finally Daddy answered, "yes, it was a blessing for sure," and nothing else was said of the matter.

Sarge was constantly up and down replenishing his platter.

Mama loved to see a good eater, so she told the Sarge before he left she'd fix him a platter to take home with him.

Things were mighty quiet in the livingroom so before Mama started serving dessert, she went in there and threw a piece of wood on the fire, collected their empty plates and told them she'd soon return with dessert.

I dearly loved my Mama's fruit cake, with its candied watermelon rind, candied figs, candied orange and lemon peels with the pecans we'd just picked off the ground the day before. Every ingredient came right off the farm except the flour, because instead of using sugar for sweetener, Mama used as much of Daddy's honey as she could when sweetening things.

Daddy ate a little pecan pie and Daddy Jim ate some banana pudding.

Sunshine never left his side, and she never went into the

living room either.

Everyone was sitting around in the dining room stuffed when Sarge reminded Daddy to follow him out to the barn and look at what he was talking about earlier.

Daddy slipped on his jumper and called for Buddy, of course Pap and I followed.

We liked to have frozen before we walked the 70 yards are so until we reached the old barn behind Sarge's house.

The old barn was still roofed with the old typed wooden shingles and near half them had blown off. There were lean-to's built off each side, and they were about to collapse.

Carefully Sarge pulled off some old lumber and card-board that was holding a tarpaulin down, then he peeled the covering back to reveal a red Farmall tractor. It was a big one, too. It had the letter "H" stamped on the side.

"Now this thing hasn't been cranked since 1948, the year that my brother died. I don't know a thing about it. Some-body told me the motor was probably froze up on it. It's got all the 'quipment wid it too. Shoot, it ain't doing me a bit of good. Maybe you can fix it up and use it since you're buying more land"

"Sarge my money is low right now, with the move, land, and all."

"What money Mr. Charles? Shoot. I'm just gonna make you a Christmas gift with it.

Daddy reached into his brand new coin purse and emptied its contents of $32.00 and some coins and handed it to the Sarge, then said, "Boys go hitch up the chains to old Pete, we want this tractor and equipment on our property before dark."

Sarge looked at the small amount of money and Daddy's empty coin purse, thinking that was all the money my Daddy had.

"I thought you wanted five more acres of land," Sarge said.

Daddy, looking at him quizzically and said, "Yes the old Lady's got that money."

Then Sarge showed his big ole horse teeth grin.

The Sarge even had an old cotton wagon he loaned us to load all the farming implements on so that ol' Pete could pull them to the new ground we were buying.

Daddy didn't stop with that tractor though until the

mule had it almost in the front door of the shop.

Sarge had gone back into our house where it was warm and was really having a time of it enjoying Daddy Jim's company.

You could hear Daddy Jim's hearty laugh clear inside the shop with the door closed.

Daddy even stopped and listened for a minute, then said, "You know boys, there's not too many true men around like your Granddad."

"Just think of the pain he's suffered from that crippling arthritis, and it started as a young man too from what your Mama told me she's the only child that can remember seeing him straight."

"Despite his health and dragging his troubles around with him, you know he hasn't done bad for himself and I can honestly say he's always been on the up and up with me. Just listen to him laughing in there. I know your Mama is enjoying her Daddy."

"You reckon why he puts up with Big Mama. She lies, hits us with her Bible and just down right hates us," I said.

"You shouldn't talk that way about your Grandma, Lewty

boy. Besides, that's none of my business."

"Has Daddy Jim always had money," Pap asked?

"He sure didn't have any to my knowledge until he moved to Redtown," Daddy said.

"Hmmm, about like us," I thought to myself, but didn't say anything.

It was nice and warm inside the shop due to the wood heater, so Daddy continued.

"I know one thing; I wouldn't want to cross that old man! He might be all crippled up, but folks know he'd just as soon kill you as not."

Daddy closed the damper on the stove and we walked back into the house.

The Sarge, Mama, and Sunshine were sitting in the kitchen, completely mesmerized with some of Daddy Jim's Moon shinning days in his youth.

I could see the admiration and sparkle in my Mama's eyes as he told the story about beating a mad dog's brains out with a claw hammer at the time that he was drawing with arthritis, even though he had to crawl to get to him.

The dog was tied to a post in the back yard.

Big Mama was in the bed in deep labor with Margie Ree when Mama came to him and told him the dog was acting crazy, foaming at the mouth and wouldn't allow her to get to the woodpile. He asked Mama to find him the claw hammer and she did. Daddy Jim crawled on his hands and knees until he got near the dog, right before he was about to hit the dog, the dog jumped, the rope broke and Daddy Jim popped him right between the eyes and kept hitting him until he was sure the dog was dead.

When he'd crawled back into the house he realized his Bull Durham smoking tobacco was missing so he sent Mama back out there, who wasn't but three years old and she found Daddy Jim's tobacco and papers lying right in the middle of that dog's brains.

Since the container was made from cloth, Mama picked the tobacco up with a stick and took it in the house to her Daddy, who took a paper out and rolled a cigarette and smoked it.

I'd never heard the mad dog story before, but I knew Mama remembered it for she would nod her head now and then as Daddy Jim told the story.

"I'd been afraid to smoke that cigarette after it had laid in them dog brains. I'd been afraid I'd go mad too, Mr. Jim," Sarge said.

"I am mad," Daddy Jim laughed then let out a ferocious roar, causing Sunshine to jump from his lap and run to my Mama.

The big Sarge even jumped back in his chair, causing everyone to laugh. Eventually, he joined in on the laughter at his own self.

We heard the long black Taxi blow the horn outside.

Mama was going to prepare a platter of food to send back with Big Mama, but Daddy Jim told her that wasn't necessary.

He gave Sunshine a long hug, while I saw him stuff some green backs in Mama's apron pocket.

Daddy Jim thanked The Sarge for everything that he'd done for us, then he hugged Mama and told the rest of us goodbye and he'd be seeing us around.

Of course we all followed behind Daddy Jim.

Willie Joe and Talmer were still sitting in the same spot they were in when Mama had taken them all dessert.

There was a strong odor of urine in the room.

"What in the hell," Mama yelled as she grabbed them by their arms and saw that they had urinated on her new floor, then found some of Sunshine crayons and drawn lewd images on the floor beneath them.

"It's the little Lambs kidneys, they're so weak and they were afraid to leave the room," Big Mama said sympathetically.

Mama went wild!

She stomped out of the room and returned in a jiffy with one of Daddy's wide leather belts, and you talk about putting an ass whooping on two boys that day, she did.

They had whelps everywhere.

Daddy Jim said she'd better check their pockets before they got away from there.

Sarge had witnessed the situation and stood in front of the door so they couldn't get out.

Finally Talmer thought about the back door and ran in that direction with Willie Joe close behind, forgetting all about their infirmities.

Of course, Big Mama fainted when Mama first started to wield away, so after she heard the back door slam she gave

Big Mama a wrap cross her behind to bring her back around.

Mama then grabbed a shocked Big Mama in the collar and told her.

"I could think of a lot worse things to say to you old woman, but I'm not, but I will say this... You'd better start taking better care of my Daddy. Quit stealing from him, get up off your ass and start cooking for him or I'm coming! You just think you read about Hell in the Bible all the time, but I will be coming and Hell will be coming with me. You mark my words!"

Mama looked at the wild eyed frightened woman to think of just the right words for her, then realized it was useless, she simply shook her finger in her mother's face and told her.

I never want you or those two idiots in my house again."

Chapter 40

I truly felt sorry for Mama that day. She was so proud of her new house, and the enjoyable visit from her Daddy. Only to have it all spoiled by Big Mama and the twins, so we all knew to step lightly around her for the rest of that Christmas day.

She did manage to tell Sarge to just help himself to what was on the table. Then she covered the remaining food with a table cloth and cut the gas heater off so the food wouldn't spoil. She then went to work on the living room floor with that concoction of homemade soap of hers.

Daddy, me, Pap and Buddy went back out to the shop.

Sarge stumbled back across the yard with his platter of

food.

Daddy, Pap and Buddy went right to work on disassembling that tractor.

I found me a warm cozy place and started reading "Robinson Caruso," one of Daddy's books, and I thought to myself, before I got into the book, that I had finally witnessed a Willie Joe and Talmer whooping, and I sure didn't want one.

That afternoon, as we made our way back into the house we were met with the familiar scent of that lye soap concoction of Mama's. I didn't see how they had managed to stay in the house.

Poor Sunshine had a towel wrapped around her head and all you could see was the color of her red streaked purple eyes.

Mama and Shelby were constantly sniffing their noses.

Daddy suggested right away to just open the windows in the living room and allow some of the strong lye odor out of the house.

"We'll just close the door to the living room and let Mother Nature take care of it tonight; besides, it couldn't be healthy for these young'uns to sleep in this house tonight with that odor being so strong."

Mama thought for a few seconds, then laughed.

"You know Charles, I've been so determined on getting, not just the scent, but the whole situation away from me and out of my house I guess I just wasn't thinking. All I knew to do was just scrub as though I was scrubbing not only the odor and crayons out of my house, but them too."

"I know that sounds crazy, but now that I think of it, I think that's what I was doing."

Mama sat down at the table and cupped her chin on the palm of her hands.

"You know it's hard to believe that woman is the mother of me and my sisters."

"Sweet Pea," Daddy said, "You are Jimmy's child, dyed in the wool."

Mama laughed, and said, "Well I've been putting the inevitable off just for Daddy's sake for years, I knew it was coming though," she said, and then she went into the living room to let up the windows before we ate supper.

We were sure thankful that Christmas night for our gas heater that Mr. Hooks had installed. With the windows open in the living room, you could sure feel the cold coming from that end of the house.

Mama got a towel and poked it under and around the door that led into the living room and that helped some.

Waiting on the time to go to bed Daddy told us all a story that night.

He said that right after him and Mama married, Daddy Jim had him in the swamps running one of his whiskey stills.

Daddy said the still was pretty close to a stream and it had rained steadily for three days, leaving the streams swollen. There was a foot log that crossed the creek and Daddy said he knew exactly where it was at.

"Well I was smoked as black as tar from being so close to that fire on the still."

"I heard a noise from up the hill from me and sure enough when I looked up it was the law. They were all around me."

"What did you do," Rum asked?

"What did I do? I ran."

"There was this one little short revenuer that was hot on my heels. Well, I knew where that foot log was, and it was about a foot beneath the water. I hit that log and run

across the stream, when I got to the other side of that hill
I looked back and every one of them law men had run into
that creek."

"I've often wondered if they thought I run across water
that day."

Sunshine went over and sat in Daddy's lap, she loved to
hear him tell stories about her Daddy.

Daddy continued.

"Well, they pretty well knew it was Jimmy's still, but I
was smoked so black from the soot from the fire until they
thought I was a black man, so I got by that and it wound my
bootlegging days up," Daddy said.

We ate a scanty Christmas supper that night, we were all
still so stuffed from dinner, and too, there wasn't the usual
frolic as there would have normally been, due to the bitter
cold weather outside, so we didn't burn off too many calories
and we couldn't go into the living room and listen to our usual programs over the radio.

Mama told the girls that night, since it was so cold, she
was going to let them forgo their baths. She then gave all us
a look over and only Pap and Buddy were required to take

a bath that night, due to the grease under their fingernails from helping Daddy with that tractor.

Mama opened all the doors to our bedrooms for about an hour, allowing some of the heat from the gas heater to warm our rooms a small degree, then we all sailed into bed under mounds of homemade quilts. Before the heater and lights were cut off I saw that Mama had the sabre on display above my bed and I knew she had discovered the old trunk under the house.

I never could fall to sleep as quickly as my brothers. They'd be long asleep, breathing deeply before I'd usually fall to sleep.

I remember that night there was a dim light from a clear night shining through our window. We hadn't been in the room too long before I could see the steam coming from my brother's breaths due to the dropping temperature in the room as they lie there asleep.

I lay there thinking of the day's events and of Big Mama and my twin uncles, wondering how they could be the way they were to such a good old man as my Daddy Jim.

"I wished that he'd move in with us," I thought.

I thought about the last thing I saw my Mama do that night before we were shooed off to bed.

She placed the fancy blue cup and the tiny silver spoon at the table where she'd be drinking her coffee the next morning.

Across town Minnie had looked and looked at the photographs that she had secretly hired a photographer to take of her family.

Her Daddy had marked them well for she could definitely see the resemblance.

Oh how she longed for her family. She had thought and thought about her situation and the only way she could let the truth be known meant her father would be going to prison for a crime, in her opinion he had honorably committed and she couldn't let that happen.

She'd did her best though to see that the family progressed, especially when she came back into town and discovered what a close call the little boy named Lew had with the pneumonia.

Lucky for her, she wasn't too well known in Hampton and Redtown for she'd been residing in New York with her

Mother until her death in 1951.

There was one thing she did know though, her Mother died calling her Father's name and she knew she'd loved him through the years and she'd made a promise to her Mother on her death bed.

Chapter 41

Thank goodness the cold weather had subsided enough for Pap and me to try out those number four's.

Daddy knew his time would be limited so he and Buddy went straight to work on that tractor.

I heard Daddy tell Sarge that morning that he and Buddy turned the engine over and the engine wasn't locked.

I don't think Sarge knew what he was talking about either for he offered Daddy his $33.00 back.

Sarge had about twenty acres of hardwood trees to the east of his house, an area we'd never been.

We asked him could we hunt it and he said we could hunt and fish anywhere on this land but just be careful and not shoot one of Mr. Norris's cows.

He also told us to watch out for bob cats, because either it was bobcats or foxes that were killing a lot of his chickens.

Black Boy was ready to go hunting on that new land, so as usual he took the lead.

We began to see trails running everywhere as soon as we reached the woods.

Black Boy went wild about 40 feet out into the woods, we heard a ferocious growl. One we'd never heard before.

We practically ran to the spot and looked up the tree.

Black Boy didn't know what it was either, for after he treed it, he came running to us as if he was in surprise at what it was he'd ran up that tree.

After looking we found it to be a big bobcat, both us showered down on him at the same time and the cat hit the ground. That thing must've weighed 30 pounds.

Well, just as soon as we shot, we heard a thunderous sound to our right going back toward the pasture. We looked, and it was a buck deer with a wide spread of antlers. We re-loaded our weapons fast and as soon as he hit a clear space we both pulled our triggers at the same time, causing the huge animal to come to a skidding halt before he also died.

"My Lord," Pap said, "the only deer and bobcat I've ever seen was in pictures."

Black Boy didn't know what to think about the unusual kills either. He had the enormous bobcat by the nap of the neck and kept shaking him to make sure he was dead.

"I don't ever recall us eating deer. Wonder what it tastes like?" Pap said.

"I don't know, but we're gonna find out," I said.

After poking and prodding the beautiful animal with our guns, still not believing our beginners luck, we began to pull on his back legs towards Sarge's house, but with very little progress because the deer was so heavy.

The only thing we knew to do was go get Sarge, because we knew Daddy's mind was on that tractor and if we hitched up Pete the deer would be bruised on one side because of Pete would have to drag it on the ground all the way to the house.

As usual, when we reached Sarge's, he was at his barn feeding the squealing hogs.

Black Boy was still dragging the bobcat.

"Well, well, well. Looks like you boys got one pretty quick. I heard all the shooting and knew you'd run into something down there," Sarge said.

"Sarge that's not all we killed. We got us a humongous deer, horns and all," I said.

"The problem is, it's so big and we can't get it to the house."

Sarge cocked his head to the side, then went inside his house and brought out a small hatchet and a skinning knife.

"Show Ol' Sarge where this monster is," he said.

It didn't take us long before we got there and Sarge surveyed the situation. He hacked a branch from a tree about six feet from the ground, leaving on the stub. Next he sharpened a short limb and ran it behind the tendon of each back leg.

You could tell the Sarge had plenty of experience at his job. He had that deer skinned, gutted, and hacked half into from his neck to his rump in no time.

He then slung one section, one across each shoulder and we headed toward the house.

We weren't down there a total of thirty minutes after Sarge got there.

On our walk back home Sarge told us if we wanted another one, the best time to be hunting would be late in the evening; and the only way we killed one this early in the morning was the deer was unaccustomed to being hunted, but you can bet they'll be on the lookout from now on.

"They'll lay around in those woods until right before dark, they'll come out to eat and that's when you can bag em, of course if you take your dog he'll run em out, but they'll be high tailing it and you'll be lucky to get him."

"I'm sure proud you got that old bobcat though. I'll show you boys how to tan these hides and you can make you a little money with them, especially them bobcat hides," he said.

Sarge smoked the two deer hams and Mama went right to work canning the rest of the deer. She said it was a first time for her to can deer, because she'd never had one to can, so she just preserved it like it was beef and she was so glad to get it.

After dinner the Sarge met Daddy at a lawyer's office and next day Sarge deeded Daddy the other five acres of land.

That afternoon we strung up the wire for Pete's lot and began to move the hog pen, piece by piece as far away from the house a possible.

Mama was one happy woman when we came in for supper that night.

She said old Bossy's stall was just fine where it was at and we didn't have to move it.

Chapter 42

Three things happened the next day on December the 27th.

Shelby turned 13 years old and Mama told her that morning she could start shaving her legs and later that day they'd go to Hughes' store and buy her a pair of penny loafers and some bobby socks, which was the rage for girls her age at the time.

Right after dinner that day Sarge was showing Pap and me how to skin another bobcat we'd killed that morning so that we could get the highest price possible.

"You boys really need to train your dog to not gnaw the poor animal so and you need a rifle. That way you'd just leave one hole and the price would jump sky high on your pelts.

He told us all we had to do was salt the back of the hides down, let them set for a day or two, then salt them down again. After that, we needed to tack them somewhere out of the weather until they were completely dry, then start running the backs of them back and forth across the top of an old wooden chair until the pelts were soft.

Sarge then tugged his head to the side and said.

"I'll tell you what; they must be fifteen or twenty guns in yonder in that house. A couple of them are them old timey muzzle loading things. I'm sure there's some rifles in there somewhere. I'll tell you what I'll do. You talk to your Mama, and if she don't care, I'll be glad to make you boys a gift of one of them rifles. Shoot, I'm scared of em anyway. They're just as my brother left them."

"Sarge, what happened to your brother? Don't you have any kin folks? I've never seen anyone here before," I asked.

A grin suddenly crossed Sarge's face.

"That brother of mine, he was a mess of a little brother. He was my Mother's baby."

Sarge had finished salting down our bobcat pelts, and we

had made our way to his front porch and were sitting on his wide doorsteps as he continued his story.

"Little Richard was what Mama called him. He wasn't like me. Whereas I was slow to catch on and my words seem to come out all backwards at times. Well, Richard wasn't that way."

"I guess what I'm trying to say is he was a lady's man.

Mama kept praying he'd find him a good woman and bring her out here so she'd have some grandchildren, but that Little Richard wasn't satisfied with just one, he wanted them all."

"I shouldn't be talking about this stuff to you boys, you're too young," Sarge said.

"Aww, go ahead, you've started now," I said.

"Well, to wind it all up, he was found dead early one Sunday morning outside one of them hoochie coochie joints on the outskirts of Redtown. He'd been shot in the back of the head," he said.

"Paw, he'd been dead ten years or more, and Mama had all her hopes on Little Richard for running this place, and we thought he was doing a good job of it until he was kilt, shoot

Little Richard had everything on this farm borrowed to the hilt."

"They come and loaded up all the cattle, even emptied all our barns of corn and such."

"Mama sold some of her old timey stuff in the house to see that Little Richard got a top notch funeral though."

"After Little Richard died... Mama, she just quit eating. I built her casket and dug her hole with my own two hands three months later."

"I didn't know what to do. All I knew wuz this heah place. Mr. Jim, your Granddaddy, bought me a hog that was gonna have some piglets. He lent me some money till them shoats got big enough to slaughter and sell, and he showed me how to do all of that stuff. Anyway, it wuz enough for me to make a poor living, then when Miss Minnie moved back heah he got her to look after my books and the land and everything. And you know, Mr. Jim never would take a penny back I offered him!"

The day was cool, but not as cold as before. We knew Sarge was lonely and just wanted to talk, so we let him talk, and we were completely entertained by the things he had to say.

"Geez, we didn't even know you knew our Granddaddy," Pap said.

"Humph, who around here don't. When that man speaks, folks knows to listen. Why he's got his finger in almost every business around here, and across the tracks too," Sarge said.

Then Sarge stood up, reached into his pocket and retrieved a loop of keys.

"Come on inside and we'll get a look at them guns, boys. You can go ahead and take one apiece, now. Let your Daddy look at 'em first before you shoot 'em, though. Them old bullets have been in there for ten years or more."

Sarge wasn't lying. In one of the back bedrooms he had two beds standing. You could tell the old room hadn't been entered in years for the old door creaked very loudly as the Sarge practically had to shove it open.

I held my nose; the place stank of rat urine and mold. Sarge peeled back the top layer of the dusty quilts and sure enough, just like brand new was an assortment of shotguns and rifles.

To Pap and me it was better than striking a gold mine.

We immediately began to plunder through the find, looking for that very special one, yet trying not to disturb the others.

We pretty well knew guns and rifles from looking through Mr. Hughes' catalogue so many times.

I finally settled on a Remington .30/.30 lever action and Pap decided on a .22 automatic rifle.

"Sarge, are you sure about all this?" I asked.

"Sure, nothing is too good for Mr. Jim's grandsons! I like your Pa too, and like I said, you let him check these guns out and get yo' Mama's approval, ok?"

Sarge wasn't lying about the guns, after he covered those back up I began to see more guns in the corners of the room and hanging from a homemade gun rack, made from a tree branch.

Sarge sat on the front porch enjoying some of the sunshine, Pap and I had made it about half way home when we saw the sheriff's car come speeding up our dirt road.

For some unknown reason we both instinctively threw our rifles in the bushes beside of the road.

The car pulled into Sarge's yard, and we ran back to see

what was going on.

Sheriff Watson and two deputies got out of the patrol car and arrested Sarge for the disappearance of Gloria Jean Snell, the mayor's daughter.

The Sarge thought they were pulling a joke on him until one of the deputies fired at his feet.

Sarge threw his hands into the air.

One of the little deputies tried to handcuff the Sarge but the cuffs wouldn't fit around his wrists.

They tried and tried to get the Sarge into the back seat of the police car but his big hulk of a frame was simply too big to fit into the opening.

By this time Mama had made her way out there.

"If you harm one hair on this poor over grown child, I'll see that you pay," Mama said, then asked, "What the hell is all this about?"

"Mind your own business lady," the Sheriff said.

I saw the bulk of Mama's pearl handle revolver from her apron pocket and knew that she had come prepared, but I shook my head at her, "No."

Finally Sarge stood sideways of the opening and the two

deputies more or less kicked him into the police car.

Sarge threw us his keys and told us our deer hams should be through smoking late that evening. He then asked us to keep an eye on things around there, and to contact Mr. Jim and Miss Minnie to tell them what had happened.

The third consequential thing that happened that day was Miss Minnie never returned to her hole.

The law was in such a hurry to get away from Sarge's that day until poor Sarge's feet and legs were still outside the vehicle as they drove away.

Chapter 43

It seemed the life that we had known just a year ago had done a complete double back flip.

It was April 1956, the Sarge was still in jail and things along the little red strip of road in town just weren't the same.

Miss Minnie had left her hole and someone had even resurrected a crucifix at the sight.

Mr. Reese had made a trip to the jail house with two of his daughters to talk with the Sherriff to see if there was anything he could do about getting Sarge out.

"My God Man, two of the girls that are missing are yours, and you're coming in here wanting to get this murderer out of jail so that he can kill again!"

"Two" Mr. Reese said and then nodded his head "Yes." Before he'd left the house that morning, Daddy said that since Sarge left, Mr Reese's business had fell off to near nothing. About all the bizness he's getting is from that new drank box. He said folks would come through Redtown just to see Sarge direct that traffic and to buy his pork, but they've quit coming, so Mr. Reese ain't selling any gas, and Miss Minnie, she's climbed outter that hole, so that's hurt Mr. Reese's bizness too, for folks would come by just to see the strange woman in the hole."

"How did they get in here, get these idiots out of my office," Sheriff Watson said, but not before he pinched the pretty little Jimmie sue on her ripe rump, causing her to jump.

The strangest turn of events was, Miss Minnie wound up being a full-fledged lawyer from New York City. She proved she had her license to also practice in the State of Alabama, and she was Sarge's lawyer.

Another thing that had happened, when the mill opened back up a fellow that Daddy was training to set up a big saw started it too soon and it cut the little finger and almost all of the fourth finger off.

Miss Minnie got Daddy $3,000.00 from the insurance company down at the mill.

Miss Minnie was also Sarge's Attorney in fact so Daddy bought ten more acres of farm land. Mama bought us a 1953 Buick 4 door and a television.

She must've had plenty money left, because after offering Daddy a wad of bills, he told her to just put it up somewhere and so she went into their bedroom with it.

The tractor was put back together piece by piece while Daddy was off with his hand healing, and by the middle of February I heard a sound that I would hear until I left home; the putt, putt, putt of that Farmall tractor.

We had already fenced in the entire twenty acres of Daddy's land.

Buddy acted as though he already knew everything there was to know about the different hookups and things that went with the tractor and in no time at all we were breaking land, getting it prepared for the spring planting.

Myrtice kept walking over wanting to play but she didn't comprehend we were just poor working folks and had to work for a living in the Spring and Summer months, so she and Sunshine wound up playing together most often.

Having the tractor was more efficient and a whole lot faster than plowing with a mule.

One night at the supper table I heard Mama tell Daddy that he had twenty acres now and from "Now on out her children wouldn't be hired out for field hands anymore. She told him to start planting twelve acres in cotton, leave her two acres for a yard, and that would leave him eight acres to plant corn for the animals and for the garden and fruit orchard.

We boys worked that tractor, Daddy felt the same about it as he felt about Mama's Buick, as soon as they cranked he was through with them.

I know it was a hard thing for Daddy to do, but after he saw we had caught on to the tractor pretty well. He turned ole Pete loose in the big pasture with Mr. Norris' Cows.

Daddy left the bridle on Pete though just in case we needed to catch him.

Pete took to that big Pond and large acreage too because pretty soon he was as fat and sleek as he could be. Of course, we'd all slip him and ear of corn here and there and if Mama thought no one was looking she'd sling some of her biscuits across the fence to him.

Ol' Pete was honorary at times but he had kept us from going hungry and we all knew it too.

Mama had bought her car from Mr. Lester, the midget. He'd about gone out of the mule and horse business, so he'd started selling used cars, trucks, and a few tractors.

Miss Minnie had tipped Mama off about the vehicle. She'd heard that Mama was looking for a good used one. She said she knew the vehicle and it had been driven just a very few miles and that it had been locally owned.

Mama looked at the car and they struck up a deal.

Mr. Lester got one of his helpers to drive Mama home in the car, because she didn't know a thing about it.

After the worker ran back toward town, we naturally all piled into our very first car.

Daddy just looked at it from a distance in the yard.

After she let us all have a gander she began to look over the Bill of Sales paper and discovered that Mr. Lester had added $500.00 to the total price.

"I'll have to bring this to his attention," she said, "but

first I'm going to teach myself how to drive this baby."

She warned us all to stand behind the house until she caught on, "Lemme at least learn how to hit the brakes," she said.

Sunshine and Shelby ran into the house and peered through the windows.

We, along with Daddy, did as Mama said and hid behind the house.

Well, it seemed that Mama did pretty well as long as she went backwards.

Finally she'd backed herself until she was right against Sarge's house and she had to do something.

We saw and heard the stripping of the gears until finally the car leapt forward. She passed our house stripping gears until she finally made it down the road and turned it around.

Mama taught herself how to drive that Buick in less than a week and she loaded us all up to make a trip to the Court House to get her license.

Chapter 44

It nearly killed me to see the big Sarge in jail.

The little cot was too short and narrow. In fact the whole room was so small that it looked as though if Sarge would lay in the floor and stretch his hands and arms he could touch it on both sides.

Daddy kept us pretty busy, but we'd try to slip into Hampton at least twice a week and talk to the Sarge, unknowingly to the Sheriff of course.

It was very easy; we'd bring one of ol' Pete's plow lines with us, then lasso the chimney, pull ourselves up and hide behind the chimney so no one could see us. We'd then walk over the roof and talk to the Sarge through his cell window.

Sarge told us over and over that he didn't have anything to do with the girls disappearing, but he said for right now he would be safer in jail than he would be at home because everybody was so stirred up about it, "but I just want to go home," he'd say.

We told him that we were feeding his chickens and hogs for him, but we weren't slaughtering any. "Miss Minnie is getting someone to pick them hogs up and selling them to use for your trial, so you won't have to sell any of your land."

"Smart woman, Miss Minnie," Sarge said.

We'd catch him up on everything around the place, he'd always tell us to thank our Mama for sending him his Sunday dinner every Sunday.

Since Pap was about a foot taller than me, I'd always climb down the rope. Pap would undo the rope and slide off the top of the jail house. Then we'd coil up our rope and hit the road running back toward the house.

On one such visit Sarge told us that he'd heard rumors the County was going out to his place and going through it to look for evidence.

"I want you to talk with your Daddy about it first then go

out there and get every gun I have, try to go tonight, you'll have to take a flash light."

"Look under my bed, son, and you'll find an old metal Army box. It has money in it; see that Miss Minnie gets it. And boys, on the other side of my bed is a box of watches; some of them are gold. See that your Daddy gets them. He might can fix 'em."

"Yes sir Sarge," we said, "Don't you worry, Miss Minnie will have you out of here before you know it."

"No, boys, she's talking like it might be this fall or winter before it even comes to court," he said.

So that night, after Mama and the girls were in bed, we sneaked across the grounds towards Sarge's house, making sure to shush Black Boy. We kept our flashlights off until we were on the other side of Sarge's house.

Daddy found a window that was in the kitchen area but was high from the ground.

He kept working at the window until he got it high enough for me to crawl through.

I crept to the kitchen door and unlocked it so the others could get in

There were so many guns and rifles in that house until it took three trips each, carrying three or four at a time to get all that we could find out of there.

I couldn't help but laugh, because everything was just in such a rush, rush, rush, when I looked out the window trying to catch my breath when I saw my baby brother Rum, who never got in a hurry about anything creep across the back yard with a muzzle loader thrown across his shoulder that must've been seven feet long.

After all the firearms were gone I showed Daddy the cash box and the box that contained the collection of watches.

The box with the cash contained a small clasp and lock at the top, but the assortment of watches didn't.

"Sarge said to tell you that you could have the box of watches if you could fix them," I told Daddy.

Mama made us put every one of those guns in the loft of that house while she and Daddy went through the box of, what they thought was just old watches, for scattered among the watches they found jewelry of all sorts.

"Most of this looks very old and expensive," Mama said until she had picked through all of it, just leaving the watches on the table.

Most of the watches were of the old pocket watch variety. One or two of them had engravings that dated back to a hundred years or more.

I could tell that Daddy wasn't interested in all those diamonds and such. He had set his eye on an old gold colored railroad watch. He didn't care whether it was gold or not. He just knew he'd always wanted him a railroad watch, and now he had it.

"I think Miss Minnie needs to be aware of all this jewelry when she picks of this cash box. And Charles, that big old simple-minded man didn't have a thing to do with those girls' disappearances! Not a piece of jewelry in here belongs to a child their age." Mama said.

By the spring of that year Elvis Presley had become the thing, He had a new hit single out called "Heartbreak Hotel."

Now, I haven't mentioned this before, but Mama was born in Butler county, Alabama, it adjoined the northeast county of Monroe [the county we lived in.] A doctor Tippins delivered my Mama, then he went right up the road and delivered Hank Williams.

Mama didn't know what to think of Elvis and his new style of music, for before him, when ol' Hank was singing over the radio, she's always turn the volume up.

Back in those days everyone drank the same brand of coffee. The more you bought the more coupons you'd get.

The first thing Mama traded in her coupons for was an electric iron and the next thing was a small plastic radio that she kept on top of the refrigerator.

There was a program that came on every day after school called "The Hep Cat" program. It was on the local station in town, so it came in loud and clear.

Mama had a bottle with a sprinkler on one end of it. Sunshine would dampen the clothes, while dancing around and around to the music, then Mama would iron them going all the way around that ironing board, really expressing herself to Heartbreak Hotel. We looked for her to throw her back bone out, but she didn't.

Shelby would be waiting with the clothes hangers and she too would be twisting in the most provocative physical positions. I thought to myself that Elvis had really made an impact on the girls and Mama.

Sometimes she and Shelby would trade places.

To me the whole affair sounded like a bunch of pots and pans being beaten together.

"Give me the music down at Pig Meat Malone's any day! By the way, I'd learned the lady that sang "Bing Bang Boom" was from New Orleans, and she went by the name of Della Rice.

Well, it was on one of these days that the girls were ironing and listening to 'The Help Cat" program when Miss Minnie pulled in front of the house, riding in the taxi.

She heard all the loud noise coming from the house and asked if it would be alright to go in?

"Sure," I said to her with a smile.

Miss Minnie banged on the door but didn't get an answer.

When she followed me into the living room, she couldn't help but sink herself into a chair and laugh.

Sunshine was the first one that noticed Miss Minnie. She walked over and tugged at Mama's dress, who was just throwing her rump out of place to the beat of the song.

Miss Minnie retrieved a piece of paper from her brief

case, put in front of her face and you could tell from the movement of her body she was having a good laugh at watching the spectacle before her eyes.

I was laughing too, but the music was so loud no one could hear anything but the blaring voice of ol' Elvis.

At Sunshine's insistence Mama finally looked up and saw Miss Minnie sitting there, all dressed prim and proper in a light purple two piece outfit.

"Miss Minnie didn't look like she came from this neck of the woods anymore," I thought.

"Well I'll be damned, I'll bet you'll knock before you come into this house the next time," Mama said.

"Quite the contraire, in fact, to tell you the truth, I enjoyed the performances.'

Without thinking, Mama turned the ironing over to Shelby, smiled at herself for being caught in such a predicament, then invited Miss Minnie into the kitchen for a cup of coffee.

On the short walk to the kitchen Minnie was amazed at how orderly everything in the house was. And that darling little Sunshine, it took every fiber of her being to keep from pulling the gorgeous child into her lap and squeezing her senselessly. She was the exact replica of a child she'd known at that age. Only the other little girl wasn't so innocent, but she had wanted to be, she thought.

Mama asked me to go into her bedroom and bring Sarge's cash box and the box of Jewelry.

I knew where Mama kept all her, what she considered to be private things, so I looked in the bottom of her dresser drawer. Not only did I see the two small trunks. I saw the sterling silver mirror and brush Miss Minnie had sent her at Christmas, still sitting in the same place, never used. On a whim and wanting Mama to break the ice with Miss Minnie, I brought the two objects along with the rest.

The brush and mirror was the first things Miss Minnie looked at.

"Why Darling, from the looks of your brush you haven't stroked your hair, not once with it," Miss Minnie said.

Mama poured the coffee. I noticed she just used the regular cups. Then she laid out the sugar and creamer.

Mama hesitated for just a second.

"No, it seems to me at the time that you had written something about me sharing my children with you, and you'll have to admit about all I knew about you was someone that lied around in a hole all day and ate bananas, and too with the disappearances of these children. I just wasn't ready to turn my boys over to a total stranger."

Miss Minnie stirred some cream into her coffee, contemplating what to say next.

She grabbed Mama's hand in hers.

"My dear sweet woman, would it surprise you to know that I learned more about life while lying in that hole than I did my entire twenty years of school."

"I have a Doctor's degree in psychiatry, a doctorate of law to practice here and New York State, a degree is social economics, but none of that compared to what I learned lying in that hole and simply observing things."

"You see I was an only child. I was born here but when I was a little girl my Mother moved away from here."

"I only saw my Mother occasionally as she was a social climber, I was raised by butlers and a variety of nannies, but oh how I longed for my Southland and my Family, so when she died five years ago and I had charge of the money I moved back home, to be near my family"

"Who is your family," Mama asked?

Miss Minnie acted as though she didn't hear her.

"Would you believe I own every building in Redtown and half the businesses in Hampton," Miss Minnie continued,

She wound up with saying, "I am a very wealthy woman, and I'm not meaning to boast, just telling the facts before you find out from someone else and think that I've hidden something from you." Mama looked her straight in the eyes then asked me to bring her the old family photograph album from the living room.

"Uh oh, this woman is nobody's fool, now's not the time to play my cards, it's too soon. It would mean a man's life. Someone she loves dearly," thought Minnie.

I returned with the old album, one that had wound up at our house somehow or other that came from Big Mama's.

I'd long since noticed that Mama had removed all the pictures of her Mother and her side of the family, leaving only Daddy Jim's family in the book.

Mama thumbed straight to the photograph of her sister Margie Ree, then showed it to Miss Minnie.

"Does this image look familiar?" asked Mama as she

shoved the heavy book over for Miss Minnie to look at.

I saw a look of tenderness as Miss Minnie ran her manicured fingernail over every detail of Margie's face.

"Amazing, the resemblance, isn't it?" Mama said.

Minnie didn't say anything for a good minute. Instead, she pinched the bridge of her nose, and then rubbed her brow, before she finally closed the album and looked away from it.

She then leaned over and whispered something in Mama's ear, too quiet for me to hear.

Mama looked in the cupboard and brought out a Goody's headache powder, stirred it in some cold water and gave it to Miss Minnie.

"Poor dear, some months it can sure slip right up on you," Mama told her.

"Exactly! So instead of a visit as I would have loved, I'm afraid I'll just have to get right down to business."

"As you know, the only evidence they have on our friend is the curly blonde hair. Well, I believe the hair in question is yours. Now, I've retained two 'snoopers.' It seems as though they know just about everything that goes on around here; those are two very bright children you have, in Lew and Pap."

Mama looked quizzical.

"After talking to my snoopers, I discovered you had them drop off an envelope at Sarge's stand that Christmas Eve morning before they came to my house for their gifts. I think that's when a strand of your hair must have fallen out from the inside of Lew's coat, into Sarge's meat contraption."

"How are we going to prove that hair is mine?" Mama asked.

"Simple. I've come here today for a single strand of your hair. I'm going to send it, along with the strand the Sheriff is holding for evidence, to the FBI lab and see what they come up with when they compare the two."

"You know, I've thought of the same thing, because the Snell girl didn't have any hair. I know, because I got a good look at her bald head the night of the contest. I just didn't know anything about this FBI lab."

"So you don't mind if I pull a hair follicle from your head, then?"

"Pull all you want. Anything to help that poor overgrown child," Mama said.

Miss Minnie used some big black tweezers and gently

pulled a strand of Mama's blonde hair from the side of her head, then dropped it into a freezer bag and folded the bag several times.

After looping the bag several times with a rubber band, Miss Minnie unsnapped her purse and dropped the wrapped hair sample inside it.

She then dumped everything in the watch box out onto the center of the table. With her fingernail file, she began to plunder through the hodgepodge of jewelry and old tie pins and clips.

After going through everything, Miss Minnie whistled. "Boy, back in the day, someone in that family must have had some money! Most of this stuff is gold with garnets, diamonds, jade, pearls . . . you name it."

"I know. Sarge told us to take whatever we wanted, but Charles just got the watches. We thought maybe you might need to sell the rest of all this to help pay his court fees," Mama answered.

"We don't know what's in the cash box, of course," she added.

"Well, I am his attorney, in fact," said Miss Minnie, "so

let's have a look." She took the nail file and jiggled it in the small inexpensive lock until it opened.

They both looked inside and their eyes got wide. The box was full of money!

On top of the big pile of bills was the neat stack of two thousand dollars that Daddy had paid Sarge for the land. Under that, there was much more. Some of it looked very old; a few of the bills were even in Confederate currency.

"Look, here's an 1862 two-cent piece. That one has been around a while," Mama said.

Miss Minnie kept counting the money, straightening it out as she went. When she was finished, it totaled a little over nine thousand dollars.

"Lord, that Sarge!" she exclaimed. "Whoever would have thought he had that kind of money?"

While Minnie was gathering up the jewelry and the money and putting them back into their respective boxes, Mama asked, "Minnie, why do you suppose that poor soul is having to spend so much time in jail? I'm telling you, the town is just not the same! It seems so deserted with him not being at that intersection. I just felt safer with him standing there, even though he really didn't do a whole lot."

"Well, to tell you the truth, I really had to fight to have his case prolonged until this fall. I knew with the temperament of the local populace they'd all rush to judgement and he'd be found guilty, and I wanted time to prove him innocent," Minnie answered.

The two talked a little longer, then Miss Minnie gave Mama one of her cards and told her if there was anything else she could think about the case to contact her.

Miss Minnie only took the box with the cash, saying that she had talked to Sarge and he still wanted Mama and Daddy to have the contents of the watch box.

"Lord have mercy, what would a common woman like me want with such do-dads as that?" Mama asked.

"You can always sell them and buy you some carpet."

"Oh, I'd never do that! Besides, I like my plain wooden floors," said Mama.

She looked at the card that Miss Minnie had given her.

The card read "S. MINERVA RAINES, ATTORNEY AT LAW."

"What does the 'S' stand for?" Mama wanted to know.

"Shelby."

"Who named you?" Mama asked.

"My Daddy," replied Miss Minnie. "And who named your daughter," asked Miss Minnie.

"My Daddy, of course," said Mama, and as she and Miss Minnie were going through the living room, they both burst out laughing. Then Mama stopped her at the door and told her she would use the brush and mirror, and they laughed again.

Chapter 45

There was always two birthdays at our house in May. Pap turned 11 May the 11th and Buddy turned 12 the following day.

Mama always just had them a cake together and it was the same that year.

I've always credited Mrs. Sessions for me making a poor living as a writer. Right before school was out for summer vacation that year she gave all the students a test to write an essay or story about someone you admired.

I'd heard most of the boys in class remark that their essay would be about their Daddy.

I didn't have a second thought about it. I knew it had to

be Miss Della Rice, the blues singer down at Pig Meat's place.

That day after school I asked Shelby to tell Mama that I was going to stop by Miss Minnie's for a few minutes before I came home. Naturally Pap ran with me even though he had no intention of doing any kind of an essay, (But I was proved to be wrong.)

Luckily for us, it was on a Friday and we had to have the papers turned in on Monday.

I talked to Miss Minnie about it.

She started talking some kind of mumbo jumbo about segregation and stuff, which we knew nothing about, so after taking a deep breath and brushing through her hair, she squared her shoulders and walked to Pig Meat Malone's with us.

After telling Miss Della my intensions, she smiled and said "And you're sure you want me to sing the Bing, Bang, Boom song."

"Yes Mam, that's probably the only one you'll have time to sing, you see, I'm going to say a short story about your life before you perform."

Miss Della grinned, showing her wide impeccable teeth.

"Show ain't much ter tells dare, been making my own way fuh as long as I can remember. Down in the quarters singing and dancing for the folks or singing for them Nanner boats when dey comes in. Ole' Della never been to school a day in my life."

"That's it, keep talking," I said, as I caught up with her scribbling in my notebook.

"What, you mean you're doing a story on ol' Della right now," she asked?

"Sure I am, keep talking.

Miss Della had sure had a hard scrabbled life, but she said she'd never took to drinking, she said she'd seen too many good people go down with it.

After listening to her biography, I shortened it to the required three pages, even though it was a hard thing to do. Miss Della was such a swell person.

Miss Minnie and Pap said that with just a little practice Sunday afternoon they could play the saxophone and guitar for Miss Della during her performance.

I tried to get Pap to at least make an attempt, and do one and make it on "The Snake Man," but he said nah, if he was to pass something they might go to expecting it of him all the time, so he let it slide.

Pig Meat was worried about a reprisal at the school house, but Miss Minnie assured him that everything would be okay.

When we reached home that afternoon I asked Mama if she knew that Miss Minnie had a picture of Sunshine sitting on a table in her living room.

"Are you sure it's my baby," Mama asked?

"Well it looks just like her except Sunshine has short curly hair in that picture."

"Ah, you know I would never cut that child's curly locks. It's probably a picture that comes with the frame," she said.

When I told Mama about the story I was doing on Miss Della, she agreed to drop us off at Miss Minnie's that following Sunday at two o'clock.

When Pap and Minnie started to play while Della sang, I'll have to admit I had my doubts there for about an hour. It just didn't sound all that great to me. Finally, Miss Della told them they were going to have to pick up the beat, that she was use to following the music and they were playing entirely too slow.

She started stamping her feet and snapping her fingers to demonstrate what she wanted. Miss Minnie caught on with the sax, then Pap joined in. By four o'clock, Miss Della asked them if they were ready to hit the road.

It sounded so good by the end of it that they even had Pig Meat snapping his fingers along with the music.

The deadline for turning in your essay was eleven o'clock. I'd asked Miss Minnie to arrive in our room with Pap and Miss Della at ten forty-five.

They arrived right on time.

Miss Della was dressed in a red feathery dress that came down below her knees. She was also wearing a wide Panama hat. It, too, was covered in red feathers and looked to be about two sizes too big. In her right hand, she had a huge white feathered fan, and she made sure she kept her huge bosom covered with it at all times.

To finish her outfit, Della was wearing white sparkly shoes on her tiny feet.

Oh, she was a sight!

The children, along with Mrs. Sessions, stared at her in

awe. She paid them no attention; she just cocked one big hip out to the side and leaned against the chalkboard while I read her life's story.

Then it was her turn to speak.

She started out with, "Gee, if I'd known I'd have started out in the fifth grade, I'd have come to school sooner! But Mr. Lew here, he's told you my story and it was a lot different than yours. So you'd better take an old woman's advice; learn all you can in school, because you may not be blessed with a God-given talent to make a living with."

Then she started to sing, with Pap and Miss Minnie going right along with her.

The song started out like a slow-moving train, but then it got faster and faster until Della's big voice thundered off the walls of that little school room.

"You just lay 'round de house and do de Bing Bang Boom!"

It wasn't a surprise to me that, like all her other performances, Miss Della owned the stage that day, and everyone there knew it. Even the coach and principal, who had heard her and stuck their heads through the door to find out what was going on, insisted she was good enough to record her own music. She would later do just that; she wound up in Chicago and made quite a name for herself.

Miss Minnie and Pap didn't miss a note, either, and for Pap's effort he got the highest grade he had ever made, other than in physical ed. Mrs. Sessions had simply torn a piece of yellow construction paper in two, and the only thing she wrote on it was "Pap Gulley, C-."

I was so proud of my brother that day! With a borrowed guitar and two hours of practice, he had mesmerized those people. And the best thing was, to him, it was just an ordinary thing, something that was expected of him and no big deal.

Mrs. Sessions allowed me to escort my "project" outside to their waiting taxi. Pap didn't ask; he just came anyway, carrying the borrowed guitar.

Once outside, I thanked Miss Minnie and Miss Della for what they had done. Miss Della was like Pap; she acted as if it was no big thing to her.

"Honey, at least I can say I made it to the fifth grade!" she said, then added, "Lawd, let me get home and pulls this outfit off. I look like a Indian on the war path, not counting these shoes are killing the bunions on my feets."

There were three seats in the taxi, and my eyes didn't fail to notice how tenderly Pap laid that guitar on the black velvet seat.

It was a great day all around; I was the only one in class that made an A plus on their essay.

Chapter 46

I hated leaving Mrs. Sessions' class at the end of the year, but I was promoted to the sixth grade, and so was Pap.

All of a sudden we became known as "Baby Boomers." I didn't see any big deal about it, though.

After school was out that year, we lost a playmate. Myrtice and her family moved across town to Dennis Street. I later learned that Myrtice got herself a baby sister, and I was proud for her, but we sure missed her in our neck of the woods. I had gotten used to her being around; she even went with us once when we decided to drink our RC colas in the shade of Miss Minnie's porch.

When Myrtice's family moved out of the house another

family moved in. They had two daughters, named Betty Jean and Joanne. Their mother's name was Imojean and was, what I considered to be, one of the prettiest ladies I had ever laid eyes on. She had coal black hair, with fair skin and was a small woman.

It didn't take long for us to be visiting each other, for they were in the same room as Pap and me.

Daddy had tied a rope around the branch of a tall sweet gum tree next to the barn and on the other end, about two feet from the ground he'd tied a small cotton sack stuffed with corn shucks. Boy did we have a good time swinging on that rope.

One would climb on top of the barn and another one would swing the sack of corn shucks toward the barn. As soon as that sack hit the barn, we'd sail off, grabbing the rope them lap our legs around that bag of shucks, and boy would it ever go so high!

Betty Jean and Joanne mastered the technique of jumping off the barn onto that sack of shucks pretty quickly!

As far as I knew, Miss Minnie had only one client for her law practice, and that was Sarge. She kept busy with music, though, and continued giving Pap his free guitar and saxophone lessons twice a week.

Then something happened that I would have never believed. Mama actually allowed Miss Minnie to give Sunshine piano lessons twice a week! Minnie had told Mama, "That child has a natural gift for the piano," and after Mama listened to Sunshine play with just a few short practices, Mama agreed to bring Sunshine for two hours a day on one of the days Pap wouldn't be there.

On my next visit to Miss Minnie's, I looked for the picture of the little girl with the short blonde curls in the pretty frame, but it was gone.

Of course, the work never stopped, no matter what else we did with our time. We all found out one thing; having that tractor made a world of difference in time spent on the garden and the fields.

Daddy's twelve acres of cotton was looking good. Mama was really canning a lot of fruits and vegetables from the garden.

The only drawback about living at the end of the dirt road was, I'd gotten use to the action of Redtown. I missed the oddball characters living and operating their businesses up and down the narrow dirt road.

Besides, Mama was just too close. Heck, you had to get her permission before you could do anything. And things just didn't seem to be as much fun if she knew about them.

We did continue with our fishing business, but either the fish were getting harder to catch, or we were about to fish the pond dry. So we decided to come up with something else. We had ninety-four dollars and fifty cents stashed away, though, which was quite a sum in those days. I'm sure Mama knew we had a little money, but I was also sure she would have never dreamed we had such a large amount.

Pap was usually pretty smart with his quick wit, but I thought he was dead wrong when he suggested we buy a mule at Mr. Lester's place and start plowing gardens for people.

"Are you crazy?" I asked. "We haven't been from behind that mule but a few months and you're wanting to get behind another one, so the answer is no!" I told him.

Pap had Mama's temper, and I knew it.

"Give me my damn money, then," he said, and I knew

better than to argue.

"Alright, but you owe me eight dollars and thirty cents."

"Fine," he said as he held out his hand for his money. Then we pulled our shirts off, lathered down good with soap and rinsed off before he walked over to Miss Minnie's.

I walked on down to Mr. Reese's and bought me a cold drink.

There wasn't anything going on; the town was dead, so it was a slow, lonely walk home for me.

When I did reach home, Mama told me that Daddy had received a letter from my Grandpa in Conecuh County and he wanted us all to come for a visit before things got so hectic on the farm. Along with the letter was a ten-dollar bill, "I guess to hire a taxi," Mama said.

I hadn't seen nor heard from any of that part of the family since we'd left from over there when I was five years old. All I could remember is, we were about to starve to death when we left.

I'll have to admit, though, my Grandpa had it made. He dressed in a suit seven days a week, and belonged to every club there was to belong to. He was a well-educated man for his day; he'd taught school for a while. He also clerked in stores around the small town where he lived, and kept the books for different businesses.

He'd go out into the fields early in the mornings and tell his three sons that still lived at home with him what he expected of them that day, and they did it.

His young wife's name was Liza, but he called her Lize, and she didn't seem to mind. She was thirty-nine years old when they married, and I guess she was just tired of being dumped from relative to relative, so she treated him like a king. There was something wrong with her feet, so my Grandpa had to hire someone to help out around the kitchen and other household chores.

Her entire day was centered on dinner, and boy, could she cook! But after Mama beat her, we weren't allowed to eat there anymore.

None of them had the smarts that my Grandpa had, and I really liked him. He had the prettiest penmanship; he wrote in large scrolling letters. He was born in 1876 and was just a walking history book. Oh, how I loved to hear him tell stories of his father, who was one of Mosby's Gray Ghost Rangers in the CSA.

Of all the people in my Daddy's family, my Mama liked him best, and I think he liked or either respected her, too.

I liked two of Daddy's brothers all right. They were just meek, like Daddy. The oldest one, John, didn't like us, though, and he watched our every move. I don't think his mind was right or something, I don't know. My Mama summed it up by saying the whole damn bunch was crazy, but then I'd learned that she'd say that about people she just didn't understand.

I still liked my Mama's Daddy best, though, and I missed going down there and listening to him play that old Gibson guitar, but I sure didn't miss Big Mama and her wrath.

When Pap came in later that day, he gave me all his money back, and nothing was said about it.

After talking with Daddy that night about the letter from his father, a trip was planned for the following day to go over there.

The next day was Friday, June 15th, my birthday. I was ten years old. Mama cooked me my favorite, chocolate cake with thick homemade icing and we all ate it for dessert that night after supper.

While we were all together, Mama warned us that we were dared to touch a morsel of food the entire time we were at our Grandfather's.

"We're going over there because he's sent for us, not for y'all to gobble like a bunch of hogs and give that she-devil something to talk about after we leave."

"Now, I'm packing us a good picnic lunch before we leave in the morning, and we can all gather under the shade of that big bay tree and eat, is that understood?"

We all nodded our heads in agreement.

I guess Daddy must have had a bad experience in a car sometime in his past, because he wouldn't ride in the front seat; he gave it up to Shelby and Sunshine.

Me, Pap, Rumby, and Daddy were packed liked sardines in the back seat.

Daddy didn't have but three fingers on one hand but he held on for dear life as the Buick pulled out of our drive way at ten o'clock that morning. We left town, turned east on highway 84, and we were there in about twenty minutes.

It was easy to spot where my Granddaddy's land started; it looked like ours. There wasn't a blade of grass to be seen, except it was about eighty acres, whereas ours was just twenty.

My Grandpa's house was a beautiful old rambling Victorian-style house. I loved it, and due to Liza's feet condition she couldn't keep up with us in the house. There was a lot to look at, especially the old family portraits and huge pictures hanging on the high walls everywhere.

There were two fences that surrounded the house: a white wooden fence that was seen from the road, then after you walked through the gate and took about thirty steps, you ran into a wire fence where you were always greeted by Ruby and Trixy, my grandpa's two pet dogs.

Needless to say; we were all dressed very nice; Mama made sure of that.

When we arrived, the first thing Mama did was kick Ruby, for jumping up on her leg and ruining her hose.

Of course, Ruby went yelping to her master for solace.

Grandpa was a small man like Daddy, and he was sitting on the front porch swing when we arrived. You could tell that he was genuinely proud to see us by the way his face lit up after he recognized who we were.

REDTOWN: A NOVEL BY L.E. GULLEY

He didn't know Sunshine had come to live with us, but he hugged her neck along with everybody else's.

Once the dog calmed down and the hugging was done with, Mama reached into her purse and gave Grandpa his ten dollars back to him.

"We drove our own car," she said.

"Oh boy, I saw that big old car coming up the road and I figured it must be a politician or something."

"No, it's ours, and it's paid for too," Mama said proudly.

I knew Daddy, and I knew that he'd stay there all day and not mention our new house and land, so I blurted it out.

"Yeah, and we have a new house and twenty acres of land paid for," I said.

Mama shushed me. "Your Grandpa will think we're bragging or something."

"Is that the truth? My goodness, I'm so proud for you, Charles!"

"Yep, it's taken a lot of hard work, plus my Daddy and poor old Charles losing almost two of his fingers, but we have a place of our own, and a nice one too," Mama told him.

"She's right, Paw. Once we got away from here, things

just seemed to fall in line. Of course Mr. Jim, he helped a lot after we got going," Daddy said.

"That Jimmy had a rough go of it with his back and all, but then, he was a lucky rascal too. He won a great big guitar shooting craps right down yonder at that creek," pointed Grandpa. "He'd take that thing to the depot station on Saturdays, pick and sing for the folks and make more money in a half a day than I could all day long clerking in the stores! Yes sir, he had a talent."

"Humph, the best move Daddy ever made, and us too, was getting away from here," Mama said.

Grandpa looked at Mama as though his feelings were hurt, but he didn't say anything.

"We sort of looked for y'all today, so Lize has put the big pot into the little one in there. There'll be plenty for everyone."

"Well, you can go in there and tell her not to cook for me or my bunch; we brought our own food. We just came because you called for us, Paw," Mama said.

"I see. Well, I may as well ring the dinner bell early and get the boys in from the fields. We'll go ahead and have the meeting and get it over with."

My grandfather's land was a fine place for a youngster to play. There were several old barns, some of which were made from logs. My ancestors had homesteaded the place in 1821.

There was cats running everywhere, and you couldn't get close to any of them. My Grandpa said he just fed them and kept them around for the snakes.

It would have been a fun place to play, that is, if it wasn't for Daddy's oldest brother. He watched us like a hawk.

We always felt he had money hid in one of those barns but we never could find it.

The men folks all had their meeting. Mama never did go inside; she just sat out under the shade of the bay tree.

Sunshine wanted to run and play with us, but Mama wouldn't let her. She told her that we had gotten too old for her to run with, so she let her draw some lines in the dirt and play hopscotch.

While our Uncle John was in the house, Pap and me slipped in the mule stable, climbed up to the highest board and emptied our bladders on the back of those two mules. We knew from experience that scent would be there for days, especially when they'd start plowing and them mules would work up a lather.

It served him right for being so damn mean.

After the meeting, Daddy's brothers seemed mighty happy. After eating dinner, they came outside and picked with us children some, all except John, who just went on back toward the fields with a hoe thrown across his shoulder. After we started eating, they too headed back into the hot fields.

I never saw Liza the entire time we were there.

After we left, Daddy told Mama that his Paw was drawing up a will, and he called the meeting to explain to all of them who was to get what.

Daddy said he told his Paw he didn't want a thing over there, and to give his part to Arthur, the brother that was nearest his age.

"Good for you. You did the right thing. If John got the upper hand of things, he's so stingy the place wouldn't hold up long," Mama said.

On our ride back home I thought how queer it was that two old bitter women kept too households so stirred up and unhappy. Liza, and Big Mama. So different, and yet so alike.

REDTOWN: A NOVEL BY L.E. GULLEY

Chapter 47

I always wondered why Buddy seemed happy just going along hammering and banging in that shop and not out trying to make extra money like me and Pap, but I was about to soon find out.

Daddy had taught Buddy to shoe horses and mules, how to file saws and how to repair tools.

Whereas Pap and me was making money any way we could. Buddy was learning a trade. Something that could last him the rest of his life.

Daddy had an old bellows that was fired with coal and the hot metal was actually hammered together until it was mended.

Mama did with Buddy as she did with me and Pap she never asked for any of the money that we earned away from the farm.

Shelby and Sunshine didn't have to worry about anything, they didn't get everything they wanted but like Rum, they got what they needed.

One night while I was lying in bed I began to think back in time and I could never remember Buddy getting a whipping, so I guess he had the whole concept figured out from the get go, I don't know. All I knew was I wished I had been born more like my brother, more tranquil, quiet and stable. Maybe Mama wouldn't watch me so closely and I could get by with more because I could sure think of a lot of things to do to make money if it wasn't for Mama. I had no idea what I'd do with money if I had a large sum, but I'd seen times when Mama and Daddy didn't have food to feed us, especially before we moved to Redtown and I guess even at such a young age I didn't want the family to be caught in such a situation again.

I know one thing, especially at nights when I was lying in bed and trying to put my brain in the sleep mode, I still thought of the pretty little Bessie and I wondered how she was doing way up there in New Jersey and I hoped she had warm clothes to wear in the winter time.

It took the Sheriff and his deputies nearly seven months but they finally made it to the Sarge's. They flew by the house one morning in a new 1956 Ford, sirens and lights going, with a pickup truck struggling to keep up with the car.

The truck had some boards on the back and before too long the workers were measuring and marking the planks to nail them across the doors and windows.

One of the little short deputies must have gotten bored just sitting on the porch and started taking random shots at Sarge's chickens, shooting them in the head.

When that one would quit flopping and flipping, he'd shoot another one.

Sheriff Watson didn't say a word. He had about a half stick of bologna that he was gnawing on.

I was hid behind the furthest barn from our house, so I ran home and told Mama what was going on.

"You go back out there and if they start shooting the hogs come in here and let me know," she said.

So I did, only I got a little closer this time. Our cotton was up high enough for me to crawl right to the edge of our property.

The Sheriff was gnawing away on that red stick of bologna and hurrying the workers to speed it up.

The Sarge didn't have electricity so the poor workers were sawing as fast as they could with the dull handsaws the Sheriff had brought. They were already soaked with sweat and they'd just finished one window in front and the front door.

The workers started to complain to the Sheriff, so the Sheriff and deputy drove to our house.

I came in the back door just in time to hear the strutting little deputy tell Mama they were going to saw some boards at our shop if we had an electric saw.

"Sure we have an electric saw and I'd be glad to let you use it but I heard twelve shots go off out there and if you're a good shot that means you owe the estate of Sarge six dollars, fifty cents a chicken.

The short little fellow looked at the Sheriff as if he wanted the Sheriff to say something in his defense.

"Just who the hell do you think you are Bitch."

That was all the short deputy was able to get out of his mouth before Mama slapped him out of the door and off the porch.

It sounded like one of our fire crackers went off.

Mama made a lunge for him but she stopped at the edge of the porch.

"Not in my house and not in front of my children," Mama said.

"Elrod, you heard what the lady said. I believe you owe her an apology; that is, if you want to keep your job and I think six dollars is mighty cheap."

"Yes Mam, I don't know what come over me, I'm sorry Mam," said the red faced deputy as he began to count out the money.

"Another thing Sheriff, while you're here, every Sunday when I take the Sarge's dinner to him this idiot deputy of yours just ruins his meal by sampling it or sticking his filthy fingers in it."

"Elrod!" stomped the heavy Sheriff, jarring our whole porch.

"It's a wonder Minnie hasn't said something about it."

"That's because I haven't told her and the Sarge, bless his heart thinks I bring them that way."

"Well, you can rest assured it won't happen again, and could I have some water?"

"Your deputy can go on back to Sarge's and send the workers over here with the lumber.

Come on in Sheriff Watson and I'll pour you a glass of cold water."

Chapter 48

After the big POP, Deputy Elrod would just leave the office when Mama showed up and the janitor would take Sarge his Sunday dinner.

We don't know who was behind it but there was an apparatus rigged up on the chimney that wouldn't allow me and Pap to throw our rope around it anymore. We couldn't get word to Sarge about it by Mama because she was unaware of our night time forays.

Daddy was keeping us pretty busy on the farm. If we weren't hoeing we were dusting for boll weevils.

Thank Goodness the tractor we got from Sarge's had some scissor like blades that attached to the bottom of the tractor and we kept his three acre yard cut instead of hoeing it up like ours.

During that summer Mama did something that really surprised me. Since Myrtice had moved, Sunshine had no one to play with but Betty Jean and Joanne. They were so much older, so she began to allow her to spend more time with Miss Minnie than I know Mama would have liked, but Sunshine always came in excited about some new tune or something that she had learned on the piano.

I do believe that Mama felt a pang of jealousy, yet gratitude toward Miss Minnie for taking up with Sunshine, more so than she did when she was giving Pap music lessons.

Maybe it was just Pap's nature to not take things as seriously as Sunshine before he was on to something else, I didn't know.

I knew that Mama would've killed to have Sunshine a nice piano sitting in our living room like Miss Minnie's but I knew we couldn't afford such extravagance.

Contraire to most folks beliefs, when it came right down to it Daddy had the last say about things, and I'd heard him tell Mama he intended to start a savings account if we cleared money with our cotton crop, so I knew a piano wasn't in the future.

Meanwhile, I don't know whether it was because Sunshine wasn't under foot as much or what it was but the ever so quiet Shelby had discovered she could paint.

With just regular enamel paint she was painting beautiful flowers on pieces of wood, which later went on to become landscapes and portraits.

Miss Minnie went to the expense of buying Shelby some oil paints and real artist brushes, which Mama insisted on paying her back.

Shelby turned the little room in the back of the house into her art room and Mama made sure she didn't have a speck of paint on her when she left that room.

On a rare occasion when I wasn't busy doing something, Mama missed me and came into my bedroom.

She found me lying in bed with my callused hands behind my head staring up at the ceiling.

It was stifling hot in the room, even with the window up. Buddy was banging away at something in the shop, Shelby was in her painting room, Pap and Sunshine were at Miss Minnie's taking their lessons.

"So there you are," Mama said, as she came over and put the back side of her hand to my forehead.

"What's the matter my little Lewty," she asked?

"I'm not your little Lewty," I replied, and turned away from her.

"It's not like you to just lay here in bed when there's so much devilment out there for you to be getting into."

I turned back over and faced my Mama, who was now sitting on the side of my bed.

"Mama, I just got to thinking, everybody's got a talent but me, excluding Rum, 'cause he's still mighty young, but I imagine he'll get him one."

Shelby had painted the old trunk I'd shoved under the house that day. She'd done a very good job with it, so Mama had put it at the foot of my bed.

She got up from my bed and opened the old trunk then brought out some old composition books that I'd written short stories about people that I had encountered and even about my family tree on both sides.

She thumbed through the stories I had written so hastily and had given so little thought about at the time when I was writing them.

"You are so wrong about yourself son, could you imagine any of my other children writing some of these things, why with just a little cultivation, you'd make a first class writer son."

I never knew my Mama read my discarded journals. To think with all her housework and running the other ones hither and fro I didn't think she had time for me.

"Lew, you might be too young to grasp this, but you try to remember this. You seem so unhappy right now, but it only takes three things to make you feel good about yourself and to be happy. Do you want to know what those three things are? She asked.

I looked up at Mama and slowly nodded my head, yes.

"Okay always try to remember this. 1. Find something to do. 2. Something to look forward to. 3. Something to love, and Lew, I pray you find these three things. I have, and I'll have to admit, it's worked for me," she said.

"How wrong I had been," I thought to myself.

"Now you straighten up my bed before you leave this room boy," She said then she smacked me on my forehead, put the note books back in the trunk and left the room.

I decided to run downtown for a cold RC, so I jumped out of bed, straightened the bedspread, told Mama where I was going and I'd be back in a small while.

I can tell you one thing, I felt ten feet tall as me and faithful ol' Black Boy trotted down the dirt road that day.

My Mama believed in me.

After getting my drink at Mr. Reese's I noticed a big delivery van at Pig Meat's place, so I walked up that way to investigate.

Miss Della usually wasn't there on Thursdays, but I soon learned that Pig Meat had hired a new piano player. He and Miss Della were having a little trouble staying in tune with each other.

The new piano player put the trouble off on the old upright piano that had been in the juke joint so long, so Pig Meat bought another used one from somewhere. The new player tried it out while it was still on the moving van and found it to be suitable.

I whispered to Miss Della that I needed that old piano bad for my little sister and to see what she could get him to sell it for.

The van was about to pull out when Miss Della threw up

her hand.

She yelled for Pig Meat to come to the door.

It took some effort but the big man wobbled his way to the front door, wiping a glass with a filthy apron.

"Pig Meats, what's de lease you can take fuh dat ole beat up piano in there?"

"A hundred dollars," he quickly replied.

"Pig Meats, you wants me to keeps singing fuh you?"

"You knows I do baby."

"Den gives dis chile five dollars ter pay dees livery folks, cause dat ol' piano is free to dis chile.

"Whatever you says Miss Della, as Pig Meat peeled off a five and called the delivery boy to him.

On the short ride to our house in the moving van I wondered why Miss Della used the black slang language that she had used around Pig Meat. She'd never used it before in my presence. I knew one thing she had found a friend in me and I knew that good people like Miss Della, Miss Minnie and the Sarge were rare and far in between.

REDTOWN: A NOVEL BY L.E. GULLEY

Chapter 49

As far as we knew, Daddy Jim had gotten completely out of the moonshining business and much to our dismay (and to a lot of other townspeople) he had finagled around and bought a small brick building years earlier and had been renting it to a watch repairman. The old fellow had decided to retire so Daddy Jim opened up a small loan company in the building.

If someone was late paying the loan, he'd hired Big Sam that ran the taxi service to run them down and collect for him or whatever it was they had used for collateral was legally ceased through the court system.

Of course Daddy Jim always made sure the collateral was

worth many times more than the amount he loaned out.

Most paid back the loan with the interest then would turn right around and borrow it right back again, so Daddy Jim had quite a lucrative business going on.

He hadn't left Big Mama, he went back there occasionally to check on things, but the little business had a small bed and bath in the back, so Daddy Jim spent most of his nights there (Or so we thought. We would later find out different).

The day the van brought the piano home Mama couldn't believe it.

As soon as they rolled the battered piano to the spot Mama designated, she went to work on it with her bottle of Old English furniture polish and after about fifteen minutes of deep scrubbing that piano shined like a new penny.

Of course her next step was to wash the keys down good with her lye soap.

"There, that'll do it. Now Sunshine can play a piano right here at home," Mama said.

Mama could hardly wait until it was time to pick up the two from Miss Minnie's.

She'd told me over and over she couldn't believe the

good fortune I'd had in getting such a beautiful piano, "And it looks like it's made of solid walnut," she said.

Mama was right Sunshine was thrilled about the piano, but she couldn't play a thing without her sheet music.

Pap, who had never done a thing but tinker around with the instrument while Sunshine and Miss Minnie was out of the room sit down in front of that piano and with just a little tinkering around, he was playing a boogie woogie tune.

We couldn't get over it, he just kept getting better and better at it and within an hour he had that thing dancing on the floor.

We all were amazed, even Daddy and Buddy came out of the shop and stood in the doorway grinning at Pap.

Mama, Sunshine and Shelby were taking turns jitterbugging in the living room floor.

Once again Pap had stolen the show, but when he felt like he had mastered that particular tune, it was no big deal to him. He simply closed the lid and asked what was for supper.

In times to come, after goading, Pap would play the piano along with Sunshine, but they played in two different styles.

Pap said the electric guitar and sax were his instruments

of choice, and along with a little banjo, played claw hammer style.

Mama loved that her Daddy was in town and she had ready access to him.

He had his usual high chair behind the counter and a couple of stools for his cronies to sit.

Mama usually didn't stay long because of her duties at home, but I could always tell by her mood when she'd made a visit to Daddy Jim's.

We didn't get to go that often because we were so busy on the farm, but we planned to make up for it as soon as cotton season was over.

Mama had written Margie Ree and Joyce, they had both written back and were elated that Daddy Jim had moved out of the house with Big Mama. They each explained they were busy with their businesses but promised they'd all meet up at our house at Christmas time.

I don't know where Daddy got the seed to our cotton from but it just kept growing and growing. It looked like we were going to have to climb the stalks in order to pick it.

First, though in the mid-summer, while the leaves were

still green on the stalks of corn, the leaves were stripped and stored in the attic of the barn to feed Bossy in the winter months.

Next, after the corn was dried, it had to be pulled from the stalk and stored in the barn.

All this was in between the never ceasing hoeing of grass and weeds over the twelve acres that was being farmed.

Last, but certainly not least was the picking of the cotton.

I remember Daddy waiting until he thought all the cotton bolls were pretty well open.

Daddy liked to start early so we could get the dew cotton; he said it would weigh more.

I remember looking out across the sea of white that morning, with the irritable strap of the cotton sack across my shoulder.

Mama had made Rum a little short red sack that didn't even drag the ground, I sure felt sorry for his back later on when he got some weight in that thing.

Like usual, Pap picked like a machine, he carried three rows at a time and never looked up,

Buddy and me carried two rows each and Rum one.

Pap picked cotton in two positions, standing up or bending over.

I picked it standing up, bending over, on my knees, and occasionally laying down.

We used the Sarge's old cotton wagon to empty our sacks in after they were weighed by the ole pea scales that hang from the wagon.

We drank about a gallon of water and hit the hot fields again until Mama called us for dinner.

I was so hot and thirsty that first day, until I think all I ate was a biscuit with honey poured over the top and I drank so much cold sweet tea that I'd occasionally burp up a mouthful the rest of the day.

When Mama called us in, right before dusk dark Pap had picked 428 pounds of cotton, I came in second at 302, Buddy was third at 275, and rum had 35, which totaled 1,040 pounds, a little over two bales of cotton.

Daddy came in from work right after we did and was well pleased at our work and after surveying the field he said we should be through if the weather stayed clear in about six or seven days.

The next day a good switching across Rum's legs and he picked his speed up again. That day he brought in seventy pounds. His little red sack was as round as a ball that afternoon when he weighed up.

None of us ever wore a shirt but Buddy. Mama said he was too old to be seen without one. We other three looked like full blooded Indians by the end of each summer.

Daddy hit the nail on the head. At the end of the seventh day we'd picked fourteen bales of cotton from our twelve acres.

I didn't know at the time how much money Daddy made off that twelve acres of cotton and seed, but whatever it was wasn't enough. Now the only thing left to do was to pull up the stalks, pile them in piles and burn them.

I heard him tell Mama that night, while we were all lying around the television, exhausted from our work, that from the proceeds of some of that cotton he was going to see Sarge about buying ten more acres of land.

"Charles Gulley, those children laying around in there in that living room are not slaves. Now, they have worked hard enough. You weren't here to see how eager they were to work, just to prove themselves to you."

"Nope, twenty acres is enough," she said.

Four days before school started for the season of 56-57 and two days before Sarge's trial was to begin Mama loaded us all into the Buick except Shelby and Buddy, who didn't want to go and took us with her to the 1ˢᵗ National bank to open a savings account. It was a big day for Mama.

Two days earlier Miss Minnie had sworn her to secrecy not to tell a soul, but the hair sample had finally come back from the FBI and both strands were definitely Mama's.

Mama was issued a subpoena the day before and she was ready to tell what little she knew.

The bank was two buildings down from Daddy Jim's Loan shark operation.

Mama deposited us all into the sterile little red and chrome chairs up front, while she went through the motions of putting all that money in the bank.

We were all nervous and wanted to leave. We soon just got tired sitting there and not doing anything.

Finally Mama came out with a cheap rope sucker for each of us. I saw a beautiful painting of a deer drinking water from a stream. I knew Shelby Rae would love to have that painting. It was attached to a calendar.

I reached up and pulled the thumb tack out, and without folding or wrinkling it, I walked out to the car with it.

We just walked over to Daddy Jim's place and when we entered we found Miss Minnie and Daddy Jim laughing and seemed to be having a good time about something.

Mama took about three steps inside, and never turning Sunshine's hand loose, she stopped dead in her tracks and looked from one to the other.

"Well, what a fool you two have played me for. Did you have to go so far as covering yourself in dirt and playing the part of a fool yourself?"

"Why couldn't you two just have come out and told me, I'm not a damn child," Mama said, as she whirled around and left the building with us in tow and Miss Minnie running to try and catch us.

We reached the car and even though it was hot Mama told us to roll up the windows.

Trying not to make a scene she said, "Bessie Rae you don't understand if things were let known your Daddy could have been sent to prison to say the least. Just have faith in me until court tomorrow.

Mama cranked the car and left. We didn't understand what had taken place between the two, and we were too scared to ask.

Chapter 50
MOBILE, AL.

Gloria Jean Snell was ready to come home.

The prostitution was easy money in New Orleans, but it was what went with the job that was bad.

Some of the clients wanted to do all manner of filthy things to her body, but she endured it. She could always take a hot bath and clean the filth off.

To start with she really enjoyed the sex with the handsome ones, but after ten or twelve a night that even got old.

The ones she hated were the ones that abused her physically.

She wasn't like Willa Dean or the Reese sisters who drank up their money or spent it on some frivolous tattoos. She'd squirreled her money away, evidently inheriting her Father's business sense about money.

The reason she was in Mobile, she'd found a good doctor to reset her jaw when a customer had slapped her.

While she was waiting on her appointment she picked up a Mobile Press newspaper and started reading it. She read about the Sarge's trial coming up the next day.

After her doctor's visit she caught the first Trailways bus to Hampton.

She arrived at the Bus station in Hampton at 4:00PM and her first call was to her Daddy then the next call was to S. Minerva Raines, attorney at law.

Mama dressed nice and made sure she was sitting in the witness room at 9:00am. She recognized the Snell girl that Sarge had supposedly killed, but they were warned not to fraternize with each other so Mama followed the rules.

At nine o'clock the Honorable judge slammed his gavel and the Court was brought into session, all the juror had already been seated. The Sarge was called into the court room in hand cuffs and leg irons; he had to duck his head as he entered the door leading into the Court room.

Mama had told us all to stay home, but naturally me and Pap ran to the courthouse as soon as Mama got out of sight.

We went upstairs to the peanut gallery and stayed hidden in the shadows but we could still see everything going on below.

Even Daddy Jim was sitting about middle ways down the aisles, and sitting beside him was Mr. Reese.

Daddy Jim was dressed in a suit and tie, but Mr. Reese looked as though he was just plucked from his service station.

Two chairs were placed together so the big Sarge wouldn't hang over.

The Court room was packed and stifling hot, especially up top where we were as we continued to crouch and hide behind the bannisters.

The frail looking old Judge finally slammed his gavel and said "Let the case of Grover Cleveland Sargent begin."

"Hmm," I thought, "So that's how the Sarge got his name."

The prosecuting attorney said he intended to prove that Mr. Sargent was a vile wicked man and he intended to prove he was guilty of all charges that had been placed against him.

He continued to strut around for a few more minutes just saying all kinds of bad things about the Sarge.

The Sarge bent his head and cried, doing his best to cover his face with his cuffed wrists.

It finally got to be Miss Minnie's turn.

She was very smartly dressed.

She turned and addressed the jury, then the Judge, and told them she was sorry the whole thing was coming before the court and it was just a waste of the taxpayers' money. I intend to prove my client is innocent in fifteen minutes or less and I'm also going to close another case that's twenty five years old while the townspeople are gathered here.

The Court house rumbled with noise and the Judge slammed his gavel.

Miss Minnie called Gloria Jean Snell's name first to testify.

The Court house went wild, the district attorney almost ran to the Judge's podium.

Gloria Jean slinked through the back door of the court room dressed in a tight fitting black dress. I also noticed her hair had almost grown back to shoulder length.

Miss Minnie asked her to be seated in the witness chair after she had been sworn in as a witness, while the Judge was still arguing with the district attorney.

Meanwhile, to some of the folks in the hot court room it was like seeing a ghost, so naturally some of them fainted.

Judge Larrimore said if order wasn't restored to the court room he would have it cleared.

The district attorney whined that he knew nothing about Gloria Jean being in court and he should have been notified,

"I just found out last night your honor and I couldn't contact our district attorney. I tried until well past my bed time and still couldn't get him," Miss Minnie replied.

"I see," replied the judge then he added, "You may proceed with your witness Miss Raines.

Miss Minnie started off with simple things then before long she got to the nitty gritty of things.

She had that District Attorney jumping up and down like a jack in the box. Each time the Judge would overrule him.

Finally Miss Minnie asked her did she know the other girls.

"Sure I know them and well. The Reese sisters and I work together.

Willa Dean, she works across town at a different establishment," Gloria Jean said.

"So you know for a fact that the other three girls are alive and well."

"I do,"

"I am through with this witness at this time," said Miss Minnie.

The district attorney jumped to his feet.

Gloria Jean acted as though she was unconcerned about the whole affair, as she was drumming her manicured fingernails on the arm of the witness chair.

"You say, you say, yet you nor Miss Raines have produced one shred of evidence the other three girls existance."

Gloria Jean looked up toward the ceiling and said,

"Try a subpoena I'm sure they'll come running."

Even the Judge snickered at this one before he slammed his gavel once again.

"You say you were working, what kind of work is it and where is this mysterious place."

"Nothing mysteriously at all, the Reese sisters and as well as myself were working for Madame Gilda's bordello on Beale St. in New Orleans.

Willa Dean worked for someone else across town, but I'd see her maybe once a week, especially on the weekends.

The attorney was shocked at Gloria Jean's words, especially her being so beautiful and being the mayor's daughter.

"I am through with this witness for the time being," the district attorney said.

Gloria Jean's rear exit was even better than the entrance.

Her rear end moved like two pistons working side by side as she left that court room.

I couldn't help but notice some of the jury goggled at her as she made her slow walk to the back door.

Miss Minnie's next witness was Mama, Mrs. Bessie Rae Gulley.

Mama stepped through that door like a queen with her head held high.

If she was nervous, she didn't show it, if anything, she looked mad, as she was sworn in.

Miss Minnie started out the same way with Mama as she

did with Gloria Jean.

Her name, place of residence, etc.

Then Miss Minnie asked Mama how she came to know Sarge.

"Same as you, through my children, he gave my son Pap some musical instruments, I invited him to Sunday dinner and it started from there."

"You have a teenage daughter don't you Mrs. Gulley?"

"I sure do."

"At any time has the client ever acted inappropriate around your daughter in any way?"

"Of course not, he's been as gentle as a lamb around all my children."

"Thank you, Mrs. Gulley. I'm going to ask you a few more questions I'm sure, but right now I'm going to turn you over to the prosecutor, now try and not lose your temper."

Miss Minnie stepped up to the Judge's podium and said, "I'd like to submit these two strands of hair as evidence. They just came in from the FBI laboratories and they prove that both strands of hair came from my witness Mrs. Bessie Rae Gulley. I've produced the supposedly deceased Gloria Jean

418

Snell. Are you ready to get this thing over with and acquit my client Mr. Sargent," Miss Minnie said.

The District Attorney didn't answer Miss Minnie.

The Judge accepted the evidence, took a deep breath and looked at the prosecutor.

"Not so fast, I'd like to question Mrs. Gulley, I'm not ready to throw in the towel yet," said the district attorney.

He started pacing in front of Mama.

"You know, I've been doing some checking on your family and it looks like your family moved here penniless just six years ago. Now you have twenty acres of land, a tractor, a brand new house, riding around in a new Buick. It seems to me like you have connections somewhere."

Mama stood up from the witness stand. Boy, was she mad!

"You listen to me you over stuffed pompous little idiot of a man, what we have, we've worked like slaves for it, and my husband lost two of his fingers at work to pay for what we have, so don't you question me."

Daddy Jim was constantly laughing, and the Judge was slamming his gavel again.

"Mrs. Gulley, watch your language," he warned Mama.

The cocky little lawyer came at Mama again.

"What is this relationship between Mrs. Raines and your children, I hear they practically live there and receiving free musical lessons. Tell me." the District Attorney insisted.

"Tell the Court what's going on here. Do you owe her a big enough favor as to get up here on this stand and you two perhaps concoct something?"

"You are a vile creature," Mama said, as she sat back down.

Mama then looked and her Daddy and Miss Minnie, she put her hands over her face and sobbed, "Because she, because she is my sister."

After a few seconds of silence, giving the spectators time for the realization to sink in, the courtroom went wild.

The district attorney didn't want to tangle with Jim Jordan and his cronies, so he turned to the Judge and said, "Judge due to the over powering evidence in this case that Miss Raines has brought before this Court I recommend that all charges be dropped against Mr. Sargent."

The Sheriff started to uncuff the Sarge immediately.

Miss Minnie couldn't stand it any longer, she rushed toward Mama. They hugged and cried together.

Miss Minnie whispered in Mama's ear, "It had to be done this way. I'll explain it all to you later, Pray Bessie Rae that we can get out of here before that dumbass DA puts 2&2 together and indicts our Daddy."

There I said it, "Our Daddy" I've waited a long time to say those two words.

The whole Court room stood up and applauded as the Sarge made his way down the narrow aisle to go home.

Mama saw us in the balcony and told us to stop the Sarge at the front door, that she would give him a ride home.

Miss Minnie was straightening papers and putting them in her satchel when Mama walked over to her.

"You know I can't help but feel like a scape goat in all this, but I knew there was something about you that I trusted, even though you buried yourself in that hole and ate all those bananas."

"Ugh, at the end of the day sometimes Sarge would leave from that intersection with 50 bananas, I never ate over three a day. I had a secret bag in that hole, and when no one was looking, I'd slip them in there. The Sarge kept my secret."

"Would you mind if I referred to Mr. Jim as Daddy? I've waited so long!"

"I would consider it an honor," Mama said, as their Daddy made his way to them and hugged both of them.

"My beautiful girls," he said.

"Daddy would you mind closing shop and let's all go to Bessie Rae's and explain this whole crazy thing to her. You can ride with me and Big Sam. I think she'll have a car full with those two cantankerous sons of hers and the Sarge."

"No need mentioning their names, it'll be Pap and Lew," Daddy Jim said.

The Sarge didn't want to take the time to go by the jail and get his personal items but Mama insisted so we stopped by there briefly.

The Sheriff and not so cocky little deputy were just entering the door as we arrived.

"I suppose you're after your personal belongings Sarge," the Sheriff said as he slapped the big man across his back.

The Sarge just nodded his head in compliance.

Sheriff Watson yelled for the janitor to bring all of the

Sarge's things out, and then added, "And you'd better not steal any of it, either."

"Sarge, I guess you already know how sorry I am about all of this, but I was just doing my job."

The Sarge didn't make a motion nor sound one way or the other.

The Sheriff continued.

"You know I'm in a tough fight to keep my job in November with that Pecker wood from the south end of the county, I'd sure appreciate your vote.

I'd never seen anything like it before in my life, but the Sarge grabbed the fat Sheriff in the front of his shirt and with one huge hand he picked him off the floor until his head was bumping the ceiling. You could hear cloth tearing and Sheriff Watson began to plead for help.

The cowardly little deputy ran out of the room.

Mama calmly began telling Sarge to turn the Sheriff loose.

The Sarge did, while the Sheriff was in mid-air, causing him to crumple to the floor.

"That's my answer as for voting for you," Sarge said, as

he got his old cardboard case from a goggled eyed janitor, turned, lowered his head and walked through the door.

"Oh, you might as well start looking for a new job Sheriff. Did you notice all the people in that courthouse today? Sarge has a lot of friends," added Mama.

Sheriff Watson was still scrambling around and cursing for the janitor to help him to his feet when we left.

Epilogue

As it turned out Daddy Jim had beaten John Raines to death with his walking stick after learning he was molesting Minerva.

Big Mama suspicioned it and held it over Daddy Jim's head for years until Miss Minnie moved back and finally got her license to practice law in the State of Alabama.

After being confronted with the news, Big Mama wasn't a fool. All she asked for was for her and her lambs to be taken care of.

Both Willie Joe and Talmer died in their early twenties from diabetes, but not before Talmer had invented a patent for an aluminum pistol that you could put together in your own living room. He didn't make a bundle of money but enough for Big Mama to give him a fine send off at his funeral.

After "Her Lambs" deaths, she died right afterwards.

Daddy Jim never moved back there again. He either slept in the back of his store, with Minerva or with us.

We never knew at the time but Daddy Jim owned the Taxi service in Hampton.

After the trial, word got out about Sarge's actions in the Sheriff's office, so Daddy Jim gave him a job collecting, riding around with Big Sam.

Aunt Minerva and Mama became very close over the years. As we got older and could do without Mama's presence, Aunt Minerva would pay for air fare for them to go to New York city to watch famous plays and such, but after a couple of trips Mama said that wasn't her world. She said making biscuits for the aging ol' Pete and her little corner was her world.

The Sarge continued eating Sunday dinners at our house until my senior year in High School. When he didn't show up that Sunday, Mama sent me out to his house to speed him up.

In line was this beautiful ebony creature. You could tell she had class.

When she approached me I asked her how she wanted the book signed.

She leaned forward just enough for me to smell a slight fragrance of her perfume.

"Just sign it "Little Bessie," she whispered.

I asked her to please sit down beside me in an extra chair that had been placed there.

My heart raced as I looked at the beautiful young lady out of the corner of my eye. Heaven knows how my signatures were, in those other signings.

Finally, after all the other customers came through, I began questioning her.

As it turned out she'd married well, and he was a white man. Of course, she had pictures to show me of her two children.

She had done a stint in the Air Force, had gone through college on the GI bill, and she taught economics at Newton High School.

I asked if she was happy.

"Very much so," she said. "That man treats me like a queen."

"You are a queen," I replied.

"And you?" she asked.

"It's a lonesome life for me at times, living out of my suit case, darting from town to town, trying to keep my name out there."

Little Bessie looked me right in the eyes. I remembered the dimples at the corners of her mouth and the small cleft in her chin. She then spoke.

"Aww, Lew, I've kept up with you over all these years. I reckon I have a copy of everything you've had published and you know what I've come to believe?"

"What?" I asked.

"It's your writing. Your writings are your queen."

THE END

Das Ende`